MASADA'S GATE

DAVID BRUNS

CHRIS POURTEAU

SEVERN RIVER PUBLISHING

Severn River Publishing
www.SevernRiverBooks.com

ISBN: 978-1-64875-547-7 (Paperback)

ALSO BY BRUNS AND POURTEAU

The SynCorp Saga

The Lazarus Protocol

Cassandra's War

Hostile Takeover

Valhalla Station

Masada's Gate

Serpent's Fury

Never miss a new release! Sign up to receive exclusive updates from authors Bruns and Pourteau!

severnriverbooks.com/series/the-syncorp-saga

1

RUBEN QINLAO • APPROACHING DARKSIDE,
THE MOON

The *Roadrunner* shuddered.

Ruben Qinlao flinched. Not from fear the ship might disintegrate around them, but from knowing what would follow the turbulence.

"This fucking thing is gonna shake apart," Richard Strunk said.

And there it was, the fear voiced out loud. Strunk's bulk, lumpy with muscles, loomed in the passenger seat behind him. It struck Ruben in that moment how closet-like the *Roadrunner* had become in the mad-dash escape from SynCorp HQ. And how Strunk's oppressive presence only added to the stress of the situation. In a way, Tony Taulke was lucky he was unconscious.

Enough of that, Ruben thought. *Not helping.*

Pushing off the paranoia, he reached forward and patted the console, muttering words of encouragement under his breath. It was the ritual he'd perfected as the shuttle's engines had spat and sputtered on the flight from Mars to Earth. The little ship's stealth design, obsolete though it might be, and lack of transponder had kept them invisible from tracking via the corporate network. Only sensors targeted right at them or a human eye watching them fly past would see them. The engines, on the other hand— those seemed to need personal reassurance. The soft touch of a friend.

"Talking to it ain't gonna help," Strunk said. Somewhere in his voice, the natural confidence of a man who'd relied on his size all his life tried to see beyond the fear of a man strapped into circumstances beyond his control.

"*Her*," Ruben found himself saying for no reason. "Not it." Then, in a mimic of Strunk's drawling baritone, "And it ain't gonna hurt."

The trick this far out wasn't staying invisible. That was the easy part, if you flew low enough. Without the help of automated guidance, though, the trick out here was to avoid crashing.

By staying below official flight paths trafficked daily by freighters and transports, they'd be fine. That meant avoiding the Moon's overlapping sensor webs used to prevent ships from crashing into one another by slaving their nav systems to control their approaches with algorithm-perfect accuracy. The sensor webs were narrow for efficiency and to avoid signal dispersion, which promoted sensor ghosts. It was easy enough to land undetected if you did it far enough out from the main docks of Dark-side proper, away from civilization.

The *Roadrunner* shook again. Strunk, for once, held his tongue.

"We're fine," Ruben said anyway. "The ship's adjusting to lunar gravity. And we're getting some wave interference from the artificial gravity genera-tors in Darkside. Old ships like this one don't have—"

Strunk made an obnoxious snoring sound, like a pig trying to breathe in vacuum.

"How much longer?" he asked.

"Just a few minutes." Ruben's answer was instinctive, distracted. He was having trouble locating the old drill sites. The latticework of lunar caves was still there, but the *Roadrunner*'s sensors, like everything else on the ship, seemed sleepy with age. "I'm coordinating the old maps in the ship's data-bank with what I can find on CorpNet to—"

The space pig made his air-sucking sound again.

"Tony needs help," Strunk said. "If he dies, I'm gonna make sure you do too. *Slowly*."

Ruben rolled his eyes. *Wouldn't want to kill your meal ticket, now would we?*

Sometimes, he swore, Strunk had no brains at all. Just more muscle, pressing on the inside of his skull.

But Strunk wasn't wrong. They'd staunched the flow of blood from the knife wound in Tony Taulke's chest, not an easy thing to do in zero-g. Keeping him unconscious, aided by a shot of painkillers, had helped keep the wound from opening back up. But Ruben had no idea if they'd merely restricted the bleeding to internal. Clotting was a notorious problem in space. You could bleed out from a paper cut under the right circumstances. And Tony was almost sixty. The wound was close to his heart. He needed more than the minimally outfitted medkit in the *Roadrunner* to survive. But first they needed to land safely.

Imaging from the ship's sensors overlaid the old maps stored in her databanks. Ruben was looking for something very specific: two vertical shafts and one thin, horizontal tunnel connecting them.

When the United Nations had first mapped potential sites for their new lunar colony, the UN engineers had dug five tunnels straight down into the Moon's surface around the Albategnius Crater. Named Alpha through Echo, four were abandoned relatively quickly when Point Charlie was chosen as the perfect colony site: stable rock foundation, nearby minerals, and enough sublunar ice to create a small ocean. LUNa City—later renamed Darkside's End by the Company and now simply called Darkside—stood over Point Charlie, a testament to man's engineering ingenuity. But connected to it by a long tunnel was one of the rejected sites: Point Bravo. Ruben hoped it, abandoned like the others, would also remain forgotten.

"And there it is," he muttered. Grateful they no longer needed them, he cut the minimal thrust of the unreliable main engines and cut in the parking thrusters to slow their descent. Their momentum should get them to Point Bravo.

"There what is?" Strunk asked.

Before Ruben could answer, an alarm sounded. A red console light flashed.

"What the hell is that?" Strunk demanded.

"We've lost the forward portside thruster," Ruben explained, mostly to himself. "We're dipping."

"Fuck that!"

Strunk's voice seemed to demand either the ship right itself, or he'd kick its ass.

"Stay calm, please," Ruben said, his fingers pushing buttons. "One screaming baby at a time." He was tempted to apologize to the *Roadrunner* for Strunk's outburst. He'd become just that superstitious.

The small ship listed to port and forward, angled by its three active thrusters in the direction of the one that had failed. The idea of cutting back in the main engines flashed briefly through Ruben's mind, but that would simply cause them to overshoot their destination. And the engines were so unreliable, reigniting them could make things worse.

Repeated attempts to reengage the dead thruster weren't working. And he didn't have time to sweet-talk the old lady. They were starting to spin. Darkside's arching dome loomed on the lunar horizon. Ruben could see a freighter being drawn in by SynCorp Central Control toward the colony docks. Then it was gone, swept beyond his view through the forward window as the shuttle's spin accelerated.

"Oh, Jesus," Strunk said, swallowing with a clucking sound. "I'm gonna..."

"Don't!" Ruben shouted. The last thing they needed was Strunk's vomit spinning around the cabin in zero-g. A quick notion drove Ruben's fingers before his brain could countermand it. He cut the remaining thrusters, waiting for the ship's momentum to circle them around until Darkside's docks circled back into view. It happened so fast, he almost missed them. The *Roadrunner* had spun nose down on its z-axis, forcing Ruben to squint through the pilot's canopy to find the docks. The shuttle's trajectory had skewed radically. The lunar surface reached upward.

They'd closed half the distance to the docking freighter. Then it spun over and behind the shuttle, beyond Ruben's view. Through the overhead canopy, the stars of deep space streaked by.

Strunk was retching behind him. Ruben ignored it. He reengaged the aft thrusters, and the ship began to move upward in a broad arc. Still listing, still perversely angled, but now directed again. Ruben's stomach turned somersaults in solidarity with Strunk's.

He didn't bother to orient himself to the landing pad or the freighter attempting to dock there. Either the semi-thrust maneuver would work or it wouldn't. Hell, they might have already strayed far enough into the approach lanes to trip Darkside's emergency encroachment alarms.

All in all, that seemed like an acceptable problem at the moment.

"What the fuck!" Strunk pleaded through a wet mouth. "What the fuck!"

Ruben felt it in his calming innards before he saw it through the forward window. They were leveling out. The aft thrusters had finally begun to overcome the spinning force of their unbalanced momentum. The shuttle flew cockeyed still, so Ruben set aside what his eyes saw through the window and focused on aiming for a makeshift landing spot outside what the computer claimed was the entrance to Point Bravo. He even had to tap the still-working forward thruster to correct their course.

They were heading in.

Hot.

"What the hell is happening?" Strunk demanded. "Where the hell are we going?"

"The crash site," Ruben answered with dark humor. As proximity alarms blared, he cut power to the aft thrusters and fired the landing rockets. "Hold on!"

The *Roadrunner* hit the lunar surface hard. Despite the cushioning foam of his seat, it felt like Ruben's tailbone had fractured. The metal hull groaned so loudly, only the volume of Strunk's terror dominated it. A plume of gray dust enveloped the plastisteel windows. The shuttle skipped and lifted, then hit again, less violently. It arced over a dune, then hit the surface again and slowed faster with the impact. All motion abruptly ceased, and the old shuttle settled on the lunar surface.

A wet, smacking sound splashed the cabin floor.

Red and amber lights blinked everywhere. One entire control panel had turned into flashing crimson warning lights. The grating sound of multiple alarms competed for human attention. Gas was escaping from somewhere.

Ruben glanced over the structural integrity readouts. The ship's hull was solid. No breaches. Then he checked in with himself—the piercing ache in his ass confirmed he was still alive. The foam of the pilot's seat had saved him a broken tailbone after all. But the bruise would be there a while. Still—no breaches for him, either.

He unbuckled his harness and slowly, achingly, lifted himself out of the pilot's seat. The light lunar gravity helped. Turning, he found Strunk, folded as far back in the protective foam of his seat as he could squeeze his massive frame. Through the frozen look on Strunk's face, Ruben thought he could see the boy the assassin had once been. He doubted Strunk had ever been a fan of carnival rides as a kid.

Ruben glanced down to the deck and found the chunky evidence of Strunk's fear. The rank, sour smell crawled into his nose.

"Anything broken?" he asked.

Strunk inhaled, as if he'd just remembered that breathing was a necessary thing. Then, he did it again.

"I'll take that as a no," Ruben said, moving to check on Tony. He pressed on the older man's extremities in various places. Nothing seemed broken here either. Being stoned and unconscious during the crash had probably worked to Tony's benefit, kept him from tensing up. With a nod to himself, Ruben returned to the forward console.

"If you say anything, anything at all," Strunk said, his voice somehow embarrassed yet threatening at the same time, "I'll fold your head through your legs and shove it up your ass."

"Say anything about what?" Ruben said, trying to reconcile the still-working tactical display of their location with the gray-fogged landscape outside the forward window. When Strunk wasn't forthcoming, Ruben turned and looked expectantly at him. "What?"

Strunk was hunched over Tony, giving him a second once-over. "Nothing. Forget it."

"Right." Ruben returned to assessing their position and, after a moment or two of verifying what he thought he knew, sighed heavily. "Well, the good news is this: we're within walking distance of Point Bravo. We'll wait there for Fischer."

Strunk grunted. "Don't keep me in suspense. What's the bad news?"

Ruben regarded him. "The *Roadrunner*'s run her last road."

"*Good!*"

"I don't think you understand, Dick," Ruben said. He relished, just a little bit, the excuse for calling Strunk by his nickname. "We're marooned here. And the Kisaans will be looking for us. For *him*." He nodded toward the sleeping Tony. He was an exile now, a Napoleon on the run. And Ruben Qinlao and Richard Strunk were fugitives right along with him.

"Yeah, maybe," Strunk said. "But we're alive. Against ... all ... odds." He glared around him at the *Roadrunner*'s wrecked interior. Then, to Ruben: "One thing you learn in my line of work—as long as you're alive, you're one step ahead of where you could be."

"Good point," Ruben allowed.

"How far is this walking distance?"

"About a kilometer."

"Okay. We got vac-suits, right?"

"Yeah."

Strunk nodded, then began loosening Tony's crash harness. The older man was sweating. Not a good sign since the *Roadrunner*'s life-support system had begun to fail. That was the flashing red light on the support systems console.

They needed to get moving. And he needed to find the Darkside doctor Fischer had recommended. Brackin.

"I'll help you suit him up," Ruben said. "I can get us through the hatch and into Bravo. There might still be a seal there. And atmosphere."

"Might?"

Ruben shrugged. "It's been thirty years since I was down there. It might be nothing but vacuum and cobwebs."

"No cobwebs on the Moon, dumbass," Strunk said, seemingly proud of himself for the knowledge.

"Right." Ruben looked up through the plastisteel of the shuttle's canopy. The dust was clearing, an infinite canvas of stars becoming visible again. He had no idea if they'd tripped Darkside's traffic sensors when the *Road-runner* spun off course. He had no idea if they'd been tracked the whole way from SynCorp HQ. Maybe Kisaan's forces, having secured the station, were already sweeping the system for them. Maybe they were inside Point Bravo right now, anticipating the capture like hunters in a blind waiting for their targets to walk into their crosshairs.

"You gonna help or not?" Strunk asked.

"Yeah," Ruben said. No use obsessing over the what-could-be's. Strunk was right. As long as they were alive, things could always be worse. "Let's get Tony suited up."

2

STACKS FISCHER • APPROACHING THE BELT

I'd had some time to think since Callisto. I usually love being alone inside my best girlfriend. Not so much this time.

I'd spent two days in the close quiet of the Hearse heading back to the inner system, speculating ad nauseum on how everything had so completely gone to shit. If all the king's horses and all the king's men ever put the Company together again, there'd be some serious after-game quarterbacking to find out who fucked up where. And then there'd be some open positions to fill...

Who the hell were these Soldiers of the Solar Revolution? More than pirates skimming in the Belt, that's for damned sure. They'd had starships going toe-to-toe with the corporate fleet at Pallas. This wasn't some reinvigorated Resistance movement gen'd up in the past few months on promises of mankind's potential. Events had been carefully orchestrated to topple the Five Factions of the Syndicate Corporation in one fell swoop. Tony Taulke: chased out of his own station. Ruben Qinlao: no longer controlling Mars. Only Adriana Rabh and Gregor Erkennen, safe through distance in the outer system, were still in power ... for now, at least. And Erkennen had gone dark, severed from CorpNet. That could be a strategy or a silent tombstone—maybe a separate SSR force had already taken Titan?

Elise Kisaan, Regent of Earth: dead. And not just dead, publicly beheaded by the golden-eyed half human calling herself—itself—Cassandra. That's a question I didn't seem anywhere nearer to having an answer for—a human body, born of her mother Elise, but with DNA integrated with artificial intelligence. Cassandra was once a baby named Cassie thirty years ago, when I'd missed my mark— and now she was a self-proclaimed savior of humanity. The rhetoric on CorpNet was pretty damned clear: Cassandra promoted the Soldiers as liberators, and she—it—was trying to convince everyone else of that, too.

Anybody tries that hard to hit a message home? They've got a pig agenda they're putting lipstick on to make it look good. And while Cassandra seemed to have a personal grudge against momma—sawing Kisaan's head off was my first clue—she'd taken Earth first. Earth, the most powerful jewel in the SynCorp crown, the source of all luxuries and still, despite local hydroponic efforts around the system, the breadbasket of Sol.

I felt my stomach grumbling already...

But that was a problem for a different day. My immediate concern was reaching Tony and the Qinlao kid. Although, I kept having to remind myself, Ruben Qinlao wasn't a kid anymore. When you meet a person, that first impression tends to stick. Despite his title as Regent of Mars, Ruben Qinlao would always be a shy teenager to me, hiding behind his sister Ming's skirts.

A big question mark hung over his new besties friendship with Tony Taulke, though. The Taulke and Qinlao Factions never much cared for each other. But Ruben had stepped up for some reason when Tony had needed him most.

Loyalty is everything to Tony. He never forgets a good turn.

The travel time alone in the Hearse had helped me figure out one thing, though—the clue in Qinlao's last message. "Bravo, Stacks!" had sounded odd. After hours of searching the Hearse's databanks, I'd finally put two and two together. They were headed for one of the old, pre-construction sounding shafts on the Moon—about as invisible a hiding place as you can find there, if you don't count The Sewer, Darkside's underbelly-of-the-underbelly. Only the poorest of Darkside's poor live there, and all of them need money to live. They'd sell Tony out in half a heartbeat. Kudos to the kid for quick thinking and not taking him there.

Since figuring that out, I'd been able to rest easier. Or doze, at least. Even the soft hum of the engines through the hull couldn't lull me to Sandman Land. When I can't sleep but I'm not visiting Minnie the Mouth's bordello in Darkside, I snuggle up with my second favorite pastime: reading. Sometimes that puts out the peepers, if the material's dry enough. I'd even called up Hampton Fitzgerald's *Complete History of Medieval Warfare* with its six appendices on siege engines and how to build them—usually a guaranteed snore starter.

Nothing. Wide awake.

This trip ... this trip was different. That dawned like a black sun in the back of my thick head. The closer I got to the Belt littering the space between Jupiter and Mars, the closer I got to regret. I could feel it coming on like a cold in the back of my throat. I'd told myself I'd just shadow the Frater Lanes as usual, keep off the grid. Get back to Tony, and then we'd take the fight to Cassandra and her snaky minions.

I'd flown this same route just a few days earlier, headed to Rabh Regency Station with the intel Daisy Brace had died for. But this time was different—no Daisy.

I glanced for the thousandth time at my longcoat and fedora sitting on the seat where Daisy left them before springing me from Elaena Kisaan's pirate cove on Pallas. I hadn't touched them in all that time since. Leaving them there, like she'd placed them, felt like I was doing her a solid somehow, like I was honoring her sacrifice. I know it sounds stupid. They're just clothes, and they weren't even hers. But I'd met Daisy less than a week earlier and run the gamut from strong dislike to outright hate—when I thought she'd betrayed me—to a pretty goddamned high peg of respect at the end. That's a lot of road to process with someone over a lifetime, much less in the too-short stretch I'd known her.

I felt goofy. I felt sentimental. I felt a little bit creepy, at my age, crushing on a woman who could've been a grand ... a daughter. She'd died doing what she was paid to do—protect Adriana Rabh's interests. She'd died helping me escape Pallas. She'd done it with style, fooling me enough to hoodwink Elaena Kisaan, aka the Dutchman aka the Pirate Queen of the Belt. Daisy had been a first-rate killer with a wicked sense of humor.

I respected all those things.

But Daisy Brace had chosen her profession and the dangers that came with it. She'd known the score. Maybe Mother Universe had shown up too early to settle up, but that's just how it happens sometimes.

Them's the breaks, kid, I thought, hating myself for thinking it. It felt icy and lacking, like words usually are. A way to distance myself from her loss because people die every day and why should she be any different? The universe is a cold place and doesn't give two shits for your preference for living cuz whether you're dead or alive, you're just stardust to the void.

The Hearse's proximity alarm shook me out of my sullen mood. I was entering the outer edge of the Belt. My girl was doing her due diligence letting me know, and she'd make course corrections automatically, steering around any potential dangers.

I muted the sound but let the red light blink, should I get distracted again. I took manual control of the engine and cut thrust. At the speed I was traveling, that wouldn't have much immediate effect, and anyway, I wasn't about to flip and decel burn to slow myself down. I needed to get to Tony. The Hearse used the maneuvering thrusters now and then to steer around debris.

Wait, *debris*?

It was everywhere.

The battle between the pirate fleet and Admiral Galatz's Company ships had been broad and deadly by the looks of things. Looking at all that scorched, twisted metal, I wondered how many ships either side had left. Dead hulls are dark, so I switched on the Hearse's running lights to get a better look. I zoomed her camera in on pieces of the floating graveyard. Bodies, frozen in death, their limbs splayed out. Thousands of them. Some in Company navy blues, yellow stripes stretching across the shoulders of officers. Some in SSR green, lined in black, the uniforms I'd seen on Pallas. Dark until the Hearse passed over them to light death's rictus on their faces.

Pallas blipped at the edge of sensor range. Its natural orbit around the sun had taken it beyond my flight path, and I wouldn't be able to reach it without going far out of my way. I considered doing exactly that anyway to recover Daisy's body. But Galatz was bombing the shit out of that place the last time I saw it, which meant it was likely breached to vacuum—that'd preserve her remains, if they hadn't been sucked into space or atomized by the admiral's bombardment. Daisy's corpse might still be lying on that flight deck.

Maybe I could swing back and pick her up and take her home to Adriana, after this was all over. Right now, I didn't have time for good deeds. Tony was my priority, and Daisy would understand that. She'd respect nothing less. I was having another moment when the comms pinged.

"Message received," the Hearse said in her sweet voice. *"Black star encryption."*

Black star! That was good news. Nobody but Tony uses that encrypted frequency. Or Ruben on his behalf, lately. Maybe Tony was still alive. I opened the message.

A man's face appeared. Middle-aged, rings of gray hair that looked unwashed. Grave eyes.

Not Tony. Not Ruben Qinlao.

"Eugene Fischer," the man said in half an accent that hadn't been wholly Russian in at least a generation. "This is Gregor Erkennen. You must come to Titan. The survival of SynCorp depends on it. I hope the missus has weathered the storm. Adriana Rabh's seal accompanies my own."

The screen went dark. I stared at it, not quite sure I'd just heard what I'd just heard.

When I closed my mouth, my uppers and lowers clicked.

"Hey, honey," I said, "replay the message."

The Hearse acknowledged. When it finished, I had her play it a third time.

Several questions competed for my attention. What did Gregor Erkennen need with me? Like all the faction leaders, he had his own stable of enforcers he could call on. As I recalled, he had a particularly soulless creature named Bruno Richter who could take care of business just fine. And how the hell had he co-opted Tony's private ... wait, of course Erkennen had access to the black star channel. His faction controlled the Company's tech. I doubted there was a single secret in SynCorp that Gregor Erkennen didn't have backed up on a server somewhere. Leverage, should he ever need it.

Okay, but the demand he'd made ... I checked the stamp on the transmission. Sure enough, Adriana Rabh's double-bar-R sat beside Erkennen's brand. I tapped my middle finger on the armrest, thinking that through. He could have faked that, I guess. Maybe Gregor had teamed up with Cassandra. Maybe that's why he'd gone dark. But I'd half convinced myself of the same thing about Adriana while a prisoner on Pallas, and that had proven to be dead wrong. Dead Daisy wrong. Maybe Erkennen was still loyal, too.

I hate not knowing what I don't know.

"Message received," the Hearse said.

Two within a few minutes? Too coincidental to be coincidence.

"Play it."

Adriana Rabh's ivory-carved face appeared. Her expression was flat, her skin drawn, like she'd missed her last meal or two.

"Stacks, Gregor's message is legit," she said. "Get to Titan. This is bigger than Tony. Gregor will explain when you arrive."

The screen went black again.

I sat there, thinking. First, a demand from Gregor. Then—because she knew I'd need it—a personal endorsement from Adriana. Without it, I'd have likely ignored Erkennen. Faction loyalty comes first, and she knows my loyalty to Tony trumps all.

One thing I found curious about both—they'd been messages, not comm requests. Cassandra owned SynCorp's comm system—she'd taken over CorpNet and filled it with her piggy-lipstick propaganda. If they'd connected to talk directly, they'd be giving away my location to anyone tracking the call. So they sent their messages into the ether, hoping I'd pick them up. But what if Cassandra had taken control of more than just the subspace network? Maybe she was aiming to seize everything else that was SynCorp in virtual form. Technologies, personal histories ... every scrap of data SynCorp had ever captured. Huh—that gave me pause. And that, my friends, is why I never got the medical implant installed—in the wrong hands, the SCI's data can lead the bad guys right to you. It's also why the Hearse didn't have a transponder. Forward thinking, that's me.

The two remaining faction leaders had just asked—no, *demanded*—I forsake Tony and head to the opposite end of the solar system. Without explanation.

"This is bigger than Tony," Adriana had said. That suggested SynCorp was at stake. Nothing was bigger, more important than Tony—other than the Company itself.

It was Tony who taught me that.

I turned off the Hearse's running lights. The floating graveyard around me disappeared.

"Nav: plot a course for Titan," I said. It was more or less five days away. I had a lot more me time ahead of me. Joy. "Start a hard decel burn ASAP."

I prepped myself for the g's. The Hearse fortified me with an injection to keep me from stroking out. The adaptive foam of my pilot's chair began to soften, preparing to counter the force that was coming.

"Well, kid," I said, picturing Ruben Qinlao in my head and having a hard time seeing anything older than that shy teen boy. "Take care of the boss. I'll be along eventually."

The Hearse flipped and started her decel burn. My old face started to stretch young again.

I didn't dare send Qinlao a message, much less a comm request. I couldn't be sure he'd be able to decode whatever cloudy language I came up with—spy stuff wasn't his thing. But I *was* sure Cassandra's people would intercept it, and they'd become pros at this business, damned near overnight. If they'd tapped the messages from Erkennen and Rabh, they could make a fifty-fifty bet I was headed to the outer system. No need to confirm it. Ruben and Blockhead Strunk would just have to make their own way.

As the g's multiplied, I wondered what was so damned important on Titan to keep me from Tony. Pretty important, I figured, since the two SynCorp regents still in power had refused to even name it in the message. And that business from Erkennen about my missus making it through current events.

There is no Mrs. Eugene Fischer. Despite my resume, I'm too kind a soul to ever inflict marriage to me on the fairer sex. But even I could figure out Gregor's meaning.

MRS.

Maintain radio silence.

Cassandra was listening.

3

REBEKAH FRANKLIN • MASADA STATION, ORBITING TITAN

Bekah Franklin wasn't sure why she was here. She really needed to visit her grandfather today, and her work schedule was already overclocked. One more meeting was one more thing she didn't need competing for her attention.

But Gregor Erkennen had asked that she attend, and so here she was. It was an unusual request for an unusual time. A frightening time, especially since Gregor had cut them off from the rest of the SynCorp network.

Bekah glanced around the conference table, gauging the temperature of the room. Rahim Zafar, her team leader, nodded reassuringly. She'd half-thought he might begrudge her being here, but he was open and generous to those who reported to him. No professional rivalry. No need to feel threatened by her presence.

Next to him sat Daniel Tripp, lead heuristics researcher and resident expert on machine learning and artificial intelligence. Just ask him, he'll tell you. Brilliant and self-confident to the point of conceit.

Carrin Bohannon entered and sat across from Bekah, offering a how's-it-going smile. They were old friends, though recently they'd spent less time together as their interests diverged. Carrin was now the Erkennen Faction's cybersecurity team leader, while Bekah had kept her programming skillset more generalized.

One seat remained vacant at the round conference table. The first time she'd seen it, Bekah couldn't help but think of King Arthur's Round Table. In the spirit of that mythical ruler, Gregor Erkennen liked his department heads to see one another as colleagues on common ground. They were a group of forward thinkers co-equal in the realm of proffering ideas, he liked to say. But when Gregor attended meetings, there was little doubt who wielded the power at the table.

When he walked in, the small talk quieted.

"Ladies and gentlemen, thank you for coming," Gregor said in his slight Russian accent. He lowered his frumpy bulk into the fifth chair. "Ms. Franklin, good to see you here."

"Thank you," Bekah said. She'd almost called him Gregor. That wouldn't do in a public setting, despite the longstanding ties between their two families.

"I called you all here to discuss our strategy for defense," Gregor said. As usual, he wasted little time on polite conversation. "First thoughts?"

"We're alone out here," Daniel Tripp observed. His voice held concern, if not panic. "Cut off, helpless."

"That is not exactly true," Gregor answered, his cadence careful like a coder's would be—attentive to syntax and its effect. "Our faction resides on Titan. We have the most advanced technology in the system. We are not helpless."

Rahim Zafar inhaled a breath, then let it out. Bekah knew what that meant. He was about to politely, professionally disagree.

"You're right, Regent, of course," he began. "But we haven't heard from the fleet since Pallas. Who won that battle? Reports are confused. We know the SSR worms are crawling CorpNet, boring holes in the Company's virtual infrastructure. They've already secured the subspace satellite network and completely control interplanetary communications."

"They're winning," Daniel whispered.

"At the moment," Gregor acknowledged. "I grant you that."

"It's like Pearl Harbor. The First Gulf War. China's annexation of Hong Kong after the Century Flood." Rahim ticked off the short history of surprise attacks on his fingers. "Shock and awe that overwhelms."

"And yet the Japanese did not prevail, despite their early victory at Pearl

Harbor," Gregor said. He offered them all a smile that required more work than it should have. "So there's still hope. Which is why we have cut ourselves off from CorpNet—to insulate ourselves until Tony Taulke organizes a counteroffensive."

"Being cut off won't help us over the long term," Carrin Bohannon suggested. "Every siege ends eventually, when the besieged starve. And Tony Taulke's dead."

Gregor Erkennen made a dangerous sound. "We don't know that."

"It's a double-edged sword, being cut off." The table turned to Daniel Tripp. "Passively monitoring CorpNet keeps us informed, but we can't affect anything without actively engaging the network—and the moment we do that, we open ourselves to infiltration by Cassandra's worms. Every technology, every dataset, every—"

"Cassandra might already have viruses trolling Masada," Rahim said quietly.

"No," Gregor said, raising a hand. He seemed very old to Bekah just then, slumped in his chair. Slumped in his confidence. "Our antivirals are patrolling the Masada mainframe now. They're the most robust security protocols mankind—or womankind—has ever produced, thanks to Carrin. And so far, they've found nothing."

"So far," Rahim acknowledged. "But to assume we're not already compromised is to invite disaster."

The idea that the Syndicate Corporation's central repository of technological knowledge might already be breached chilled the room. This eventuality was why Viktor Erkennen, Gregor's father, had established the family faction's research and development hub on Titan in the early days of SynCorp's expansion—far beyond easy access, or easy meddling by the other factions. Saturn was the boonies of the solar system.

Gregor let the room breathe. Bekah had seen it before on projects. He was fine with the uncomfortable silence, wanting it to spur his senior staff to offer up constructive suggestions. Daniel flitted his eyes at Bekah like he hoped to crib the answers to an exam. Carrin studied her fingers, which seemed to be typing what she was unwilling to say aloud.

"Ms. Franklin, what do you think?" Gregor asked finally. "You've been very quiet."

Rahim made a soft, amused sound. "She's always very quiet."

A nervous, light laughter passed around the table.

Smiling, Bekah glanced around without making eye contact. "I'm just listening," she said, hoping that would be enough. She hated talking in meetings, especially when Titan's regent presided.

"I've noticed that about you," Gregor said, not unkindly. The smile on his face was less weary now, more familial and lived in. "But when you speak, you always have something intelligent to say." His compliment, unexpected in a public setting, seemed to open up a box inside Bekah. She was surprised by the quiet pride she found inside it. "Speak your mind."

"Come on, Bekah," Rahim prompted. "Cut through the code."

Bekah's expression relaxed. It was what Rahim always said when he wanted her to use her fabled ability to see past the eye-crossing clutter of programming to find an error obscure to everyone else yet obvious to her. He called it using her Oracle's Oculus.

"Sometimes it's better to look at what we know first," she said. "Or at least what we think we know. To keep from building on a foundation of faulty data."

Gregor nodded. "Start at the beginning, then."

"The Masada mainframe contains every R&D project we've ever conducted," Bekah said. She ignored Daniel's and-then-the-dinosaurs-came look of impatience. "If Rahim is right and the SSR has already infected the mainframe, then it's only a matter of time before they steal everything in it."

"Even the experimental stuff," Carrin said. The significance of that was obvious. "The new stunner prototype that penetrates first-generation MESH. The folding-space jumpgate simulation model. The—"

"Yes, that is what is at stake, Carrin," Gregor said. "But our analytics have found no breach. I'm asking all of you how we can best protect our data."

"We first have to identify the threat," Rahim said. "Aberrant code, maybe, newly introduced as a virus."

"Or code that looks old and legit because its timestamp has been forged," Daniel added.

"We must assume the firewalls we have in place—sophisticated as they are—will be breached at some point," Gregor said. "This Cassandra, the leader of the Soldiers of the Solar Revolution—she is the result of human procreation and artificial intelligence. The AI that controlled the New Earthers thirty years ago was destroyed, but not before altering Elise Kisaan's DNA. Cassandra is the hybrid child resulting from that experimentation."

"You're saying we're not just fighting another group of programmers working for the SSR," Rahim said. "We're fighting an artificial intelligence that's sophisticated enough to gene-splice human DNA?"

"One whose thought-to-action processes aren't as limited as a human's," Gregor said.

"But how can we outthink an AI that can process trillions of operations per second?" Carrin asked.

"We can't," Bekah said. "We can't think faster, so we have to think smarter."

"What does that mean, though?" Carrin asked.

"It means," Gregor said, "we have to think beyond the standard anticipate-counter model of viral response."

"All right, sir," Rahim allowed in a way that said he was again trying hard to be cordial. "But what does that really mean in practice?"

"Buried treasure," Bekah said.

Gregor's head tilted. "Explain, Ms. Franklin."

"Every viral attack has a purpose," Bekah said. "To steal data, compromise the data holder ... *something*. Cassandra has secured CorpNet to cement her power by controlling the means of communication with citizens across the system. It makes sense she would target us next."

"Once she steals the Company's tech secrets, she can build the next-generation stunner," Carrin said soberly. "Or the next-generation warship."

Gregor pursed his lips. "Knowledge is power."

"But what if our goal weren't simply to keep Cassandra out," Bekah continued. "We already agree—it's almost impossible. Over time, the processing power of her AI brain will breach the best security we can offer —no offense, Carrin. You said it yourself: sieges always end. It's only a matter of time."

"So, we should just let her in?" Carrin asked, her security expert's ethics clearly offended by the idea.

"Not *just*," Bekah said.

The three team leaders around the table shared impatient expressions. Gregor Erkennen seemed intrigued.

"What if we created thousands—millions—of buried treasure sites across a mirrored backup of Masada's databanks?" Bekah said. "If we can convince Cassandra that the fake mainframe is the real one by fighting hard enough to protect its fake secrets..."

Rahim tapped his finger on the table. "It's a cool idea, but her attacks could number in the billions. Cassandra can always think faster. We'd never be able to keep up. We're back to the speed issue again."

"A Holy Grail," Gregor said.

"A what?" Daniel asked.

"A Holy Grail. A decoy so convincing, you believe it's real because you *want* to believe it's real." Gregor leaned forward, his voice alive with the idea. "We already have a backup site for the mainframe at Prometheus Colony, in case of a catastrophic event up here. Let's invert that reality, ladies and gentlemen. Let's turn the backup from a perfect replica of the mainframe into a perfectly *flawed* replica that appears to be the *real thing*. With thousands of flawed fakes of every technological innovation we've ever produced, going back thirty years. No, not thousands, *millions* of flawed fakes—Holy Grails. And around each one, the highest level of security— the moat of code around the castle, yes?" Gregor's enthusiasm was shining from his eyes. "We put millions of Holy Grails behind the strongest of castle walls—the toughest, most robust security protocols we can produce. Innovations so well protected, Cassandra will identify each and every one as must-have tech."

"So you're suggesting," Rahim said, "that the AI's own prioritizing algorithms will sucker her into thinking they've found top-level tech behind top-level security. Lead her down rabbit holes."

"Rabbit holes full of Holy Grails." Carrin's earlier incredulity had turned predatory.

The excitement of the idea seemed to pass from person to person.

"Millions of Holy Grails," Bekah said.

Daniel raised his hand before speaking, as if in school again. "But what about the real data? The *actual* tech secrets, especially the experimental stuff. How do we protect that?"

"We cut Masada Station off from outside contact," Gregor said. "The station goes dark and stays dark. Nothing but passive network monitoring. The station will seem abandoned. Cassandra will think we've turtled up on Titan to protect our data. And we'll build a data history showing the station was never anything more than an outpost—that all the real discoveries made in the last thirty years happened at Prometheus. Not up here."

"So all Cassandra's efforts will be aimed at Titan," Carrin said, her tone what a smile must sound like. "And its millions of moats surrounding millions of coded castles with their millions of fake Holy Grail artifacts."

"We don't have time to create the tens of billions of yottabytes of code we'd need to pull off such a masquerade," Gregor said. "So we'll have to adapt existing code."

"You mean, use actual discoveries as bait? Even the experimental stuff?" Daniel asked. "Isn't that dangerous?"

"Yes, but we can build in critical errors and gaps in the code," Gregor said. "We hide the new stunner tech, the folding-space gate, and the rest in plain sight. But with the code fatally flawed in such a way that the tech would never work."

"Turn alphas into gammas," Rahim said. "Null sets into factorial expansions. Divide by zero now and then. But we have so little time ... it would literally take years to do all that."

The quiet that followed was strange in the wake of the excitement that had permeated the room.

"We write our own worms," Bekah said.

As one, the table turned to her.

"We fill the Prometheus decoy d-base with our own programming worms specifically aimed at changing equations, cutting lines of code, and blowing out all the performance thresholds," she said.

Gregor Erkennen pushed his seat away from the table and stood. "We need two teams. We'll need the vast majority of our staff on Titan, creating the fake mainframe and its security protocols. It doesn't just have to look good, people. It has to fool the most sophisticated AI that's ever existed.

Cassandra's worms *must* be convinced that Prometheus Colony is home to SynCorp's secrets. And that fake history of the colony itself I mentioned—work schedules, meal orders, the number of times the toilets have flushed—thirty years of data documenting human existence, tied to all of your names, which Cassandra may very well know by now. And another thing—the Prometheus decoy must be entirely detached from Masada. We can't take a chance on Cassandra finding a back door to the real data—one open data port could compromise everything." He scanned the table, emphasizing that fact. Then, "I'll head the Prometheus team myself. A second, smaller team will remain here on Masada Station, monitoring what's happening and prepared to defend the *real* treasure chest of SynCorp secrets, should Cassandra discover our ruse. Bekah, I want you leading that team."

She looked up sharply. "Sir?"

"It's your insight that helped us determine a viable defense. I want you and your insight here, protecting our most sensitive data."

"Okay," she said with an awkward glance at Rahim. To her surprise, he wore a proud expression. He didn't seem jealous at all.

"We'll need to fast-evacuate the station to Titan," Gregor said. "I'll oversee that effort. Rahim, you're in charge of setting up the greatest diversion in human history. I want hourly updates on your progress. Local network only. No CorpNet connection."

"Of course, sir. I'd be honored."

"Get to it, ladies and gentlemen," Gregor said. "We're already behind, and we have no idea how far."

As chairs scraped the floor, Rahim beamed warmly. "Time for the big leagues, Bekah."

"Doesn't get much bigger," she answered. Gregor was already on the station's comms, ordering the evacuation.

"What's wrong?" Rahim asked. Then, as realization dawned: "It's your grandfather, isn't it?"

Bekah nodded. "I doubt he's healthy enough to move to Prometheus."

"You should go see him."

"Yeah. And now, this ... it's a lot to take on."

"Hey, Bekah," Rahim said, reaching over to squeeze her hand, "you're the best natural coder I've ever seen. You're like a savant or something. If anyone can protect Masada, it's you."

His belief in her was almost enough to inspire the same confidence in herself.

"Thanks."

"Tell your grandfather I said hi," Rahim said over his shoulder. "And that I miss his hummus!"

Bekah watched him go. She should really get her team together. To prove to Gregor that his faith in her wasn't misplaced.

But first, she needed to visit her grandfather.

4

KWAZI JABARI • VALHALLA STATION, CALLISTO

"Again!"

Kwazi Jabari got to his knees on the deck. More slowly, this time. More carefully.

The endurance training he'd undergone after signing his contract to work in the Qinlao mines on Mars hadn't been this rigorous. Then again, it'd been in a point-four-g environment, not the variant half- to one-and-a-half g's Carl Braxton was inflicting on him. His stomach felt loose, suspended on rubber bands. Braxton appeared to take a grim delight in literally jerking him around by varying the gravity in the training room without warning.

"Tell me again why this is necessary?" Kwazi asked, standing up.

"Need to know. And you don't. Not yet, anyway," Braxton said, arms crossed. "But I'll tell you this much: you never know when artificial gravity will fail. Grav-reaction skills are good to have. I'm training your body to keep you from losing your lunch. It's like riding a bike on Earth. Once you muscle-memory VG, you never forget."

Braxton leaned against the padded wall of the training arena, his magnetized boots firmly clamped to the metal floor. A permanent expression of distrust painted his face. "Now, back on your feet, Hero of Mars. Back to first position."

Don't call me that, asshole.

Kwazi resumed his place at the start of the obstacle course.

"Course setting: alpha-two," Braxton told the tech outside the arena. Then, to Kwazi: "Don't try to anticipate. You can't. That's where you're going wrong. That's what the pads are for."

"Okay."

"Ten second warning."

Kwazi adjusted the strap of his left elbow pad, trying to cinch it tight without cutting off his circulation. Either he'd master the course without the pads eventually, or he'd be off the strike team. Braxton had made that much clear. What he hadn't made clear was the target of their strike.

"Go!"

The lighting changed from the amber of Callistan norms to the shadowed crimson of a starship on alert. Kwazi didn't fall for it this time—Braxton's "Go!" and its implied start to a race. Instead of sprinting forward, he moved at a measured pace toward the first small shipping container along the course track. His step was light but cautiously so, and for good reason. The half-g gravity doubled suddenly, making his extremities feel thirty pounds heavier. It was like the weight of the iron in his blood was being dragged downward.

Expecting another gravity shift at any moment, Kwazi knelt behind the container, ready to adjust. He reconned the corner to clear it, then rose. The shift came and his limbs lightened, his stomach floating like a suspended balloon, a fluttering giddiness tracking up his gullet. He leaned into the feeling, didn't fight it, like Braxton had taught him. Turning the nearly non-existent gravity to his advantage, Kwazi stepped quickly, springing upward to launch from the top of the container. Twisting to redirect his momentum, he caught the wall with his right kneepad, wincing as the shock reverberated up his leg. Bouncing off, he redirected toward the course's center, propelling upward with near weightlessness. Using his arms to deflect the ceiling, Kwazi angled back to the floor.

Gravity reengaged, and the shift snatched him from the air, but once again he embraced the pull instead of fighting it. Drawing his limbs in, Kwazi angled toward the cover of a second cargo container. His feet touched the floor and he rolled, halting only when his back flattened against the crate's hard edge.

Now, that's the way you do it.

"Better!" Braxton barked, sounding almost impressed. "But you're dead anyway."

The momentary heat of joy at finally besting the course evaporated, becoming instead the familiar blanket of Braxton's disappointment. Kwazi stood and turned to see his trainer pointing at a console jutting out from the wall at the eight o'clock position relative to his own. It wasn't really there of course, just an optical illusion painted by the skinning tech onto the wall. But in the training scenario, it was a 3D reality Kwazi should have seen easily when he'd gained enough height to deflect from the ceiling.

But he'd been so intent on performing the low-g maneuver, he'd neglected to clear the area hidden by the corner of the console. The jutting shadow created by the faux alert's red lighting was a dead space where an enemy could easily hide. In a real action, Kwazi could very well have been shot in the back while he congratulated himself for conquering the demands of gravity manipulation.

The arena's illumination snapped back to Callistan norms. Kwazi met Braxton's eyes. For once, they were surprisingly non-judgmental.

"Maybe I should go in the second wave," Kwazi said.

"Stow that," Braxton said, cutting a thumb across his neck at the tech outside. They were done for the day. "No time for tiny violins. You're the face of this thing. You won't be point guard, but you're going in early. And going out live on *The Real Story*."

The face of this thing.

That had a familiar ring. But at least this was a choice Kwazi was making. Fighting with the troopers of the SSR—this was him, taking back his ability to make choices. This was him making a difference.

"You've earned some downtime," Braxton said. Attempting to sound empathetic was strange coming from him. Like a boxer quoting poetry. "Get some food. We go again in eight hours. No pads, then."

"Okay. I'll be in my quarters for a bit, then."

"Set an alarm! We've got priorities here, Jabari. I don't want to have to pull you out of Dreamscape again."

Kwazi gave a lazy wave of acknowledgment, already anticipating his time alone with Amy.

Entering his temporary quarters beneath Loki's Longhouse elicited, as usual, mixed emotions in Kwazi. Braxton's bar, like the rest of Valhalla Station's Entertainment District, was built over the remains of the graveyard of Earth's first attempt at domesticating Callisto.

That early base had been carved right out of the moon's surface. The first expedition to Jupiter's least-radiated moon had ended tragically when an uncharted asteroid impacted Callisto's surface. The rock missed the colony by half a lunar diameter, but the resulting moonquake had fractured the plastisteel dome. Earth's first humans to venture beyond the Asteroid Belt had perished without so much as a goodbye to their inner system relatives.

The people had died, but the buildings survived. The dome had been rebuilt with new tech from the Erkennen Faction that could autoseal minor cracks. A heavily reinforced, rapidly deployable testudo shield—named for the ancient Roman formation of overlapping shields overhead, tortoise-like, to protect soldiers from enemy arrows—could be erected in under sixty seconds. The testudo had certainly proven its worth a couple of weeks ago, when a shuttle smashed into the orbital ring around Callisto, raining debris down and threatening to repeat history by destroying the colony's three domes.

Below the Longhouse, that first, doomed group's storage units now served the Soldiers of the Solar Revolution as quarters, meeting rooms, and training grounds. Whenever Kwazi entered the oversized closet that housed his bed and a lone nightstand, he discovered both relief from Braxton's arduous training schedule and a sinking sense of depression from the close confinement—every time.

The room, windowless being underground, was cramped. Even at his modest height of five-foot-eleven, Kwazi had to stoop. Entering the small space reminded him of working a double shift in the Martian mines—eventually the rock felt too close, the air smelled too recycled. You got tired of seeing rusty-red dust everywhere, and a feeling of claustrophobia set in. Your life felt too dependent on technology you couldn't control. Paranoia, a racing heart, a short-fused temper—Miner's Mania, they called it.

But that was the downside. The upside was that, once the SSR cut him loose, Kwazi could do whatever he wanted, as long as he did it below the surface. Away from the eyes of Callistans who would no doubt recognize him from SynCorp's propaganda broadcasts. And away from Adriana Rabh's faction agents, searching for him high and low on Helena Telemachus's orders.

He sat on his cot and stretched upward, luxuriating in the simple act of extending his neck. Calling up Dreamscape in his implant, Kwazi lay back against the chilly wall of his quarters. Before losing himself in the program, he set the alarm Braxton had requested. He couldn't risk being denied Dreamscape again.

He closed his eyes.

The reality of his dark quarters disappeared, replaced by a sweeping vista of the Martian surface, muddy crimson and stretching to a semi-blue horizon, the color the result of the setting sun's rays dancing along the thin atmosphere's edges. He'd always hated having to wear a vac-suit during his walkabouts on Mars, but here in Dreamscape, breathable air was a given. Food and water—no need to worry about either. Dreamscape was about experiencing the unexplored limits of imagination, not attending to life's mundane necessities.

The flat disc of Olympus Mons stretched to the edges of his vision. It seemed to comprise the entirety of the Red Planet. The highest point on Mars, Olympus Mons appeared from orbit as a cloudy plateau with a single eye stamped at its center. But the eye was really just a depression, and the plateau's contours the ancient engravings of the largest volcano in the solar system. A favorite thing to do when vacationing from his work below the surface had been to sit on a cliff's edge of the grand plateau, marveling at Mars's endless emptiness.

Amanda Topulos sat there now, her back to him. The light, Martian breeze played with her blonde hair, the reddish haze highlighting its hint of strawberry. Kwazi thought it complemented her cheeks, which seemed just a tad bit windburned. So odd, seeing her without her vac-suit out here. Odd and wonderful.

"How's the training?" she asked without pulling her eyes from the view.

Kwazi walked to the edge of the outcropping and sat down next to her. The wind tasted gritty, but it was more a sensation than dust entering his mouth. On Mars, everything felt gritty, all the time. That was one detail Dreamscape always fashioned exactly right from the fertile plains of his memory.

"Painfully," he said, a touch of wryness in his voice. "But better."

"That's good. Better is good."

He glanced over at Amy. Kwazi still felt self-conscious sometimes about staring at her, like he hadn't yet earned that intimate privilege. But he so enjoyed the simple pleasure of watching her admire the view he'd never had the chance to actually see with her when she was ... but no, he wouldn't think of her that way. She was alive to him, still. More alive, in some ways, than ever before. So he enjoyed watching her enjoy the view.

From orbit, Mars could seem uniform and homogeneous and featureless and cold. Up close, especially from the heights of Olympus Mons, it was anything but. The wavy, red dunes gave the landscape character. Randomly scattered, innumerable rocks hinted at a past with a story behind it—a story of building and breaking down and rebuilding. Uniformity became consistency, reassuring in its predictability. Like the mild smile tugging at the corners of Amy's lips now was predictable, but not boring for being so. Quiet and comfortable. Kwazi thought it was his favorite of her expressions.

"What are you thinking?" he asked.

Her smile ticked up a notch. "How lucky I am," she said. "To be here with you."

Kwazi snorted. "*You're* the lucky one? You have no idea how long I wanted to ask you out. To spend time with you like this."

"Like this," Amy repeated, gazing across Olympus Mons. Her tone—it was odd, he thought, as her gaze remained fixed on the horizon. It was almost like she was trying to avoid looking at him.

"Something wrong?" he asked in the way you ask a question out of obligation. In here, nothing was supposed to be wrong. Everything was supposed to be exactly, unbearably right. Shaped from the perfection of the dreamer's own desires for what they wanted the real world to be. What they wanted their relationships to be.

Amy placed her hands on the dusty rock and adjusted her seat.

"Well, we could have pillows," she said.

The relief rolled out of Kwazi as nervous laughter. He reached over and placed his hand lightly on the rock face, his fingers extending, shy and tentative, over hers. Being able to touch Amy in a way he never had in real life had proven something to Kwazi—that it was Dreamscape that was real, not his life outside it. Out there he'd been a miner, a mouthpiece for SynCorp, and now a member of the SSR. This was where he chose to exist as himself and not the Kwazi Jabari everyone else expected him to be. He merely walked through a door and found Amy, alive with her half smile.

She rotated her hand, intertwining her fingers with his in a grip that was as human as any he'd ever felt. Fleshy and soft in the palm, bony and harder near the knuckles. He could feel the tendons working when she squeezed his hand. What wasn't *real* about any of that? And when she turned to face him, her strawberry smile warmed him from his core like a tiny sun; the heat, the feeling of life moved outward along his limbs. Kwazi wondered if she felt the same life force pulsing through his palm, his fingers. If she felt the same sharing of togetherness.

"I love you, Kwazi," Amy said. The breeze snatched a length of blonde hair across her eyes, and she reached up to brush it aside. She turned to face him, the view seemingly forgotten. "I don't know how you did this, but I love you for it."

Her voice was like a scream heard from miles away, a reminder that this was *other*.

"You don't..."

But before he could finish his thought, Amy reached over and caressed his cheek with her thumb, wiping away the Martian grit. Then she leaned in and kissed him with lips he'd only ever imagined kissing before. The substance of this reality was overwhelming, and Kwazi forgot the scream of doubt and surrendered to this singular, perfect moment on Mars he was sharing with the woman he loved.

5

RUBEN QINLAO • POINT BRAVO, THE MOON

Richard Strunk laid Tony on the gray-dust ground inside Point Bravo sounding station. Ruben spun the wheel of the access door's locking mechanism clockwise, sealing out the airless surface, then wiped the thick lunar powder off the atmo gauge. Slowly, like mercury in an old-fashioned thermometer, the digital level began to rise again.

Strunk was watching the gauge too. Through the visor of the enforcer's snug vac-suit, Ruben could see the uncertainty on Strunk's face. Even after the indicator phased to green. Strunk tapped the side of his helmet with an index finger, then engaged comms.

"You first."

Ruben decided the situation presented them both with a perfect teaching moment. Richard Strunk liked to lean on his bulk and baritone voice for authority—even when talking to Ruben, a regent who was every bit his boss Tony Taulke was. Ruben verified his own suit's readings, then double-checked the digital display next to the bulkhead's door. Unsnapping his helmet, he removed it and took a deep, dramatic breath. The air was there, but it tasted like dust feels—coarse and dirty. Ruben kept that off his face, offering Strunk a smile instead.

"All clear."

As he slowly unfastened his helmet, Strunk mumbled something he wasn't sharing over comms. He took a tentative breath and set the helmet aside.

"Lucky the damned seals still work," he said. "Why would they keep air in this place, anyway? Ain't it abandoned?"

Ruben stared out the porthole of Point Bravo's access door. The *Roadrunner* rested, half buried by lunar sand. Between her rough landing and her unreliable engines, he couldn't see how she'd ever be spaceworthy again. In losing the *Roadrunner*, Ruben realized he was losing one more thing that tied him to his sister Ming's memory. The small ship with a big heart had helped him shoot a middle finger at Cassandra's attempted assassination of Tony. It had provided a way around the Company's tracking system controlled by the enemy. Now the wreck outside was just another footnote in SynCorp history.

A history that might soon come to a bloody end.

"Hey, Qinlao, did you hear me? Why's there even air down—"

Ruben turned away from the window. "It's *Regent* Qinlao." Ruben set his sentimentality aside and gave Tony Taulke's bodyguard his full attention. "We should get something straight. In the shuttle I indulged a certain familiarity warranted by circumstance. Now is different. Now you need to understand something: as long as Tony's unconscious, you work for me. Am I clear?"

Strunk stared, nonplussed. Was he about to pull his stunner and shoot, or did the old ways hold? Ruben imagined him considering Cassandra's need for an oversized enforcer and the compensation for providing such services. But when he spoke, Strunk's voice was contrite: "Yes, Regent."

Nodding and hoping his relief wasn't obvious, Ruben advanced across the small space between them. He took a little satisfaction in seeing Strunk, a man twice his size, fall back a few inches, allowing him access to Tony. Ruben didn't care much for the hierarchy demanded by SynCorp's leadership, but in Strunk's case he'd needed to reaffirm who was in charge. Ruben cringed at how elitist his own thoughts sounded in his head.

"To answer your question, when the United Nations built LUNa City, they embraced the 'waste not, want not' philosophy." He knelt to unfasten Tony's helmet. With a *phish*, suit atmo mingled with the musty air. "Since Point Bravo was tied to Point Charlie, where the city was finally founded, they used the tunnel connecting the checkpoints as part of the oxygen recycling system for the new colony. Water beneath the surface is mined for its oxygen, made into the hybrid of breathable air, and piped into the city. Thanks to the tunnel connecting the two sounding points, we have air to breathe."

"Uh-huh," said Strunk. "How do you know all that?"

"My sister Ming was the lead engineer for the United Nations when LUNa City was built," Ruben replied. "We lived here for a while when I was a kid. She taught me all about that stuff."

"Okay." Strunk's tone expressed a compromise between respect for the answer and a layman's desire that he hadn't asked the question in the first place. "How's Tony?"

"Stable," Ruben breathed. Tony Taulke's color was sallow, but his breathing was strong. The antibiotics and pain meds from the *Roadrunner* seemed to be doing their job despite being way past their expiration date.

Strunk stood up, and Ruben felt the size of the man's shadow extend over him. The enforcer moved off to conduct his own overwatch of the lunar surface.

"Your little ship took it hard on the jaw," Strunk said. Ruben heard it as an attempt at casual conversation. So, the big man was trying. Maybe it was Strunk's way of apologizing for having broken decorum earlier.

"Like I said before," Ruben answered with more sadness than he'd expected, "she won't fly again."

"I don't like that we're stuck here without transportation." Ruben could hear the tactician's judgment in Strunk's voice. "I don't like it at all."

"Neither do I," Ruben said, rising. "And there's worse news still."

"Yeah?"

"Our medical implants? They're like homing beacons to SynCorp Central."

Strunk took a minute to process that. "You're saying they can track us."

"Yeah—if Cassandra has access to Gregor Erkennen's databases."

"Through our SCIs?"

"Yeah. Once she matches a frequency with a DNA profile... But it's possible she doesn't have access yet. All we've seen is a lot of talk on Corp-Net. So she's got control of the subspace network. But Gregor's security protocols for the Company's databases are tight. It's possible, maybe even likely, she doesn't have access. Yet."

"That's likely only a matter of time, though." Strunk exhaled. "Moth-erfucker."

"Yeah."

"They find us, they find..." Strunk paused, staring at his helpless boss. "Tony's got one too."

"Everyone does."

Strunk edged closer to the two regents, clenching and unclenching his fists. Like he was preparing for an attack. "We have to turn them off."

"My thinking, too."

"Know how to do that?"

"Nope. I'm not a doctor."

Strunk's eyes moved while he thought. "I could cut them out."

Ruben eyed him.

"I'm serious."

"Oh, I don't doubt it."

The enforcer began casting around, looking for useful tools. He moved toward an old, wooden workbench.

"Yeah, we're not going to do that," Ruben said.

Strunk halted. "We have to—"

"Even if I was comfortable with you cutting into Tony's head, we can't deactivate *his* medical implant. It's helping to keep him alive."

"Oh. Right."

"And we need to supplement his care with something else if we do deactivate it. Fischer gave us the name of that doctor in Darkside: Brackin. I'll go get him and bring him here. You watch over Tony till I get back."

But Strunk was shaking his head. "Too dangerous. You'll be recognized."

Ruben reached down and filled one palm with moondust, spat in it, then worked it with a finger like stirring soup before applying it to his face.

"Facial rec will see past that," Strunk said. Ruben continued roughing up his look. "I should go."

"I'll find a hat or something. You forget, I used to live here. I went to school here as a kid. I know the place."

Faced with logic, Strunk closed his mouth.

"All right. How long will you be gone?"

"Several hours, at least. The lunar gravity will help me quick-travel through the tunnel. Once I come up in Darkside, I'll need to be more discreet."

Strunk reached into his pocket and pulled out his stunner. Ruben wondered if he'd suddenly reconsidered signing up with the SSR. The assassin turned the pistol over and held it out butt-first. "Take it."

"I don't need it," Ruben said. He ignored Strunk's raised eyebrow, a wise guy's amusement at a rich man's arrogance. "It'll only raise questions if it's found. In fact, here," Ruben said, reversing the offer and handing Strunk his own stunner. "Take mine."

Strunk took it.

"I have other, quieter options." Ruben pulled out the katara daggers he'd taken from Elinda Kisaan, the clone-assassin he'd left a prisoner on Mars. "And I know how to defend myself."

Richard Strunk nodded. "I remember the fight on the station." Ruben could see a grudging respect in his eyes.

"Best get going," Strunk said, settling down next to Tony. *He looks like a worried son*, Ruben thought. "The sooner, the better."

"Right."

Ruben stared through the horizontal louvers of the air duct. His journey from Point Bravo to Point Charlie, then up through the air tunnel and into the bowels of mankind's first off-planet colony, had gone as smoothly as he'd hoped it would. Now he stood in an accessway reserved for maintenance personnel that ran parallel to the public thruway, awaiting his chance to slip in among the foot traffic of Darkside's population.

Boy, had LUNa City changed.

Make that Darkside, he reminded himself. The "pride of the UN," as the colony had once been called, had long ago ceased being that.

During his twelve-kilometer hike to Point Charlie, Ruben had wondered how he'd feel once he entered the city proper. Somehow, he'd never visited the Moon since briefly living here with his sister Ming. Their stay had ended rather abruptly, but Ruben was still able to unearth fond memories when he looked hard enough inside himself to find them. Of school friends and schoolwork and the life of a teenager, each day both excruciatingly boring and more fiercely significant than the last. Of being incarcerated briefly for breaking a bully's nose. Of a red-haired girl named Angel, and his first kiss in a 3D sim-parlor.

The people passing in the corridor beyond the louvers, murmuring their daily lives to one another, seemed both warmly familiar and utterly foreign at the same time.

The United Nations had founded LUNa City as the indelible footprint of humanity's first giant leap off the Big Blue Marble. When the Syndicate Corporation expanded into the solar system, the Moon and the newly renamed Darkside's End were the diving board the Company leapt from to colonize the outer system. Darkside's End: a bright city on a dull, gray hill that showed what the collective brain of Man could conquer with a little innovation spiced with muscle, grit, and determination. It had been a privilege to live here then, a goal parents touted to children—if they worked hard enough in school and dreamed beyond the limits of an Earth dying from a world climate stretched to the breaking point.

It had been a city of white and silver then, a lunar Gondor. Now there was grime everywhere. The Moon had encroached on human ambition one grain at a time until it stained the clothes and faces of the old city's inhabitants like a permanent tattoo. Over the years, its name had simplified to its current, less aspirational Darkside, the backwater dumping ground for the Company's poorest and least productive inhabitants.

The lack of noise in the corridor chased away Ruben's daydreaming. His patience had paid off. The foot traffic beyond had finally tapered off, making the corridor momentarily deserted. He slipped the grate from its braces and crawled through, then carefully replaced the covering. More feet were headed his way. As shadows approached from around the corner, he struck off at a leisurely pace, unsure really where he was heading. Whenever he spotted an observation camera, Ruben coolly averted his face. Strunk had been right to warn him about the face-rec tech.

The hallway opened up into a central foyer, where other thruways led to other parts of Darkside. People passed by, none sparing a look his way. Instead, they worried over finding their next steps, as if walking a tightrope over a breezy canyon. The crisp, snap-inspection clean of UN uniforms had given way to faded, dirty jumpsuits. Ruben remembered a brightness everywhere from when he was a boy, from the walkways to the residents' smiles. Everyone had been glad to be here, had appreciated the privilege of being away from Earth and all its problems.

Despite the dour people around him, Ruben realized his ad-hoc makeup job of Point Bravo dirt wasn't enough. Strunk had been right about that, too. He needed to find a cheap vendor to buy clothes that would allow him to better blend in.

"Hey, buddy, can you help me?" he asked, keeping his voice low.

A passerby shook out of his detachment, wariness crossing his face. He eyed Ruben. The wrinkles on his forehead reached up to a receding hairline. "What do you want?"

"Directions. I'm new here." Ruben tried to avoid looking directly at the man. It was unlikely an average Darksider would recognize him, but not impossible. Especially with his face transmitted all over CorpNet by Cassandra with the promise of a reward bigger than any ten of these people would earn from the Company in a dozen lifetimes.

"Who'd you piss off?" asked the little gray man in gray coveralls.

Ruben smiled, trying to make it unremarkable and genuine at the same time. The man's curly-Q salt-and-pepper locks reminded him of Gregor Erkennen's. "You don't want to know."

"You're right."

"I'm looking for a place called the Open Market. I hear it's beyond the barrio."

The man blew out a breath. "Look around you, bub. All of Darkside is a barrio."

"No argument here."

The gray man nodded, apparently judging Ruben a soul in common. "The Market's past the Fleshway. All manner of diversion there, if you get my meaning. Cheap rooms, too—rented by the hour." His right eye twinkled beneath a bushy eyebrow.

"The..."

"Fleshway. Truth in advertising, that. You'll see."

"Okay." Ruben gestured at the spokes of hallways exiting the foyer. "Can you get me started?"

Indicating a corridor to Ruben's 10 o'clock, the gray man took his leave. "Follow the signs for the old Entertainment District," he said over his shoulder. "That's the Fleshway now."

Ruben watched him go.

The Fleshway, huh?

He set off in the direction the man's bony finger had pointed.

Yes, LUNa City certainly had changed.

6

REBEKAH FRANKLIN • MASADA STATION, ORBITING TITAN

Bekah strode the nearly empty corridor of Masada Station, forcing her hands to stop making fists. If Daniel Tripp told her one more time how important it was that the main firewall protocols be robust enough to be self-adapting, Bekah swore she'd brain him. The man was a genius at programming bridges to endow applications with near sentience.

His people skills, though? They sucked.

But Gregor had insisted Daniel join Bekah's Masada team, citing that very skill set. Should Cassandra turn her worms against Masada, Daniel's specialization could mean the difference between success and failure in protecting SynCorp's future. Personalities couldn't rule choices now.

Most of those who'd needed to evacuate had already done so. Rahim Zafar and his decoy team had been the first down the well. They were already rewriting the data on the backup mainframe, creating the millions of Holy Grails for Cassandra's worms to find, all of them useless versions of actual tech specs held safe in Masada's main databanks. Guided by Carrin Bohannon's expertise, Bekah's team had reinforced the station's cybersecurity. And, Bekah had to admit, Daniel Tripp's practical quick-fixes had come in rather handy in that time-poor, high-stakes process. If only he could be less of a dick while being so brilliant.

Bekah set aside her frustrations as she approached her grandfather's room. She heard voices holding pleasant conversation. One was her Opa Simon's, speaking in his quiet, sunny way. The other sounded familiar and slightly out of place at the same time, like a teacher you've only heard lecture in a classroom might sound if he were telling an off-color joke. She found Gregor Erkennen sitting casually on the edge of her grandfather's bed, holding Opa Simon's hand. When she knocked lightly, both men looked toward the door.

"Hello, Bekkalleh," Simon Franklin said, using his Yiddish nickname for her. Hearing him call her that recalled memories of being a little girl, her mouth watering at the rich smells of food cooking for Hanukkah. He sat up a little taller against the pile of pillows propping him up. "We were just speaking of you."

The Regent of Titan rose to his feet. "Rebekah," he said in formal greeting. "I was just taking some time to visit with your opa before I leave."

Bekah nodded with a light, self-conscious smile. Gregor and her Opa Simon had enjoyed a long and happy association, ever since Gregor had been a young boy in his father Viktor's workshop. Gregor credited Simon Franklin with teaching him to think three-dimensionally about the invention process. Once he'd established his primary R&D labs on the asteroid orbiting Titan, Viktor Erkennen had employed a whole stable of non-engineers—psychologists, sociologists, cultural archaeologists, even philosophers like her grandfather. It was his way, Viktor said, of helping mankind avoid its past mistakes of creating technology without a conscience or an eye toward consequence. No more Manhattan Projects here, no more Lazarus Protocols. Not if he could help it, Viktor had pledged.

"Of course," Bekah said, suddenly embarrassed at interrupting their private moment.

"The regent was just telling me what a wonderful job you're doing," her opa said. He always used Gregor's formal title when Erkennen was in the room.

"Indeed," Gregor added gently. He returned his attention to the ailing man. "I'd like to speak with your granddaughter a moment. I promise not to keep her too long from you."

"Take your time," Simon said, smacking his lips. "I'm not going anywhere."

Gregor shared a look of appreciation with Bekah, one that respected the courage of the dying man in the medical bed. Patting Simon's hand, he rose.

"I will be leaving soon," he said, pulling Bekah aside. "I've asked the doctors again, but they still insist he can't be moved."

"I know," she said. The words caught in her throat. She'd been so focused on fortifying the Masada mainframe, on dealing with Daniel and the rest of her team, that she'd had to wall off her feelings about what was coming. Her grandfather's illness had been whittling away at him for so long, she'd experienced a kind of low-grade sadness for months now. A combination of pre-mourning grief, existential fear that the last member of her family was passing from her life, and the certainty that she would let her Opa Simon down in the one area that meant the most to him.

"He wouldn't want to be apart from you anyway," Gregor said. "Family is very important to him."

I know.

"It's important to me too," Gregor continued. "Your grandfather taught me to think beyond the invention itself. I've never forgotten the lesson."

Bekah nodded.

"It's why I chose you to lead the team that's staying here."

It took a moment to register what he'd said, to connect the dots Bekah hadn't even known where there until she'd connected them.

"I thought—"

"Don't get me wrong, Bekah," Gregor said, her nickname sounding warm and natural, all the more intimate for its rarity coming from him. "You are gifted. You might not know this, but Rahim is your biggest fan." That surprised her. If asked how Rahim Zafar would describe her after observing her work as a member of his coding team, Bekah would have picked a safe adjective like *competent*. "But you have something else. You have your grandfather in you. It's what we need here now, leading the team that's protecting the mainframe. Talent and conscience, yes?"

She nodded from reflex. "I think Daniel Tripp might disagree about who should be leading this team."

Gregor grumbled. "Daniel is, perhaps, the most talented heuristics specialist I've ever seen." His face became thoughtful. "Sometimes his ego gets in the way. You'll just have to be patient with him."

I'm working on it.

"Here's what I need to tell you, and this is for your ears only. Understand? No discussion with anyone. Compartmentalize to preserve secrecy, yes?"

"Okay."

I've gotten good at that lately.

Gregor reached into his pocket and withdrew what looked like an oversized platinum key. It had a long, corrugated body, or bit, and a broad head with a hole through it. A thin, golden chain was looped through the hole. He held it up with the clear intent of draping it around her neck.

"This is a failsafe," Gregor said as she leaned forward. "I call it the Hammer."

"The Hammer?" Bekah stared down at it lying against her chest. It seemed heavier than its small size should warrant.

"It was Adriana Rabh's idea, actually. She's got Vikings on the brain."

"I still don't—"

"Viking warriors wore a hammer around their necks as a holy symbol. They touched it before battle, asking Thor to protect them," Gregor explained. "Now that I think of it, it's a perfect name for the thing."

"Okay. What does it do?"

"It has two functions. First, it's an engrammatic representation of the mainframe. A quantum-level memory map of everything the Erkennen Faction has ever invented and licensed to SynCorp. Only someone with specific data keys can unlock it."

"I don't understand," Bekah said.

Gregor thought for a moment. "You know the dehydrated food we eat? All you have to do is add water to recreate the original foodstuff."

"Yes."

"The Hammer is the dehydrated food. The data keys are the water."

"Okay. Where are the data keys?"

Gregor smiled. "Compartmentalization, remember?"

"That's dangerous, Gregor. If this is the only record of Erkennen inventions," she said, touching the Hammer, "then everything could be lost..."

His eyebrows arched. "That's why it's a failsafe. Not my first choice for preserving our faction's technological history."

"Okay," she said.

"Also, should Cassandra see through us on Titan, you must use the Hammer to keep Masada's data from falling into her hands, Bekah." Gregor's face became solemn, almost soulful. "Insert it into the quantum data port of the mainframe. In micro-seconds, it will update the content in the engrams. Turn it clockwise, and everything in the mainframe itself gets wiped."

"Wiped?" she said. Her skin prickled with goosebumps. "But then we'd be reliant entirely on—"

"—the Hammer to reconstitute the data, yes. At least until we plugged it into another mainframe and, er, *rehydrated* the data again." To the look on her face, Gregor said, "It's better than letting the knowledge fall into the enemy's hands. Think about it, Bekah—the medical implant records alone. We have the serial number of every SCI tied to the individual DNA profiles of billions of humans across the system. If Cassandra gained that information, she could track down everyone on her enemies list. Potentially, she could even take control of the implants, use them to infect a person with illness. We can't let that happen."

"But why would she do that?" Bekah asked, horrified at the thought.

"She beheaded her own mother and stuck Elise Kisaan's head on a pike. Not the most stable individual, I think. And this Dreamscape algorithm addicting all those mindless hackheads... They'd rather die than give up their fantasies. Is that merely coincidental with everything else going on?" Gregor's eyes were suspicious but lacked answers. "Who knows what she's capable of, really?"

The weight of her new responsibility settled onto Bekah's shoulders.

"I understand," she whispered. "I won't let you down, Gregor."

"Hey, you two!" Simon Franklin called from his sickbed, his voice rough. "Moloch Ha Movitz says hurry up, he hasn't got all day to wait on me waiting on you two."

"Tell Death he can wait anyway," Gregor replied. His fingers touched Bekah's elbow, and together they walked to Simon's bedside. "But we were just finishing our discussion. Bekah's all yours." Leaning in to her ear, he said, "I'll remain here until Fischer arrives."

"Okay," she said.

"If I didn't know you better," Simon said, "I'd think you were trying to date my granddaughter."

"Opa!"

"She's too smart for me," Gregor replied, like they'd rehearsed a routine.

Simon coughed long and labored. It sounded wet and dry at the same time. "That is true," he said when the fit had passed.

Bekah stood there feeling gossiped about, complimented, and mocked in the same instant. Gregor departed, leaving the two of them alone.

"That wasn't funny, Opa," she said.

"Life is short, Bekkalleh. No sense making it any less fun."

She sighed a long-suffering sound and sat down in the groove Gregor had left in the bed. "That's never an issue while you're around," she said. She realized too late what she'd said without meaning to say it, a blush forming on her cheeks.

"And it shouldn't be when I'm not, either," he said graciously. Then his tone turned serious. "You've been studying? What to do, I mean."

She gave a half nod. "I have. I've memorized the *Kaddish* you wish spoken. I've got a checklist for the ritual to prepare the ... your ... body." Bekah hated the way her voice sounded, like a programmer reciting the deployment plan for a new application. "But the *kevura*—I don't know how I'm going to do that." Ritual burial was perhaps the most sacred rite among the Jewish people. How was she to accomplish that on a space station?

Simon's face became attentive. "Burial soon after death is a *mitzvah*, a commandment of God," he said. She could feel her face contorting, her lifelong failure to be a studious Jew welling up inside her like bile.

"I'm having fun again, Bekkalleh," he said, squeezing her hand. "I apologize. No, I take that back—I don't apologize. I'm a dying old man. I get to do what I want."

"Oh, Opa, I wish..." She wasn't sure what she'd meant to say, then was absolutely sure what she needed to say. "I wish I'd been better at all this. For you."

The hard humor left his eyes. "Better at what? Being a Jew?" He laughed, and the wet-dry sound returned. "You're feeling guilty at not being a better Jew? You're better at being a Jew than you think!"

Bekah managed light laughter. She considered how much she'd miss this irascible old man, the last member of her family left to her. Her heart hurt.

"I still don't know what to do about *kevura*," she said, trying to focus.

"See, this is what you'd know if you practiced our religion and not merely studied it for a one-time performance." The old, reactive shame flooded Bekah's limbs, a conditioned response to the old disappointment in her grandfather's voice. "So much of the rituals, the laws, the *thou shalts*—I call them the common-sense commandments for a reason, Bekkalleh."

"I don't understand, Opa."

"I know you don't," Simon said. More disappointment from him. More self-conscious bitterness from her. But then his tone softened. "So much of our teachings derive from who we are, Bekkalleh. A transient people— nomads always moving, always *forced* to move. Don't eat that dead animal on the side of the road—it could be poisoned! Eat only the food you know is clean. Bury your dead quickly! Corpses spread disease."

Nodding, Bekah said, "You've told me this before, Opa."

"Yes, but apparently you weren't *listening*," he answered. Then his voice calmed again. "What I'm telling you is—the *mitzvahs* are important because they unite our people with culture and ritual when we don't have land and home and country to do that. And they keep us alive. They're a stranger-in-a-strange-land's guide to survival, do you see?"

"Yes, Opa," she said. "But I still don't know how to accomplish the *kevura*—"

Simon tried to raise himself in the bed, and Bekah helped him sit up straighter. She held him through the coughing fit that followed.

"You're still not listening," he said from a tattered throat. "*Listen*, Bekkalleh. *Kevura* is important, but not for the act itself. My body—put me in the damned freezer! Shove me out into space! Just don't leave me lying around for disease to take root in, or *you* could die too. Well, maybe not here on the station, maybe disease isn't such a worry in space—but do you understand my point? *You* must survive, Bekkalleh. *You*, the next generation. *That's* being a good Jew."

Her face twisted. Put him in a freezer? Shove him into space? Her grandfather never ceased to establish a new line of decorum—usually a step and a half past the old line.

"You really just have to remember one thing," Simon said, reaching out to take her hand. "We're put here to do good, Bekkalleh. That's really what loving God boils down to. Anything else is just Man placing himself at the center of the universe."

Bekah nodded.

"I'll do my best to be a good Jew for you, Opa," she said because she had to say something. Then, with a wicked look because she felt wicked in that moment: "Just this once."

"Well, Bekkalleh," Simon said, settling back into his stack of pillows, a smile of contentment creasing his lined face, "that, as they say, is a good start."

7

RUBEN QINLAO • DARKSIDE, THE MOON

Ruben smelled the Fleshway before he stepped onto it.

The double-wide corridor reminded him of an image of an Earth river teeming with spawning fish—frenzied and frantic to keep moving. Body odor rode atop the smell of reconstituted food stuffs simmering in the open-air bazaar lining both sides of the corridor, which was dotted by dark, grayish puddles. Lit up with every man-made light source, from solar-celled to neon, signs flashed easy access to cheap diversions. Exotic names like Persephone's Underworld and the Arms of Artemis. Ruben got why they called it the Fleshway, and it wasn't just that sex peddlers dominated the landscape of businesses. The constant press of moving, mingling bodies made any other name simply inaccurate.

A man stumbled nearby, cursing, then turned and kicked what had tripped him: a second man sleeping in the muck along the wall. Something yellow and dried stained the ground beside the unconscious man's head.

Ruben tried breathing through his mouth, but that didn't help. It only gave him the impression he was tasting the reek. Knowing he'd simply have to get used to it, he clamped his teeth shut and stepped onto the boulevard, avoiding elbows where he could.

"Watch it, buddy," a man nearly Strunk's size warned.

"Sorry," Ruben replied.

The lights flashed, bright and quick. Persistent, over-the-top advertising? No, that was there too, but this was different. The wall lights on both sides of the Fleshway went dark in a rolling wave. A low murmur of irritation came from the crowd.

Emergency lighting engaged, casting the entire corridor in dull crimson.

Appropriate for a red-light district, Ruben mused.

Another man bumped into him hard and nearly lost his balance. Ruben reached out to steady him.

"Thanks." The man was thin, unshaven. He might have been in his mid-twenties but looked twice that age. "Fucking brownouts. If Cassandra can fix the power grid, I'll vote for her for fucking queen."

The main lights reengaged. The crowd shared a communal, unsatisfied sound of complaint.

"These brownouts, they happen a lot?" Ruben asked.

"Yeah, all the time." The man looked at him funny. Looked at him closely. "You're not from here, huh? But you look familiar. We met before?"

Ruben's eyes darted away. "Don't think so."

"Yeah, but you look familiar."

"In this place, how can you tell?" Ruben said, attempting a joke. "Everyone looks the same."

Unamused, the man grunted. "Yeah. Fucking SynCorp. Can't even keep the power grid stable. Wait till the gravity falls to lunar norm for a few seconds and you lose your lunch, newbie. *That* takes some getting used to. If that Cassandra bitch can fix all that, she's got my vote."

Ruben nodded, feigning a keen interest in a distant shop. "Best place to find a friend here?" he asked to change the subject.

"Arms of Artemis," the man answered. "Minerva Sett's place. Warm, wet, and modestly priced. I'm not talking about the drinks!" Cackling, he walked away. Then, over his shoulder: "Price is the only thing modest in that place!"

The man was soon lost in the crowd. Had the guy recognized him? The possibility that he had was enough. Ruben spied a narrow alley next to a restaurant advertising dishes made not from reconstituted protein paste, but with real chickens imported from Earth.

Above the restaurant and the other shops were tenements where Fleshway business owners likely lived. Close to their wares, a natural deterrent to thieves. And practical, if what the man said about Darkside's gravity generators was true. No one likes a commute where the artificial gravity randomly fails. Clothes hung on a line between the two narrow alley walls, drying in the fetid air.

The alley was barely lit and appeared deserted. The lemmings on the Fleshway behind him were minding their own business.

A good way to stay alive.

Ruben slid into the space between the buildings. There was a brown, hooded cloak hanging on the line. He pulled it down and put it on. It smelled of must and moondust. Covering his head with the hood, Ruben stepped quickly to the mouth of the alley again, then reentered the river of people navigating the boulevard.

Fischer's directions to Brackin's back-alley practice had been both specific and murky. Beyond the Fleshway, Ruben found what Fischer had called the barrio—a multistoried, open rotunda of shacks and rundown tenement housing with causeways arcing across a great open area piled with refuse. Ruben recognized the open area as Challenger Park. In his teen years, the green space had been bright with sunlight reflected through the solar collectors built into LUNa City's massive dome. He remembered residents laughing there, pretending they were still on Earth, surrounded by its green grass and leafy trees but without worry for the weather. The park had once been a place for picnics, and Ruben had relaxed there with friends. Looking at it closely now, he could see movement beneath the refuse. Rats, maybe. The residents in the surrounding shanty levels seemed to discard trash by tossing it down into the park. Like people centuries before had once emptied chamber pots into the public street below their windows.

Challenger Park, where he'd shared picnics with friends, now stank of rotten food and worse.

Worse than the Fleshway, if that's even possible.

Darkside had been known as "a SynCorp shithole" for years. The place where those who were too sick or unwilling to work called home, collected and housed there by the Company. Before today, Darkside's reputation as a literal dumping ground for SynCorp's castoffs had been abstract, a theoretical construct in Ruben's mind. The old-young man's endorsement of Cassandra was making more sense. Ruben wondered how many other sympathetic souls her Soldiers would find among Darkside's dilapidated tenements and shanty towns.

He ascended one of the arching causeways and strode over Challenger Park below, fighting the temptation to look down. Ruben exited the barrio along a corridor much narrower than the Fleshway, and it led him to a slightly more upscale neighborhood of homes and businesses.

A woman leaned against a narrow storefront with a sign reading *Eros Erotics* overhead. Smoke rose from a cigarette perched between two fingers. She was dressed in what passed for provocative in Darkside—a man's shirt tied up to draw attention to her breasts and fishnet stockings full of holes.

Noticing Ruben, she stood up and dropped the cig. "You look the mysterious one," she said, licking her lips and grinding out the butt with her stiletto. "I like mystery. Name's Ionia."

There was no one else in the corridor. Definitely a quieter quarter of Darkside. Brackin's practice should be around here somewhere, if Fischer's directions were right.

"I hope you can help me, Ionia," Ruben said from beneath his hood.

She reached out and touched his shoulder. "I hope I can too."

"I'm looking for a doctor."

She removed her hand. "Are you, now?"

"Name of Brackin," Ruben said.

The woman clasped her palms together as if trying to restrain her hands. It was an odd pose for a member of the oldest profession. In different clothing, she might have been a nun.

"He's about half a block north," Ionia said, jerking her head. "He's got one of those swirly snake staff thingees next to his door."

"A caduceus?"

"Yeah, the med symbol that sounds like a sneeze." She leaned back against the shop wall again, reached inside an invisible pocket, and withdrew another cigarette. "Only it's upside down outside his door."

"Okay, thanks," Ruben said, striking off in that direction.

"Hey, Robin Hood," she said, her free hand extended. "Information ain't free. Nothing here is. How about some consideration for a working girl?"

Ruben paused. Best to pay her and avoid a scene.

"Of course. I should've thought." He brought his wrist up, and she did the same, ready to transfer SynCorp dollars between their two syncers.

"Hey, what is this?" she asked. "What are you trying to pull?"

He stared at his bare wrist. His syncer was gone.

Had he lost it in the crash? If so, he'd also lost access to the millions of dollars in the Qinlao cash reserves. Or maybe it had been the big guy on the Fleshway, the one with the attitude. Or the old-young man he'd asked for directions. Maybe one of them had stolen it. Or any one of a hundred others he'd brushed against to get here.

"Oh boy," Ionia said. "I've seen that look before. You're new here, huh?"

"Everyone keeps saying that."

"Well, honey, you just go on down to the doc's, then. But don't expect much. He don't work for free neither."

She turned away, her eyes searching for another john, and stowed the cig again without lighting it.

Ruben restrained his step as he walked to Brackin's door. The double-snaked caduceus, the symbol of medicine, hung next to the door—upside down, as Ionia had said. Ruben knew nothing about Brackin, but if he were practicing among the beggars and thieves of Darkside, he wasn't sure he could trust the man. That Brackin came on Fischer's recommendation did little to improve that opinion. But, Ruben realized, he was a beggar himself. Not many choices here. He knocked.

A small window slid open at eye level.

"Yeah?"

Ruben cleared his throat. "I'm looking for Isaac Brackin."

"Okay," the man said. "He ain't here. I'm his assistant. No new business today." The small panel began to close.

"I can make it worth his while."

The man made a sound in the back of his throat. "Everyone says that. No one pays that."

"Hey, Doc!" came a voice from inside. "*I* already paid that—so switch it on!"

The man in the tiny window grimaced.

"Dr. Brackin, I presume," Ruben said. "Fischer sent me."

Brackin regarded him a moment. "Should've led with that." Multiple locking mechanisms disengaged from the other side of the door. Brackin swung it open. "Hurry up, get inside!"

Ruben entered the small room. It was both a receiving area and a living room. A screen hung on the wall with a constant feed from *The Real Story.*

"Doc..."

"Yeah, yeah," Brackin said, returning to his first customer. He passed a device next to the man's forehead. "Better? That should hold you another week."

A smile spread across the young man's face. "Oh, yeah. Yeah, yeah, yeah..."

"Hold it, don't go into fantasyland in my place. I don't want to have to drag you out of here and dump you in the alley."

"Okay, yeah. Okay." The man shuffled out on his own. Brackin secured the door behind him.

"You're a Dreamscape dealer," Ruben said.

"Who isn't? Cash is cash."

"I can see why you hang that symbol upside down outside your door."

"If you're from the Morality Police, you should have a badge or something," Brackin said. "Now, what do you want?"

"I need you to come with me," Ruben said. "I have a friend who's hurt. Requires a doctor."

Brackin scoffed. "Bring him here. I'm not going anywhere."

A katara knife appeared in Ruben's hand. He turned it to catch the light.

"Now, hold on—" Brackin began, focused on the knife. Then his eyes flattened, and Ruben was sure he was focusing on his sceye's display.

"Don't call for help, or you're dead for sure," Ruben said, advancing. "The alternative is more wealth than you've ever seen before."

Brackin's gaze refocused on Ruben. "What do you want?" he asked again.

"I told you. I need you to come with me."

"I'm no idiot," Brackin said. "I go with you, I'm as good as dead."

"Fischer said to remind you of Jack Hade. Said that memory should overcome any reluctance you might have to help. Said to tell you this would clear that score."

Brackin swallowed. Hard. "Come where?"

"Pack your medical bag."

The return journey to Point Bravo was close, intimate. A compromise in two men quick-stepping among crowds and walking slowly in sparser areas to avoid unwanted attention and security cameras. Brackin wasn't in a talking mood. It took a couple of long, silent hours to reach the abandoned sounding station.

They came up from the mouth of the tunnel and entered the small room where Tony Taulke lay. His color had become more ashen since Ruben had left. Beads of sweat dimpled his forehead. His mouth hung open, slack in sleep.

"Where the hell are we?" Brackin asked.

Waking from a doze, Strunk rose to his feet. "This the doc?"

"Yeah." Ruben removed the heavy cloak and hood. Though the tunnels weren't on Darkside's gravity grid and only exerted the pull of lunar nominal, his feet were killing him.

Brackin stared at Strunk, who'd stood up. He seemed fascinated by the barrel-chested assassin, like he'd discovered a new species. Or maybe a missing link.

"I'm not the patient," Strunk said.

"Okay."

Ruben tugged on Brackin's elbow, pointing him to Tony's unconscious form.

The doctor tossed his bag on the ground beside Tony. "His color looks bad. That's a nasty knife wound." He looked at Ruben. "You do that?"

"Not me."

Brackin stared more closely at his patient, trying to see past the cloudy skin and grizzled face. "He looks familiar. Where do I know him from?" His gaze found Ruben again. "You look familiar too, without the hood."

"Let's play catchup later," Strunk said, hovering over Brackin.

But the doctor's eyes had gone wide. He jerked his gaze back to Ruben, then back down.

"That's Tony Taulke! Holy shit!" Brackin started to rise, but the weight of Strunk's hand kept him kneeling. "You want *me* to help Tony Taulke?"

Ruben put a hand on Strunk's arm.

"And you're Qinlao! You're both all over the newsfeeds. You're wanted men!"

"It's nice to be wanted," Strunk snarked.

Ruben ignored him. "Treat Tony, and you'll go free. With more cash than you've ever seen."

Brackin was shaking his head. "Even if there weren't bounties on your head, I wouldn't treat this sonofabitch." Strunk hissed, shaking off Ruben's restraint. Brackin continued, "SynCorp's who took my license away, stuck me in the bowels of Darkside to—"

A stunner touched Brackin's temple.

"It's time to forgive and forget," Strunk said.

Ruben gave Brackin a moment to think through his options. Then, "We can all get what we want here. But first things first."

The doctor seemed paralyzed. "If they know I'm helping you, they'll kill me."

"They aren't here," Strunk said. "But we are. Fix Tony or die trying. Or refuse and just die."

Brackin opened his bag.

8

KWAZI JABARI • VALHALLA STATION, CALLISTO

Kwazi walked into the training arena and was surprised to find it filled with chairs. After Carl Braxton summoned him, Kwazi had half-expected an unscheduled VG simulation, another attempt to literally keep him on his toes. Or, at least, off his ass. Their last session without the pads hadn't gone well, and Kwazi had the still-forming bruises to prove it.

But this was no variable gravity exercise. Standing inside the doorway, Kwazi took it all in. The long gauntlet he'd run so many times had been converted to a long, narrow briefing room. That made a certain kind of sense. The training arena was the biggest underground space beneath Braxton's bar, so if you wanted to conduct a major briefing to the troops, this was the space for it. A mobile display stood at the far end, its screen frozen with the mirrored-serpent image of the Soldiers of the Solar Revolution. Twenty or so members of the SSR milled about in quiet conversations. Kwazi recognized some of them, but the majority were strangers to him. Braxton stood near the front, talking with a man and woman. The tech who'd managed Kwazi's simulations, what's-his-name, was laughing about something with another Soldier.

"Hey, Kwazi."

He turned to find the familiar face of a man he hadn't seen since escaping the *Pax Corporatum*.

"Abrams?"

"Yeah, man. You remember Faelin, right?"

Kwazi shook the woman's hand automatically. "Yeah, of course," he said. Abrams had introduced him to Dreamscape. He'd made it possible to reconnect with Amy, to resurrect her, to have a relationship with her at all. He owed Abrams. The woman, Faelin, had been there too that night, deep in the bowels of Tony Taulke's flagship, high on Dreamscape.

"Good to finally meet you," she said. It was strange, Kwazi thought, meeting her for the first time after they'd almost died together, lost in their separate Dreamscape fantasies. "This is going to be an amazing day."

Kwazi nodded, unsure why he was doing it.

"Ladies and gentlemen, take your seats, please," Braxton said with the deep authority of his stage voice. "We need to get started."

Abrams clapped Kwazi on the shoulder. "You're a hero, man. Remember that."

Jesus, why do people keep saying that?

Braxton caught his eye and motioned him to the stage end of the converted arena. Kwazi made his way through the crowd, sliding between densely placed chairs. A few of the people he didn't know placed a hand on his shoulder as he passed. Some offered kind words, others *oo-rah* sounds of pent-up excitement. All of it began to feel like a surprise party would to someone who hates surprise parties.

Kwazi shook Braxton's hand when it was offered, and it felt odd and put on for public display. Braxton motioned toward one of the chairs facing the long room. Kwazi sat, taking in the now-seated crowd of enthusiastic Soldiers he'd just passed through. All of them were looking at him.

"This day has been long in coming," Braxton said. "The end of the Syndicate Corporation is at hand."

Spontaneous applause.

"Today we implement Operation Trojan Horse. A brilliant plan, designed by Cassandra herself. Today we wrest the symbol of Company authority away from the oppressor. It will serve as our platform—both literally and symbolically—as we complete our mission to liberate the solar system from the tyranny of SynCorp's control."

Calls of approbation. Abrams and a few others cupped hands around their mouths and whooped.

Braxton waited patiently for the cheerleading to pass. Kwazi tried to get ahead of him in the front-channel of his brain. This was what his training had been leading up to, obviously. This was the big day. But he had no idea what Operation Trojan Horse was.

"Let's get to the details," Braxton said. The screen above and behind him came to life. "Three fire teams of six Soldiers each will board the *Pax Corporatum*, secure engineering and the bridge, and take the ship."

They were going to take Tony Taulke's flagship? With just eighteen Soldiers?

How could eighteen Soldiers, no matter how well trained, take an entire starship of elite Taulke Faction loyalists?

"Once the ship is secured," Braxton continued, "we'll embark the rest of our troops and phase two will begin. The taking of Valhalla Station and Adriana Rabh's head!"

Laughter and shouts erupted from the room. It took longer than before to die down.

"How?" Kwazi asked before realizing he'd even spoken. Braxton turned to him. The whole room was looking at him again, in fact. Kwazi cleared his throat. "How?" he asked a bit louder.

"The plan couldn't be simpler," Braxton said, smiling at him. It was the friendliest expression Kwazi had ever seen on the harsh taskmaster's face. Red flags went up in the back-channel of his mind. "You're a wanted man, Mr. Jabari. And we're turning you in."

What? What had he just said?

Braxton winked. "Don't look so concerned." A few Soldiers laughed. More and more, this was feeling like an unwanted surprise party.

"Sir, you should tell him."

Abrams's voice.

"I will, but..." Braxton stepped away, and the screen came alive. Gasps went up from the briefing room. After turning to the screen, Kwazi stopped breathing.

"Assembled Soldiers, welcome to this day of destiny."

The woman behind the coup of Tony Taulke's reign sat in a chair on

Earth: Cassandra herself, the queen of the revolution. The background of blue sky shone in the clear, crystal windows behind her, though that could have been skinning tech adorning the walls. But Cassandra had taken her mother's office—and her mother's head—when she'd risen to power, and that office had been in the penthouse of the former UN building in old New York. Her mother's head rested in front of Cassandra's elevated chair, staked on a pole. Its mouth hung slack in death. The silver tresses of Elise Kisaan's once-shining hair dangled around the stake, stringy with the mottled brown of dried blood. Gravity and decay had dragged the skin downward on the skull.

"Today! Today, we take away the power of those still *in* power," Cassandra said with the cadence of a preacher in the pulpit. The camera eye zoomed in. Her golden-almond eyes seemed to glow from within. "Kwazi, our story is your story. *You* are the symbol of our revolution. And your story is going out to the masses right now."

Her image faded, replaced by Kwazi's face.

"I'm Kwazi Jabari, and this is why I fight."

The Kwazi on Callisto stared at the Kwazi onscreen. It was *his* face he was seeing. It was *his* mouth working. The voice even sounded like him. He heard it speak words he'd never spoken.

"I worked hard on Mars," the image said. "And the Syndicate Corporation took everything from me..."

The video played for two-and-a-half minutes. The Soldiers in the room sat, quietly and respectfully, watching Kwazi tell a story he'd never uttered before. His trials on Earth, losing his parents to the Drought Wars in Africa. His dedication to hard work in the mines of Mars for SynCorp's Qinlao Faction. The murder of Amy and Aika and Beren to create the fiction of the Hero of Mars.

When it was over, Kwazi sat in shock, unable to speak. When he'd been Helena Telemachus's spokesman, he'd felt trapped by destiny—a mouse in a maze directed right and left and forward and back. He'd been a symbol for her, too.

The walls of the maze felt near again.

The Soldiers sat unmoving in their chairs as Cassandra's face reappeared. A few of them wept.

"Today! Today, we take the starship that sailed the system as a symbol of Tony Taulke's power. Today, it becomes a herald of freedom!"

The briefing room erupted with enthusiasm. Every person in the room stood. Some wiped their eyes. Others began a chant, quickly adopted by the others.

"Free-dom! Free-dom! Free-dom!"

The Soldiers exchanged handshakes and embraced. The positive energy washed over Kwazi, and the walls seemed to recede a bit. If this is what it took ... if the lie he'd just witnessed onscreen led to a greater truth, the truth of retribution for how the Company had murdered Amy and his friends, well ... so be it. And was the story he'd just seen really a lie? It was a kind of truth, wasn't it? The truth of his experience. Even if he hadn't said the words himself, he'd lived the life they'd spoken of. Their truth was his truth. They could have been his words.

Braxton moved to stand in front of him, once again offering his hand. Kwazi stood slowly and took it. The man who'd once threatened to kill him with his bare fists pulled Kwazi into a bear hug.

"First Taulke's flagship, then we take out the old lady," Braxton whispered into his ear. "Now you're *our* hero."

Two shuttles climbed high over Callisto headed for the *Pax Corporatum*. One contained Kwazi, Braxton, and four Soldiers dressed in Rabh Regency uniforms. The other carried the remaining SSR troops from the briefing, disguised as Taulke supporters in black uniforms with the Taulke Faction logo prominent on their chests.

When Helena Telemachus had been informed that Rabh troops had found and taken Kwazi Jabari alive, she'd demanded immediate extradition to the starship. Adriana Rabh complied, seemingly happy to be rid of him. Kwazi had monitored their exchange via comm lines tapped by the SSR. Seeing the hungry smile on Helena's face had been particularly satisfying. He couldn't wait to wipe it off.

"I still don't see how we can take an entire starship with only eighteen guys," he said.

Braxton nodded, happy to explain. "For one thing, they won't see it coming. But we're not just eighteen guys."

The shuttle bumped them in their seats, and Kwazi clutched the arm rests until the turbulence passed.

"You've kept me in the dark on the details," he said. "I get that. After what you saw on CorpNet, when I was Tony Taulke's spokesman. But now we're entering the lion's den. Think you could share?"

"Well," Braxton said, teasing, "what do you think's gonna happen?"

Kwazi turned his head. "I looked it up."

"Looked what up?"

"'Trojan Horse.'"

"And?"

"It's how the Greeks took Troy. For ten years they'd besieged the city, but they couldn't breach the walls. One night, they left a huge wooden horse outside the gates and sailed away."

"So far, so good," Braxton said.

"The Trojans, so full of pride in their apparent victory after such a long war, pulled the trophy horse inside the city. In the middle of the night, thirty Greeks leapt out and opened Troy's gates. The Greeks, who'd sailed back to the beaches in the night, flooded the city with soldiers and overwhelmed the Trojans."

"Right," Braxton said. Then, almost wistfully, "Humans never learn the lessons they teach themselves, that's what Cassandra says."

"You're taking advantage of Telemachus's ego," Kwazi said. He could hear the admiration for the plan in his own voice. It was simple, elegant, and relied on the foibles of human nature for success. Telemachus was so desperate for a public relations win, dangling Kwazi in front of her had been too much for her to resist. That it could be a ploy to take Tony Taulke's flagship—would she even have considered that? "They'll bring our shuttle aboard Taulke's flagship, already tasting victory," he said. "Just like the Trojans."

"See?" Braxton said. "You didn't need *me* to tell you the details. You figured them out all on your own."

"Not all of them."

"No?"

"Eighteen guys…"

Kwazi waited. The *Pax Corporatum* loomed in the forward window of the shuttle, still docked with Rabh Regency Station. The amber light of Jupiter lent the starship's skin a golden hue. Though it was only her hull shining with dust and distance, the ship seemed to ripple with power.

"The other shuttle's carrying two fire teams in Taulke uniforms. They'll board as part of a shift rotation. They'll be in place before we even get there. Besides, like I said, we're more than eighteen guys." Braxton smiled. Then, "Where do you think Dreamscape comes from, Kwazi?"

The *Pax Corporatum* drew nearer. The front-channel of Kwazi's mind dawned with what Braxton was suggesting.

"Invented by the SSR?" he asked.

"Cassandra invented it." Braxton's tone was almost reverent. "To liberate human minds from the shackles of SynCorp's brainwashing."

A curious kind of certainty sank into Kwazi's gut, a queasy concoction of thankfulness and caution. It was a déjà vu ghost of how he'd felt in the briefing room after seeing his doppelgänger share his, Kwazi's, story with the billions of humans inhabiting Sol. He felt excited and just a little bit afraid.

"You've got hackheads on the ship," Kwazi said. "You've got control of them through Dreamscape."

And control of me.

Braxton nodded.

"They'll fight for us?"

"No, Dreamscape isn't that developed yet," Braxton said, his tone musing. "But they'll be otherwise—occupied."

Otherwise occupied.

Not that developed—yet.

"The whole ship's complement?"

"No, there'll be resistance," Braxton said. "But don't worry. Cassandra's mapped it all out. First, we cut off Tony Taulke's giant, floating space dong. Then we cut off the old lady's head."

Those walls felt near again. Claustrophobically so. How many minds across the system could Cassandra now control through Dreamscape? Or if not control exactly, nullify to her advantage? And yet Dreamscape had given him back Amy in a way he'd never had her in the so-called real world. How many others' dreams had it made come true?

"Approaching the *Pax Corporatum*," the pilot said. "Docking protocols initiated."

Braxton turned to Kwazi, who jumped when the fire team leader rapped him on the shoulder.

"Buck up, buckaroo," Braxton said. "The ship's as good as ours."

9

MILANI STUART • ABOARD THE PAX CORPORATUM

How many days had it been? Milani had lost count.

After Helena Telemachus switched off Milani's implant, cutting access to CorpNet, time had become a homogeneous, vanilla thing. A concept without meaning. Before Kwazi had jumped ship, day and night aboard had been shaded in regular, circadian cycles approximating Earth norms. But now, held as a prisoner in her own quarters, light was constant—sometimes dim, sometimes bright, but never absent. Time ran together, a principal weapon in the arsenal of sleep deprivation. Overwhelming the senses and denying the mind its ability to recharge and reboot were common torture techniques, unproven in their effectiveness. In her more lucid moments, Milani remembered this from her medical training.

Telemachus was nothing if not a perfectionist.

Every time Milani's eyelids began to droop, the thrash music blared from the walls. Or the temperature in her quarters rose to sweltering. Or the lights would briefly brighten to sunspot brilliance, then return to nominal. Or the rotting smell of days-old, decaying organic material would be filtered through the air vent. Randomly but regularly, her five senses came under assault, especially when she tried to sleep.

During her internship at Wallace Med, when half the point seemed to be simply surviving thirty-six hour shifts without killing a patient through fatigue or incompetence or incompetence bred of fatigue, Milani had learned to day-sleep with her eyes open. To catch a few minutes of zombie wakefulness here and there when real, REM sleep wasn't an option. She revisited that inner island now, when she could. Recalling that skill was a tiny victory on a tiny battlefield in a multi-front attack on her sanity.

It was getting harder to concentrate, but if the music was absent, she could still achieve a semblance of cognitive focus. When the music assaulted her eardrums, when Milani could no longer hear the thoughts in her own head despite screaming them, she'd turn her focus to something simpler. Her mother had taught her their family's ancestral hobby of cross stitching. She'd hated it as a child, but now Milani used the stitch counting and pattern recognition to anchor her mind. Sometimes the repetition worked against her and lulled her exhausted mind to sleep. Then the harsh, clashing music would boom again, begin the cycle again.

Convinced Milani knew where Kwazi had gone, Telemachus blamed her for aiding Kwazi's escape. Milani had become convinced that only Telemachus's obsession that Milani knew Kwazi's whereabouts—and the testimony of the colony's med-tech, Drake—had saved her from summary execution. Kwazi had acted on his own, Drake had said, citing the choke marks on Milani's neck as evidence.

Damn him, Milani would think, when she *could* think. *Goddamn him.* Then: *Goddamn you! I hope you're all right...*

The emotion wheel inside her would turn and rest its pointer on *anger*, and she'd curse Kwazi and remind herself what a dupe she was for ever having cared for him at all. Then the wheel would turn again and point to *concern*, and Milani would wonder where he was, if he was safe. Had Telemachus or Adriana Rabh caught him and locked him in a cell? Were they torturing him too? Keeping him alive with protein hypos and water?

No, that didn't make sense. If they'd found Kwazi, captured him, Telemachus would have no reason to torture her.

Or keep her alive.

When the emotion wheel stopped on *empathy* for Kwazi, Milani fretted over his addiction to Dreamscape. It wasn't a jealous thing, she'd tell herself

—not envy of a dead woman who still held Kwazi's affection. That was mostly true and partly untrue. But Milani's real concern, her worry and fear, centered on Kwazi losing himself permanently in a fantasyland that kept him from eating and caring for himself. She'd seen it happen already, when they'd discovered him and the others in Engineering, lost in Dreamscape without regard for food or water, or personal hygiene. The basics of life, ignored and neglected, in favor of a heaven that shone with its own artifice.

How long ago had that been? How many days? Weeks? Surely, not years.

The light normalized. The door to her cell opened.

Helena Telemachus stepped through.

Milani had the fleeting thought to attack her. Not like a human being, not like a trained physician, but simply to launch herself off the bed, fingernails extended like claws, her teeth ready to sink into Helena's neck before she could react. But she had no strength. And she wasn't sure if it was really Telemachus or just her brain, helping her survive again. Giving her an image to anchor her sanity to something hard and unyielding, like hate.

"You look like shit," Telemachus said. The words ran together, sounding to Milani's calloused eardrums like language submerged in liquid. She turned her head, willing her ears to focus. "But no matter. Your time here is done. We've got him."

It took a moment to register. Milani tried to interpret the words through a deaf fog.

"Kwazi?"

Telemachus moved closer, a satisfied expression on her face. "Yes, dear doctor, Kwazi. His little escapade is over. And now that we have him, we need you cleaned up." She turned and motioned behind her. Milani recognized the ship's medical staff who'd helped her care for Kwazi a few years ago. Days ago?

"The enemy is using his image to whip up rebellion in the system," Telemachus said. "We'll use the real thing to counter that. With your help."

The medical staff pulled Milani to her feet. It was like she was outside her own body, watching this play out like those stories of people who die on the operating table and float above while the surgeons fight to save them.

She smiled. But from Telemachus's reaction, it wasn't a pleasant thing to see. A rasping, grating sound came from a sandpaper throat. A generous description might have called it laughter.

"You want me to help you?" Milani asked. "After this?"

"You'll be helping yourself, Dr. Stuart," Telemachus said calmly. "You'll be helping Kwazi, too." She jerked her head, and to the attendants said, "Clean her up. Pump her with stims and saline to hydrate her. I need her presentable ASA—"

Klaxons began blasting shipwide. The ambient lighting changed to crimson.

Now Milani knew she was dreaming. They were still torturing her. She'd started to doze, started to dream a perverse dream of rescue by her own captor, and they were trying to wake her up again, to start the cycle over.

"Wake up," she said aloud. "Wake up and make it stop!"

Helena Telemachus spoke to someone through her sceye. A shipwide broadcast interrupted the red alert.

"Intruder alert! Intruder alert! All hands, repel boarders. This is not a drill."

Milani clapped her hands together, applauding her own creativity. All this detail was a healthy sign. They hadn't broken her. She could still construct elaborate fantasies, right down to the emergency lighting, the overwhelming anarchy of a ship being boarded. And best of all? Milani's mind offered her the sweet satisfaction of watching fear descend over the features of Helena Telemachus.

"Payback's a bitch, bitch," Milani said.

Kwazi Jabari • Rabh Regency Station

The vator doors opened. Kwazi's fire team stepped onto the station.

Rabh Faction personnel went about their business. And why shouldn't they? Kwazi, Braxton, and the other four members of Fire Team Alpha were dressed in the same maroon overalls with the double-bar R of Adriana

Rabh over their left breasts. They were all part of one big, happy corporate family.

"Do I have to wear these?" Kwazi asked, hoisting his wrists. It was an effort. The gravity cuffs were set at two g's.

"Gotta make it look good," Braxton said. "Won't be for long. The docking ring is close. Fire Teams Bravo and Charlie are offloading there now. Mario, take point."

Kwazi nodded like he understood. A young, thin squad member and his partner led the way. Braxton and Kwazi came next, with the final pair from their six-man team guarding the rear.

"Stay next to me," Braxton ordered as they walked. It wasn't quite a march. "Shit starts flying, you just hunker down. We'll take care of any business needs tending to."

When they took any notice of Kwazi and the others at all, the personnel passing nodded and smiled. Until their eyes lit on Kwazi, when the smiles would fade, replaced by expressions of betrayal. There might even have been hatred. It made him feel outside himself again, like he was his doppelgänger from Cassandra's video, not Kwazi himself. The lines of reality and fantasy and deception had begun to blur. It was like his life had become an Impressionist painting, colorful and blurry and indistinct.

They halted at the airlock connecting the station to the *Pax Corporatum*.

"Well, well, if it isn't the Hero of Mars," said a soldier wearing Taulke black. Kwazi had seen row after row of troops just like him from atop the platform where Tony Taulke had given him his medal in front of the whole solar system. The yellow stripes on the man's shoulder made him a lieutenant. "Back from being AWOL, I see."

Braxton faded to the front. "Not without some help." He nodded at Kwazi's gravity cuffs, sounding half offended. Frenemy competition among factions.

"I heard it was a Taulke man spotted him," the officer said. His assistant was tapping commands on the screen in front of her.

"You heard wrong," Braxton said.

The officer smiled. "He's back. Guess the details don't matter."

"Don't," Braxton acknowledged.

The portal opened, and the officer stepped aside. "Helena Telemachus will be glad to have him back. And maybe quit riding the rest of us so damned hard."

Mario led the team again. As Braxton passed, he said, "I wouldn't want to be ridden by Telemachus for any reason."

The airlock door shut behind them, cutting off the officer's laughter.

"See?" Braxton said, leaning in to Kwazi. "Piece of cake."

10

KWAZI JABARI • ABOARD THE PAX CORPORATUM

"Hold up there."

Braxton, Kwazi, and the other members of Fire Team Alpha kept walking.

"I said, hold up there!"

Braxton lifted a closed fist. "Stay frosty," he whispered. Then, "Can I help you, friend?"

Like the soldiers at the airlock, the man who'd spoken and his partner wore uniforms of Taulke Faction black. Military, not civilian personnel. Part of Helena Telemachus's escort, maybe.

"We're here to take custody of the prisoner," the man said. He was in his mid-thirties, like Braxton, with gray lining his brown-black hair. He had a scar on the left side of his face that made his jawline seem slender. "Orders of Helena Telemachus."

"Ah, I see. Hang on a second," Braxton said, then looked away to a point on the ceiling. "Checked my sceye. Nothing about that in my orders from the old lady."

"Maybe it's delayed," the man suggested. He didn't seem to believe it himself. "You know, those fucking rebels have taken over CorpNet. Local network could be compromised or something."

"Could be," acknowledged Braxton.

The man placed his hands on his belt. Kwazi tried not to stare at the holstered stunner there. The leather loop securing the weapon was already unsnapped.

"In any case," the man with the scar said, "Regent Rabh has surrendered all claim on him. We'll take him now."

Braxton bobbed his head, like releasing Kwazi would just be one less pile of shit he'd have to shovel today. "Works for me," he said. "Let me get you the key to the cuffs."

"Appreciate it," the man said. His thumbs were hooked into belt loops now. As green as Kwazi was, he still recognized a mistake when he saw one.

"Of course," Braxton said, smiling. Then he quick-drew his stunner and shot the man in the forehead. Before the second Taulke soldier could respond, Braxton shot him in the head too. "Cat's out of the bag," he said as the second body hit the deck. He passed the electronic key to Kwazi's cuffs over them, and they dropped. "Won't be needing those anymore. Bravo, Charlie, report status."

Two members of Team Alpha moved to drag the bodies out of the corridor.

"Leave 'em," Braxton said. "It's too late for that."

"Intruder alert! Intruder alert! All hands, repel boarders. This is not a drill."

"See what I mean?" Braxton said.

"What happened?" Kwazi had almost let himself believe it would be as easy as the story of the Trojan Horse made it seem.

"Dead man switch, likely," Braxton said. When Kwazi stared, uncomprehending, he continued, "Mod to the implant. Soldier dies, lack of vitals triggers an alarm."

Two ship's personnel, non-military by the look of them, rounded the corner at the end of the corridor. They seemed in a hurry to get away from something. Mario and one of the other SSR Alphas shot them down. Civilians weren't wearing military, MESH-woven uniforms like Taulke's soldiers. A hit anywhere by a stunner set to kill would electrocute them.

"Bravo Team in place. Engineering secured."

"Well, well, that's half the battle right there," Braxton said. "Bravo Team, cut the cord in twenty seconds." To Alpha Squad, he said, "Let's keep moving. Mario: point."

"Charlie Team here. Meeting heavy resistance in the penthouse. Could use some backup."

"On our way, Charlie," Braxton said. As they quick-marched, he pulsed the ship's layout to the Alphas' sceyes, a red dot showing their current location, a green dot showing Charlie's. "Sounds like the Queen of All Media is putting up a good fight." Then, with relish, "Wouldn't have it any other way."

The corridors were practically vacant of shipboard personnel. That made sense to Kwazi, if what Braxton had said was true. They were probably in their quarters or a dark corner of the ship somewhere, lost in Dreamscape. This was a civilian ship, so most souls aboard were there to serve the officers and, of course, VIPs like Helena Telemachus. The minimal military complement the *Corporatum* had shipped out with from Earth would be there partly for show and partly to handle any hiccups Tony Taulke's flagship might encounter. They were stationed in sensitive areas of the ship—Engineering and VIP quarters—or guarding the airlock to the station. The two Telemachus had sent to retrieve him, the ones Braxton gunned down had been unexpected. Which begged the question: what other surprises might they stumble over along the way?

"Down! Down!" Mario shouted. Before he could heed his own warning, multiple shots from an old-fashioned projectile weapon sped down the corridor at them. Mario went down.

Fifty feet further on, the barrel of an automatic rifle pulled back around a corner.

Braxton snapped two fingers toward cover in each of the nearby hallways flanking the main corridor. Mario's partner and the two guards behind them went left. Braxton pulled Kwazi right.

Mario was bleeding out in the middle of the corridor. Kwazi could see his battle buddy wanting to pull him into cover, but the other two Soldiers in their fire team held him back.

"Well, now it's getting interesting," Braxton said. "They—"

He felt it in his stomach first. Kwazi's center of gravity became untethered, like he'd just crested the hill of a rollercoaster. Someone had switched off the ship's artificial gravity.

"Excellent work, Bravo," Braxton announced over comms. There were shouts of confusion and fear from the end of the corridor. "Charlie, we're near your position. Hold fast."

Acknowledgments checked off from the other squads. Braxton threw Kwazi a toothy grin. "Here's where your training comes in." The three men in the opposite corridor had slung their weapons and were squatting, braced against the wall. To Kwazi they looked like armed baboons in their maroon uniforms. Braxton said, "Give 'em hell, boys."

Two of the men launched themselves upward, turning to land gut flat against the ceiling. Each began to pull himself along, finding handholds in the fire-retardant tiles and processor vents and recessed lighting panels. A burst of stunner fire sounded from the Soldiers on the ceiling, and the rifle that had shot Mario floated, minus its owner, toward the middle of the T-intersection down the corridor. Braxton followed along the near wall with Kwazi close behind. Elongated drops of Mario's blood hung in the air as he passed. Mario wasn't moving, and his partner had abandoned the mission to tend to him.

At the T-intersection, the two Soldiers swung themselves around, readied their weapons, and looped around the corner, one to cover either direction.

Punk! Punk!

The odd, muted sound of two stunner shots dispatching one Taulke combatant. The other came spinning past them, swimming like a man on a wire, trying to get away. The second Alpha took him out.

Braxton grabbed from the air the M24 rifle that had felled Mario and slung it across his back.

"Never know," he said.

The two Alphas who'd cleared the corridor were already moving down the eastward hallway of the T-intersection. Kwazi checked his sceye, finding Alpha Squad's red dot nearly on top of Charlie's green. He could hear the *punk-punk-punk!* of stunner fire nearby. Braxton motioned him to stay to the rear. The corridor turned left, and four members of Charlie Squad were hunkered down behind bulkheads. Braxton joined them, ordering the Alpha Squad Team to guard the rear.

"Like I said—"

"You never know," Kwazi finished. The sophistication of what was happening, the power of planning that Braxton and the others had done, dawned on him like new knowledge blessed upon the ignorant. The bulkheads were the shipping crates in the simulations, natural cover you'd find aboard any ship built to protect the rest of the vessel in case of a hull breach. The random pair of Taulke soldiers earlier, the M24 that had taken Mario out—unpredictable factors in an otherwise elegant and disturbingly simple equation to take Tony Taulke's flagship. It was impressive, not to mention frightening as hell, when Kwazi realized just how unprepared he'd been for combat.

"Shraz," Braxton said. The leader of Charlie Squad turned. "Throw one past the catcher."

The man smiled, nodded.

"What does that mean?" Kwazi asked. Not knowing what to expect next, he felt exposed. Despite Braxton's attempts to keep him to the rear of the action and alive, it was almost like he didn't really care if Kwazi survived or not. In point of fact, it was really starting to piss Kwazi off.

Ignoring him, Braxton engaged comms and said, "Engineering, would you be so kind as to override the Queen Bee's door? And reengage gravity in twenty seconds, ship norm. From my mark. *Mark*."

Kwazi recognized it as a flash grenade, perfectly spherical. Shraz eyeballed the angle, then arced the grenade overhead. It ricocheted off a far wall, but redirected without gravity, bouncing off a second wall before exploding. There were screams from the team defending the entrance to the VIP quarters.

The door to the quarters slid open, and Shraz threw a second grenade at the deck halfway between their position and the VIP quarters. It bounced, its momentum carrying it forward, then careened at a thirty-degree angle into the room. Its burst was bright and severe, and more screams followed.

Kwazi felt an elbow in his ribs, then the pull in his gut of gravity reengaging.

"You first," Braxton said. "We'll be right behind you. Here, take this." Braxton handed him the M24. "It'll play well on the 'net. Remember: Helena Telemachus is in there. Make it good."

Ahead of him, the chaos from the two grenades was subsiding. Human suffering was the only sounds he could hear. The woman who'd killed Amy and the others was in there. Kwazi didn't care about Cassandra or the SSR or what they thought they could make of him. But he did care about exacting justice for murder.

Taking the rifle from Braxton, he stood up and strode forward with purpose, ignoring the groaning, flash-burned Taulke soldiers as he passed them. Once inside the room, he found two more defending troops blinking hard, trying to recover. Two women were sprawled on the floor. He raised his rifle at the first one and pulled the trigger.

Click.

In the aftermath of battle, the sound of an empty rifle was like a rimshot after the stale punchline to a bad joke.

Braxton walked up beside him, holding up a magazine. "Can't kill her yet, Jabari. Emphasis on the *yet*." He moved past Kwazi and knelt beside Helena Telemachus, who was jabbering about being blind.

Robbed of his justice, Kwazi took what satisfaction he could find as Braxton jerked Tony Taulke's mouthpiece to her feet.

"Jabari?" someone said. The second woman in the room. "Kwazi?"

He sought for the source of the familiar voice. She was still on the floor. Her color was pale, her face lined in a way that it hadn't been when he'd last seen her.

"Milani?" he said, moving to her side. Her arms groped for him, finding a shaky purchase.

"I'm good, I'm still good, this is so real," she said. He didn't understand. "They didn't break me. You're alive, and this is so real!"

"It *is* real, Milani," he said as she pressed against his chest. Her arms wrapped around him. "I'm here now."

"I forgive you," she said. "I know why you did what you did."

"I—I..."

"It's okay," Milani said. "Even if this isn't real, it's okay."

Kwazi looked up to find Braxton standing over him, Helena Telemachus in the gravity cuffs he'd been wearing earlier. There were burns around her eyes, like someone had tried to put them out with a burning torch.

"What'd I tell you?" Braxton said. "Piece of cake."

He dragged Telemachus to a wall and engaged the ship's comm system.

"Crew and passengers of the *Pax Corporatum*. Your ship is now forfeit, claimed for Cassandra and the Soldiers of the Solar Revolution. Your Engineering section is ours. Your Queen of All Media is ours. Any further resistance will be met with summary judgment and extreme prejudice. Lay down your arms and present yourselves in the ship's assembly room. Failure to do so will result in the immediate execution of Helena Telemachus."

"You wouldn't dare kill me," she said, eyes wide and bloodshot and full of doubt, despite her bravado.

"Don't bet on it," Braxton said. "That man there? I could hand Jabari a butter knife and he'd slit you from naughty bits to gullet."

Helena tried to pull away but was held firm by Braxton. "Jabari?" she said, sightless but defiant in the face of capture. "This is your doing?"

He stood, remembering the line Braxton had taught him to say for the camerabot.

"The Company is done, Helena. Justice has come home."

11

RUBEN QINLAO • DARKSIDE, THE MOON

The whir of the scooter sounded weaker, sicker somehow. Being weighed down with supplies and food stuffs was part of it, but Ruben was fairly certain the maintenance bike wouldn't last much longer. He'd begun to wonder if it was simply his new destiny to only drive antiquated vehicles soon to fail.

He gathered the bundles from the passenger seat. Protein powders and water, meds from Brackin's list, and a spare vac-suit for the doctor. All of it had cost SynCorp dollars, and it was only by the grace of Brackin's syncer they'd been able to make the purchases.

"I'm keeping track," Brackin had said the day before. "It's going on my bill."

Ruben mounted the short, sloping entrance from the tunnel to Point Bravo, hands full of Brackin's grace.

"Did you see this?" Strunk demanded by way of welcome. The enforcer took the load from Ruben and indicated a screen on the wall with his elbow. They'd made it functional with some skill, luck, and a boost from one of the power conduits in the *Roadrunner*. Old LUNa City's castoff tech had become their lifeline.

"See what?"

Standing by the screen, Brackin swiped up the volume. Cassandra, the hybrid AI-human, was talking from her throne. On her right hand, the pilloried head of her mother, Elise Kisaan, stood on a pole. It had been days since Cassandra took her life. That fact was evident.

"...have renamed the symbol of oppression *Freedom's Herald*," Cassandra was saying. The screen split, the right half showing Tony Taulke's flagship in orbit around Callisto. "We are reshaping Tony Taulke's empire: its symbols, its stations, its reason for being. The people of Sol have waited long enough for deliverance. We, the Soldiers of the Solar Revolution, are the instrument of that liberation."

"Can you fucking believe it?" Strunk said, filling the small space around them with fury. "They took the *Pax Corporatum*! They renamed the goddamned ship!"

It's only a ship, Ruben thought but didn't say. But he understood Strunk's anger. It was coming from a place of fear. Fear at just how widespread, coordinated, and seemingly unstoppable Cassandra was. If she could take Tony Taulke's ship...

"You might have heard stories about the Taulke boy escaping," Cassandra continued. Strunk continued to rage, cataloging the explicit methods by which he intended to extract suffering from Cassandra.

"Quiet!" Ruben yelled. He ignored the shocked gargoyle stare from Strunk. "Brackin, turn that up."

"Like his father, he's a coward," Cassandra said. "It's the instinct of all tyrants to run when facing justice. Anthony Taulke III is no different. This is his image." A motion photo of Tony Three-point-one replaced the starship. He wore a sneering, self-satisfied look, the default expression of a teenager. Likely the best photo they could find to cast him in the worst possible light, Ruben thought. "He and his father will soon be in my custody. They will both be tried for crimes against humanity. They will both answer for those crimes. If you see either of these men"—Cassandra's image faded to be replaced by a likeness of Tony—"report these enemies of freedom immediately to the network node at the bottom of the screen. You will be handsomely rewarded for your help in ending the tyrannical rule of the Syndicate Corporation once and for all."

The screen faded, replaced by a flash-ad. Not a SynCorp product, now. But an ad recruiting citizen-workers into the ranks of the SSR. Cassandra's image dominated the short message. Her symmetrical beauty, often cast in shadow, was rarely absent from CorpNet now. Whether preaching, recruiting, or promising a life unshackled from SynCorp, Cassandra's face was a constant presence on the network.

"Turn it off," Strunk ordered. Brackin complied instantly. "Can you fucking believe that shit?"

"Calm down," Ruben said, feeling anything but calm himself. They'd all become edgier over the past three days, and Strunk's overbearing fury wasn't helping. Cooped up in this tiny sounding station, the air had grown heavy with impotent dread. "It's just a ship. And you missed the good news."

"Good news?" Brackin asked.

"Tony Junior got away," Ruben said. "Somehow, somewhere. They don't have him. They didn't mention Tony's mother, though."

The room was quiet until Strunk spoke.

"She's not a prize," he said, his tone less strident. Almost apologetic, in fact. Ruben had given him something to think about, to reason out. It seemed to settle him. "Not like Tony Junior."

Ruben nodded. "In their narrative, Marissa Taulke is probably a victim. She never really fit with Tony's image as the godfather of the solar system. That's paying dividends for her now, maybe."

Tony moaned from the dusty floor. Ruben knelt beside him. Had his color become sicklier? Was that even possible?

"That's the other good news," Strunk murmured. He went to stand beside the portal window. Leaning against the wall, he stared at the wreckage of the *Roadrunner*. "Tell him, Brackin."

Ruben looked up at the doctor to find a pained expression on his face, like he'd just stubbed a toe.

"Well?"

"He's developed a massive infection. There could've been poison on that knife. From the patchy skin, it could be sepsis. If that's the case, I could stimulate his microbiome with a catalytic regimen of bacterial consortia introduced through the gut. I'm just not sure, and down here there's no way to—"

"I don't know what the hell you just said, but if you're doing anything to make him worse, I swear to God, you'll wish I'd spaced you." The fact that Strunk said it quietly, gazing out the porthole, made it all the more menacing.

"Okay," Ruben said, trying to understand Brackin's diagnosis. "Are you sure his implant can't help? Maybe it just needs to be rebooted. When I met you, you were hooking that hackhead up with Dreamscape. You seemed to know your way around—"

"I told you before," Brackin said, "Taulke's SCI must have been damaged in the crash. I'm no micro-tech mechanic. You're lucky I was able to deactivate yours and Strunk's. We're stuck with my training and what old-school meds I can scrounge up."

"He says we need to move him to his clinic," Strunk said. "Ain't happenin'."

Ruben looked from one to the other.

"Moving him *could* kill him," Brackin acknowledged. "But my equipment's back at the clinic. I brought a medical bag, and the antibiotics I've given him are helping, but not enough. The bacteria are too resistant. We're fighting a losing battle down here. It's only a matter of time before the infection, if that's what it is, overwhelms—"

"Tony's tough," Strunk said, like repeating that enough times would help cure his boss.

"Tony's human," Ruben replied.

Strunk stared out the porthole.

"Wouldn't we need to take him to a hospital?" Ruben asked. "Not your clinic?"

Brackin had the grimace on his face again. Like he wanted to speak but was debating it.

"Apparently, Doc there's got lots of black-market equipment in a back room," Strunk said. "We had a nice, long talk about options while you were out."

Ruben nodded. "Your clinic, then."

"We ain't moving Tony!"

Standing, Ruben faced the enforcer. He mustered his best board meeting voice. "That's not your call. It's mine."

Strunk and Ruben stared hard at one another, the enforcer's index finger tapping out a rhythm on the butt of the stunner stuck in his belt. The dust shifted behind Ruben as Brackin backed away.

"It's too risky," Strunk said. "Not just to Tony's health. Being spotted. His face—and yours—are all over CorpNet. We'd be clipped as soon as we stepped into Darkside. We'd already be clipped, if you hadn't remembered this hidey-hole. And what about Fischer? I thought we were—"

"Fischer should've been here by now. Something must've happened to him."

Brackin cleared his throat.

With a lingering look at Strunk, Ruben said, "Yes, Doctor?"

"Maybe I wasn't clear, but he'll die for sure here," Brackin said. Strunk turned away again to stare at the lunar surface. "The infection or poison or whatever it is—I can't properly diagnose it out here, much less treat it. We've got to get him to better facilities. I know a back way to the clinic, a black-market supply trail through the tunnels. We can use that joke of a scooter to get there. But if we stay here—he'll die for sure. *That* I can guarantee you."

"Motherfucker," Strunk said.

Ruben waited a beat. "Strunk, it's why we brought him here. If Brackin says—"

"Not him." Strunk's eyes peered through the porthole. "*Them.*"

Ruben covered the distance in two strides. Outside the bulkhead door, kicking up lunar dust near the half-buried *Roadrunner*, a dropship marked with the mirrored-snake brand of the SSR had touched down. Someone must have finally noticed the wreckage and called it in. It had only been a matter of time before that happened.

Time, it seemed, was their newfound enemy attacking on multiple fronts.

"Discussion's over," Ruben said. "We have to go."

"I still say—"

Ruben grabbed Strunk by the front of his shirt. It was like taking hold of a bag of concrete, already set. The big man barely moved.

"Listen to me, Enforcer. As the sole member of the SynCorp board in the room, what I say goes." Strunk's eyes smoldered, but he made no effort to pull away from Ruben's grip. "We're done debating. It'll take all of five minutes for that strike team to track us to this door. We have to go. *Now*."

Ruben heard Brackin's rapid breathing behind him. Strunk held the eyes of the Regent of Mars a moment longer. He wasn't used to backing down. But he understood hierarchy. And his place in it, so Ruben hoped.

"Okay then, Boss Man," Strunk said, his voice subdued. "You and the doc there get Tony out of here. I'll hold them."

Ruben cocked his head. "There'll be a dozen Soldiers coming through that door."

"Less than that," Strunk said, "eventually."

"Strunk, it's suicide."

"For them, maybe."

Ruben opened his mouth, but Strunk cut him off. "The priority is getting Tony out of here and healed. You're right about that, Boss Man. We need him if we're gonna save the Company. But what's about to happen here—this is my kinda show. Let me run it."

Outside, the strike team had descended the dropship's ramp in five pairs of two, rifles at the ready. Dressed in military-grade vac-suits, they spread out, cautiously approaching the crashed ship.

Ruben released the enforcer, then extended a hand to Strunk.

"Your show, your way," he said.

Engulfing Ruben's hand in his own, Strunk nodded.

"We'll need to get him into a vac-suit," Brackin said, jerking his head to Tony. "It'll help keep his vitals stable, help me monitor him as we move."

"We should all get in vac-suits," Ruben said. "When they blow this door, the air's gonna vacate the tunnels."

Strunk went to the pile of pressure suits, recovered the biggest one there, and began sliding it on. Brackin was next while Ruben monitored the enemy outside.

"They've blown the hatch on the *Roadrunner*," he reported. A Soldier had already crawled inside. A few moments passed before he extricated himself. One of them, the team leader Ruben guessed, gestured with two fingers. He could imagine the orders over their comms: *"Look for tracks."*

Ruben looked over to find Strunk holding Tony while Brackin worked him, one limb at a time, into a vac-suit. Tony's vital signs came online. All the indicators were orange or red.

"Strunk, take the door. I have to get the scooter going."

Brackin nodded to the enforcer, whose movements were heavy and cumbersome in his suit.

Ruben slid hurriedly down the short access tunnel to the scooter waiting below. Remarkably, it started on the first try. He patted it anyway, his superstitious need to thank the machine getting the better of him. He left it idling and crawled back up the access tunnel, where Brackin was securing Tony's helmet. Its seal engaged with a soft *phish*.

"They're making a beeline for the door," Strunk said, fitting his own helmet in place. He engaged their local comms channel. "You need to go."

Strunk had backed away from the door. He was piling supplies and old equipment that had been left behind in the tiny maintenance station. He was getting ready for a blast. Through the metal bulkhead door, Ruben heard the strike team working. They were trying to open it.

"Help me," Ruben said. The air in the suit smelled sour. Or maybe it was his days-old sweat stirred up by airflow. Brackin moved to his side, and together they lifted Tony to the slope leading down to the tunnel. Brackin went first, and Ruben fed him Tony's body. They both slid down quickly.

"Hey, Strunk," Ruben said. "I'll make sure Tony knows."

Strunk grunted. "Fuck that, Boss Man. I'll tell him myself when I catch up."

Ruben smiled. The man was an asshole, but he had balls like asteroids.

"Good luck," Ruben said.

"Don't need it."

At the bottom of the slide, Brackin was securing Tony in the scooter's side seat. Under his weight the antigravs were burdened, barely holding the maintenance bike above the tunnel floor. With three of them aboard, Ruben wasn't sure it would move at all.

"You're driving," Brackin said, indicating Ruben should get aboard. Ruben mounted the scooter, and Brackin boarded behind him. The doctor wrapped his arms around Ruben's torso. "Nothing personal."

"Right."

Ruben revved the throttle. His feet were still touching the tunnel floor.

The small nook that was Point Bravo above them shook, a massive blast overloading their comms. Moondust and fractured rock rolled down the slide followed by a hazy cone of gray fog. All that suddenly reversed course, yanked upward again by the *whoosh* of evacuating atmosphere. Ruben gunned the scooter's engine, and they headed for Point Charlie at a floating crawl. The lower bulkhead door to Point Bravo slammed shut behind them in the tunnel. The last thing they heard was Strunk's voice cutting through the screeching static in their headsets.

"Come and get it, you sonsabitches!"

12

STACKS FISCHER • APPROACHING MASADA STATION

The Hearse's proximity alarm woke me from my semi-slumber. So, I was able to sleep after all. Five days of staring out into space kinda makes that inevitable, I guess.

It's funny how today's circumstances can make you rethink yesterday's choices. As if somehow you can hop back through time with what you know now and change things. Maybe it's how we deal with regret. Or maybe our minds are into S&M, and we enjoy tying ourselves up for a little self-flagellation.

I'd been dreaming of Daisy Brace and those last moments on Pallas—not an unpleasant thing as it turns out. In the dream, I hadn't left her to suicide. I'd snatched up Daisy from the flight deck and hauled her into my ship with a strength I ain't had since there was hair covering my whole dome. Daisy protested, of course, and there were some close calls with stunners, but we got to the Hearse okay, and she didn't make a single crack about my age, not once. That's how I knew it must have been a dream...

We'd make a beeline straight to Erkennen on Titan, I told her. He'd make her well again if anyone could. And if he couldn't, well, we'd crash land on that pad when we got to it. When we lifted off from Pallas in the dream, I had that same, sweeping view of the pirate base under heavy fire from Galatz's corporate ships, and the bad guys giving back as good as they got, that I'd seen in real life. But instead of an empty hat and coat on the seat next to me, I had Daisy, half of her body slack with maybe-permanent paralysis, but at least alive and looking just a little like she maybe appreciated my effort.

Then the alarm went off and woke me up. Titan was close. Took me long enough, but I'd made it.

Saturn's comeliest moon appears out of the void looking like a smooth, underdeveloped Earth. When the seas reflect sunlight, you can even see clouds. After most of a week of breathing my own air, it was good to see something, *anything* that wasn't man-made and blinking on a console. Even if I'd sacrificed my Daisy dream to see it.

I'll give Gregor Erkennen this—he's made Prometheus Colony on Titan a home away from home for his tech types. His daddy, Viktor, started the colony as a lure to bring people to the ass-end of the system, so far out they might never make it home to Mother Earth again. Titan is a luxury destination for exploration, the most habitable body in Sol next to Earth, really, and homier than Mars. An atmosphere, even if it ain't exactly breathable. Plenty of water. Plenty of lakes, even if they are methane and ethane. Mountains. Dunes. Tides and caves below the surface, perfect for doming and settling.

Viktor turned a moon with a pretty face into the system's most enticing excursion park. Gregor took daddy's idea and upgraded it to an overpriced resort. The well-to-do from across Sol take vacations there, if they don't mind the week-plus travel time (one way) from the inner system. Erkennen Faction eggheads have access to Prometheus anytime they want—free. Take a tour of cryovolcanoes that shoot water and methane tens of thousands of meters high! They make Old Faithful look like Earth's spitting at the sky. Haven't lost your lunch lately? Hop a balloon ride over Lake Kraken Mare. Those whacky atmospheric currents will keep you on your toes, neighbor! Need some exercise? Book an expedition across Xanadu's rarely solid surface. Pack your vitamins! It's the size of Australia... Got a death wish? Strap on a pair of Erkennen Wonder Wings® and dive off one of the mountains in the Mithrim Montes range.

Speaking for myself, I can get the same heartbeat acceleration from half an hour at Minnie the Mouth's Arms of Artemis in Darkside for a lot cheaper and minus the two-week travel commitment. And the most medical aid I'll ever need there is a course of antibiotics.

As you approach Titan, though, you don't see any of that. You just see its flat orange-aqua atmosphere. But based on *The Real Story* vids and the flash-ads from Erkennen, you can imagine how perfect everything is below. The dense, foggy atmosphere makes the moon's surface inviting from a distance, like Adriana Rabh's face in all the Company missives—smoothed by technology, regal instead of old—flawless.

Somehow, I doubted I'd have a chance to sample any of it. Gregor hadn't invited me here to enjoy the carnival rides. And I wanted to get my business with him boxed up. I was worried about Tony and entirely unconvinced Ruben Qinlao could keep him safe, even with that knuckle-dragger Dick Strunk doing the heavy lifting. Plus, sitting on my ass for so long had made me antsy. I needed to be doing something.

Masada Station sits atop a vertical rock orbiting Titan. Its body rises into a wide plateau, a perfect, flat foundation for the research station Viktor Erkennen stuck there during Tony Taulke's big system expansion initiative a few decades back. It's named for a Jewish stronghold during the first-century war with the Romans, and the asteroid *does* look a whole lot like that old Judaean Desert fortress, I have to say.

The odd thing as I came nearer the rock was how dark it looked. Running lights lit up the approach to the small hangar, but the plastisteel windows were dark. Masada is a relatively small experiment station, where Gregor Erkennen and his elite eggheads do their heavy thinking when they weren't shore-leaving to Adventures-R-Us on Titan. The dark windows reflecting those running lights felt eerie. Like I'd arrived a day too late to find anyone left alive.

The hangar itself was the polar opposite of the busy craziness of Pallas from my dream. There was only one shuttle parked, lonely, in a slip meant for a larger vessel. It looked ready to launch. Two men waited on the deck as the Hearse settled onto her struts. Gregor Erkennen rocked on his heels, like I was a waiter who'd forgotten his table. The other man seemed familiar, but I couldn't put a name to him.

"Took you long enough," Erkennen said, doing his crossed-arms, heel-rocking thing. His almost-Russian accent always sounded put-on to me, but

I knew he came by it honestly. His pop had been Mother Country, born and bred.

"Invent a better drive," I shot back. Realizing I'd just barked at a regent of SynCorp, I took off my hat—a sign of respect to take the edge off my cheekiness. Being Tony's chief enforcer, sometimes I forget my place in the Company pecking order.

"Working on it," Erkennen said.

"Figured."

"I assume you know my man, Bruno Richter?"

Erkennen jerked his head to the left. The man next to him was thin and weedy. If a ferret could walk upright, it'd be named Bruno Richter. Mid-thirties: old enough to be confident, young enough to think he could still do what he'd been able to in his twenties. Richter was known for assassination by poison. Unlike me, he was an indirect sort of fellow.

"Never heard of him," I lied, careful to look Bruno in the eye when I said it. "How's it hangin', Bruno?"

Richter ignored my outstretched hand, which was really only offered as part of my penance to Erkennen for being a smartass when I'd landed. Bruno hid his hands under his armpits, where most assassins store at least one weapon of choice. That stance is universal enforcer code for *don't fuck with me.*

"Glad to see we're getting off on the right foot," I said, smiling at him—my go-to expression for putting my professional colleagues off their feed. Let's establish who's who here.

Erkennen seemed annoyed by the dick measuring.

"Come to my office, Mr. Fischer. Time's short, and there's a lot to discuss."

"Lead the way," I said. Erkennen turned to oblige, and Richter and I hesitated to move a moment longer. "Oh, after you," I said, motioning forward and widening my smile.

He didn't move.

"Bruno!" Erkennen called over his shoulder. With a lingering stare of warning, Bruno came when called. Like a good rat terrier should.

I decided, whatever this was, it was gonna be fun.

"So, let me get this straight," I said. Erkennen was being patient. I was a blue-collar type. I couldn't be expected to grasp the strategic intricacies of the Company's technology faction all at once, now could I? "You've got a decoy database on Titan chocked full of fake inventions, flashing 'open for business' like a Darkside hooker behind in her rent. You're hoping ... *hoping*, mind you ... that your little charade pulls all Cassandra's attention away from the real treasures here on Masada Station."

Richter cleared his throat, a warning to watch my tone. I pretended it was just phlegm and ignored him.

"The deception will buy us time," Erkennen said. "Time to find a cure for Cassandra."

"A ... cure?"

The Regent of Titan nodded. "She's an AI. True—a unique form of life, to be sure. But at the end of the day, half of her is still just synthetic code married to nature's original code—the human genome. And all code, whatever its origin, can be compromised."

"I thought you were spending all your resources on defense," I said.

"That would only ensure defeat, Mr. Fischer, as you yourself have suggested. What we're really doing is delaying Cassandra until we develop a way to defeat her." Gregor Erkennen looked at me straight on. "Your mission is simple, Mr. Fischer. Help Bruno protect Rebekah Franklin and her team, so they can protect Masada Station. Fail in that effort, and the Company will be lost."

I let that sink in a minute. Sometimes I have to boil down the cryptic into something actionable.

The huge decoy mission happening on Titan: Erkennen and his people jumping up and down on a hill, waving their arms, daring Cassandra and the SSR to charge. She—it, I had to keep reminding myself—would hopefully take the bait. Meanwhile, Erkennen was looking for a tech miracle to undo her. But if Cassandra got wise and managed to steal the data from Masada Station, that effort wouldn't matter a bit.

"If I'm going to protect your supercomputer, I need a tour of the station," I said. "And I need to meet your prodigy programmer."

"She's indisposed at the moment," Erkennen said.

"Unacceptable," I replied before he'd finished. "You want me to protect your geek crew here or not?"

Erkennen sighed. "Rebekah Franklin's grandfather passed away two days ago. He was a dear friend of the faction—of mine—and she is grieving."

I gave that news the couple of breaths of respect it deserved. Diplomacy isn't my strong suit, but sometimes I surprise myself.

"I understand," I said, not really caring. Then Daisy's face popped into my mind's eye, and I felt like a heel big enough to fit on a clown's floppy shoe. I adjusted my attitude. "Regent, here's the thing—"

"Gregor," he said. "Call me Gregor."

I paused. Invitation to intimacy was not something easily offered by a regent of the Syndicate Corporation. Especially to a competing faction's chief fix-it man.

"As I was about to say, Gregor, I work alone."

"Not dis time," Richter said, reminding me he existed. His German accent was thick. His smile was skinny, amused. Well, Daisy Brace had worked out, hadn't she? Maybe Ferret Face would surprise me too.

"The old lines," Erkennen said, "they're meaningless now. We have a common enemy."

I nodded, understanding for the first time, I think, the real stakes. This was for all the marbles. And, especially, one Big Blue Marble.

If Cassandra stole SynCorp's tech secrets, the Company would end. Understanding that is why I'd set my personal loyalty to Tony aside and traveled in the exact wrong direction to reach Titan. But here's what I hadn't realized, not till now—not till Gregor said what he said the way he'd said it.

Life under SynCorp had provided purpose for billions after near extinction at Mother Nature's hands. Was it a life of value? You'd have to ask them. Each and every one. But it was life.

Cassandra promised freedom. But what did that mean, really? To lift the booted heel of the Company off the neck of humanity and restore its free-willed destiny to do whatever the hell it wanted to itself? Seemed to me we'd tried that already, and it wasn't all that and a box of chocolates. The she-bot's promise sounded like a line to me.

Was Cassandra offering a better life than Joe and Jane Average already had under SynCorp? Maybe. For me, it all boiled down to this, though: what would a half machine know about what's best for mankind? Maybe a lot. Maybe nothing. Maybe, like all of us, it was driven by pure self-interest. Maybe it didn't give a hoot in hell for mankind at all. Thirty years before, the New Earthers and the original Cassandra—a true, pure artificial intelligence housed in a mainframe, I reminded myself, tasting the irony—had murdered tens of millions.

There's the devil … and there's the devil you know.

"You two are Rebekah Franklin's guardian angels," Erkennen said to fill the silence. I'm sure it had sounded inspirational in his head. But what he'd said almost made me laugh out loud.

Richter's grin became a smirk. He looked my way, and we shared the joke. For my part, it went something like…

Stacks Fischer, an angel?

What in God's fiery hell had the universe come to?

13

REBEKAH FRANKLIN • MASADA STATION, ORBITING TITAN

Bekah drew the sponge across her grandfather's forehead. She had the pleasant thought that it was soothing him, cooling a life's worth of cares from his time-worn brow.

In death, the worry lines seemed less. Opa Simon had seemed ready to go. Or, at least, contented to meet God on God's own terms.

Like I have a choice, she heard his rueful voice say in her mind.

The peaceful expression on his face belied the cancer that had so virulently, so quickly riddled his body. Faster than his medical implant had been able to catch up and viciously outwitting the experimental therapies the Erkennen Faction's best medical minds had applied. Sometimes—more often than not—nature bested technology, reminded you that creation's original architecture, for all its apparent frailties and imperfections, was better than anything mankind's mind could create from any combination of fire and thought and the empirical method.

Though expected for weeks, Simon's death had come abruptly. A few days earlier he'd been joking with Gregor Erkennen, praising Bekah as he always did when he was within earshot of Titan's regent, strategic and obvious in his adulation. Then, less than twelve hours ago, the automated alert tied to his vital signs had called her away from the adaptive nested-loop functions she'd been working on. Not recognizing—or, perhaps, not wanting to acknowledge—what the alert meant, Bekah had been angered at first by the interruption. But her frustration had melted away when the truth hit home.

Bekah's loss had consumed her then, a strange combination of physical numbness and acute emotional pain. Her grief had ripped open a hot, yawning emptiness inside her.

It was like someone had doubled the station's gravity. Simply dipping the sponge in the water of the medical tub, then drawing it over Simon's skin, was difficult. Downward, along each limb, as prescribed by Jewish law. The forced intimacy of washing her grandfather's body as she performed the *taharah*, the tradition of ritual washing, was uncomfortable. Seeing him naked made her self-conscious, but she knew that was merely society's conscience in her head, judgment not based in Jewish norms. The ablution was meant to cleanse the body, to return it to the pure state in which it entered God's physical universe. It wasn't something needful that Bekah had believed herself. But she respected her opa's final wishes, and so she ignored the disapproving societal finger wagging in her head.

Bekah dipped the sponge in the water and drew it along her opa's skin. She thought he'd appreciate the irony of the medical tub—science providing a clean, germ-free environment for the *mikveh* preparing his body for burial. And the water, as pure as any in the solar system, scooped up for study from Saturn's rings. She could hear Simon's chuckle, see him nod his appreciation for the absolute appropriateness of this contemporary expression of an ancient ritual adapted to life in modern times. A common-sense commandment obeyed in the only way she knew how to obey it.

She drew the sponge along Simon's skin. Old, yes. Withered and rung out by life and disease. But also peaceful. What was left of God's loan of life, Opa Simon would say, the final note now called in to balance the books. A gift once wrapped in pretty paper and now removed from the box, but leaving the box and weathered paper behind, a reminder of the transient nature of the soul-gift itself.

When she'd finished washing her opa's body, Bekah lowered the relative gravity in the infirmary and lifted him from the medical tub. As she laid him on the white sheet covering the mortician's gurney, she had the odd thought that he must be cold. And while she knew intellectually that such a concern was silly, she pulled each side of the sheet over his body anyway because it made her feel better to do so. Bekah left his head and neck open so he could hear—another silly assignment of human need to a corpse that didn't have needs. She read *El Malei Rachamim*, the prayer for the dead, taking her time to get the Hebrew pronunciation right for him. Then Bekah picked up Opa Simon's Torah and read Psalm 16, his favorite: "Keep me safe, my God, for in you I take refuge…"

Then she read Psalm 90. And two more psalms after that. She wasn't even sure if he'd liked the ones she was reading now. But that wasn't important, not really. What was important was that she was reading them in his name and remembering him to their ancestors—that she, the next generation, was performing this ritual as a continuation of thousands of years of Jewish tradition.

Bekah could hear Opa Simon's warm laughter at that.

It's a good start.

She was entirely alone now, Bekah realized, without family. She didn't want the ritual to end because when it did, that fact would be true. Set in reality's concrete forever.

Her sceye pinged with an incoming message from Daniel Tripp. She was supposed to meet him ten minutes ago. More algorithms. More debates over how robust they should be.

She muted her sceye and set the Torah aside. Carefully, she wrapped the sheet more tightly around her opa. When he was completely covered from head to toe, Bekah opened the door to Masada Station's medical storage unit and slipped Simon Franklin's earthly remains inside. The temperature made her shiver. Or was it the feeling that this was inadequate to the demands of Jewish death rituals?

God, I really am putting him in the freezer.

Her sceye pinged again. She flicked an eye to open the connection.

"I'll be there in ten, Daniel, okay?"

There was a delay. "Okay," Daniel said. "I'm sorry to interrupt. It's just that—"

"I know, I know," she said, aware she was taking her anger at herself out on him. "I'll be there in ten."

She closed the connection. The white, enshrouded feet of her Opa

Simon stuck out from the storage drawer. Cold seeped out around them in whispered clouds. Bekah pushed the tray the rest of the way into the unit and closed the thick door. Its rubber seals *shunked*.

Airtight.

"Goodbye, Opa," she said. Then, almost like an *amen*: "Gravity: normal."

Her limbs adjusted, but her heart felt no lighter.

Bekah left the infirmary.

"But that's the whole point!" Daniel was saying. He took a breath. He was trying to control himself, though to Bekah, he didn't seem to be trying very hard. Maybe she was being unfair. Maybe he felt sorry for her grief. "If we don't give the algorithm the ability to screw up and self-correct, all it will ever be is programming."

They'd been arguing for at least fifteen minutes. The old argument. Daniel had circled back to his obsession over creating computer code that was a damned-near conscious thing.

"And that's a good thing?" Bekah asked, calculating her words, trying to keep her mind on the technical point she was making. Her thoughts wandered back to the infirmary and the foolish concern that her grandfather must be freezing. "Look, Daniel, we need predictability here. We need reliability. Today isn't the day to strive for the next generation of machine learning. We need to use what we know and find a hack for Cassandra, not take a chance on giving her a back door into Masada's mainframe."

His shoulders sagging, Daniel sat down on the smartdesk. The 3D biomechanical diagram hovering over it shook, then steadied again.

"You're missing the point," he said.

Something tickled the back of Bekah's brain. Daniel could have been her Opa Simon, lamenting her lack of interest in the Old Ways. Making that connection led to another about how Daniel's devotion to adaptive heuristics was so like her grandfather's faith. Daniel seemed unable or unwilling to see the flaws in his own concept of what perfect programming could accomplish, or could be perverted into accomplishing against the interests of the greater good. He failed to see the dangers. Daniel Tripp was a zealot, and self-aware code was his god.

"How can we fight an AI without weaponizing the way she thinks for our own purposes?" he insisted. "We can turn the tables on her, Bekah, fight fire with fire!"

She was nearing the end of her patience. They'd wasted too much time debating this. The door to the lab *swished* open, saving her the need for yet another rebuttal. Her mind relaxed when she saw it was Gregor Erkennen. Maybe she'd make a personnel exchange request after all, despite Gregor's desire that Daniel stay on Masada Station and support their defense of the mainframe, should that become necessary. Maybe she could convince him that Daniel would better serve the cause as part of the team on Prometheus Colony. She could get Mrissa Seldan or Kim Dillon back up here in his place. They were both talented. They were both capable. And neither were self-important, closed-minded pr—

"Ms. Franklin," Gregor said, formal as usual when they weren't alone. "I'd like to introduce you to someone."

Bekah noticed then the two men filing in behind Gregor, and she shelved the reassignment request for later. The first man she knew: Bruno Richter, Gregor's bodyguard. A quiet, frightening man. His angular face always held a perennial, flat expression approximating smugness. But it had something else in it too, a kind of willful detachment. In all her time on Masada Station, she'd never actually heard him speak.

The other man was older, nearing sixty she guessed. He wore old-fashioned clothing, a fedora hat and longcoat. He looked out of place among the Erkennen Faction's blue uniforms and the sterile white, traditional lab coats she and Daniel wore. The salt-and-pepper scruff of his days-old beard growth fit the clothes.

"This is Eugene Fischer," Gregor said.

"My friends call me Stacks," the man said, offering his hand first to Daniel, then to Bekah. His palm was rough. Old and full of history. "Bruno here calls me Mr. Fischer."

Gregor smiled politely.

Bekah wasn't sure how to read Bruno's expression at the obvious snub. Indulgent, maybe. Patient, within limits.

"I thought you were leaving this morning," Daniel said.

"I was," Gregor replied. "I am, soon. Stacks here and Bruno—I'm leaving them on the station. To protect you."

"Protect us?" Daniel said.

Gregor shared a look with Bekah. His eyes were hard, and a little bit sad. The mission he'd given to her and her alone was in them. She touched a fingertip to the Hammer around her neck.

"To protect your work," Gregor said, shifting his gaze to Daniel. "To make sure you accomplish what needs to be done."

"Of course." Daniel's eyes lingered on Richter.

"What do you do in here anyway?" Fischer asked. "Make robots?"

Gregor's breath came out in a *bah* sound. "Bekah is my most insightful programmer," he said. "She sees code in her head like Mozart saw music. Now, Daniel here is a visionary. I'm convinced he'll produce the next-generation AI that will make us all obsolete!"

Bekah blushed, while Daniel beamed.

Fischer raised an eyebrow. "Really," he said. "Robots, then."

"Oh, nothing so crude," Daniel began. "Bodies are so unnecessary to the experience of—"

"Cassandra would disagree, I think," Fischer said.

Mouth open to continue proselytizing, Daniel seemed to have forgotten his next word. Bekah noticed Fischer watching him closely.

"Let's leave that there, then," Gregor said, turning to Bekah. "How's Carrin doing on her special project?"

"Still working out the kinks," Bekah said. "But she's close."

"Special project?" Fischer said.

"She's beta-testing a way to block the Dreamscape algorithm," the regent explained. "We're now almost certain it was an early infiltration strategy by Cassandra. A way to render personnel inert, as it were."

"Huh," Fischer said. "Why bother fighting when you can make the enemy lie down?"

"Something like that," Gregor said. "Bekah, can I talk to you a moment? Alone?"

She nodded. Gregor walked them both a short distance away from the others before speaking.

"Remember what I told you," he whispered. "Fischer and Richter are here to protect you. They're the best at what they do. If they tell you to do something, you do it."

Bekah looked him in the eye. "Why do I—*we*—why do we need protecting?"

Gregor's smile was more hopeful than reassuring. "Cassandra will come here. Maybe not herself, but she will send agents. They're probably already on their way. If we're lucky, they'll fall for our ruse and attack Prometheus Colony, and we'll be ready for them. But if our deception fails, you have what used to be called a long time ago *the nuclear option*. And you have Fischer and Richter to make sure you can use it, should circumstances warrant doing so."

Bekah swallowed the fear rising inside her. It had never occurred to her that Masada Station might be physically attacked. If that happened, a few programmers and two men, no matter how skilled, wouldn't be enough to keep them safe.

"How was the *taharah*?" Gregor asked.

Bekah stumbled over the sudden change in topic. "Difficult," she said. "I hope I did it right."

Her Opa Simon's former student took her by the shoulders. "Your grandfather was very proud of you," he said. "You are exacting. Attentive to the tiniest detail. I'd put my last SynCorp dollar on it—you did fine."

She smiled her gratitude at him. The Regent of Titan leaned down and engulfed her in a Russian bear hug. His warmth felt like family.

"All right, everyone," Gregor said, "it's time for me to head down the well. I wish you all the very best of luck up here. Keep it quiet, eh? No one will even know you're here." He spoke briefly and quietly to Fischer, handed the enforcer something, then walked from the lab without looking back.

"I'm going to my quarters," Richter announced.

"I need a break, too," Daniel asked, standing and stretching. "I'll be back for the next shift."

Both men exited together. When they were gone, Fischer turned to Bekah.

"What did Gregor give you?" Bekah asked, curious.

"He called it a skeleton coder," Fischer said, holding up a small device. "Gets me in anywhere on the station I want to go."

"Oh. Okay." That knowledge made her nervous, and a shade self-conscious.

"Now that it's just you and me," Fischer said, "show me this dead man's switch the regent told me about."

Bekah hesitated. She didn't know Fischer. He looked like a human from another Earth, maybe a parallel planet or pulled from a different time. Everything about him seemed foreign. A man of her grandfather's generation, true, but nothing at all like him. As earthy as her opa had been elegant.

The difference made her uneasy, like his unlimited access to the station made her uneasy. But Gregor Erkennen trusted him. And his judgment would have to be enough.

"Okay." She walked to a computer console and pulled the Hammer out from beneath her shirt. Fischer eyed the oversized key hanging from the gold chain. "This is how it works…"

14

MILANI STUART • ABOARD THE FREEDOM'S HERALD

Her sleep had been restless. Disturbed and random. The sweat from her body slicked the sheets.

Milani turned over again, her hair worrying the back of her neck. Her joints ached. There seemed to be no such thing as comfortable anymore. No such thing as relaxing. She did her best to embrace the merciful darkness of her cabin, to wrap herself up in it while it lasted. Milani had prayed for the dark almost as often as she'd prayed for freedom. Along with silence and the sterile, recycled air of the starship and a comfortable temperature —welcome islands of relief among the constant illumination, the thrash music, the stink of rotting meat, the extreme heat.

She'd almost come to believe her liberation was true, not merely her mind's strategy to help her survive. Any second, she expected the lights to flare and Helena Telemachus to barge into her cabin and begin the whole process over again.

"You thought you were free?" she'd say. "You'll never be free."

The door chime rang.

Milani's eyes snapped open.

Telemachus had never bothered with the courtesy of requesting entry.

She sat up in her bed. "Lights." The room brightened, Milani shying away instinctively. This cabin wasn't the adapted quarters-cum-prison cell they'd caged her in before. Her eyes began to adjust, finding the 3D motion portrait of her parents. They smiled and waved from the small table at the foot of her bed. Milani released a breath she didn't known she was holding and found herself grounded again.

"Come," she said.

The door slid aside.

"Mind if I come in?" Kwazi asked.

Milani's feet touched the floor. Something inside her heart ached, though it wasn't a physical sensation. Odd, that. "Thanks for asking."

He stood in the doorway with a questioning look, framed by light from the corridor.

"Sorry," she said. "Come in."

The door slid shut behind him.

"They sent me to fetch you," Kwazi said. "For the announcement."

"Announcement?"

Milani made room for him on the bunk, and he sat down next to her.

"The ship. Telemachus's trial. You know ... you. Your deliverance from SynCorp custody."

Milani stared at her parents, smiling and waving in the moving portrait. They stood in one of the carved channels of the Antoniadi Crater on Mars, where she'd spent most of her childhood being bored to death while they studied the mineral formations in ancient riverbeds. Touching on the memory accented the ache behind her breastbone. It made her miss them.

"I appreciate all you and ... your friends ... have done for me," she said. "I really do. But, Kwazi, I don't want to be a part of this. I never wanted to be a part of it. I just want my life back. I want to go back to helping people at Wallace Med."

He put his arm around her. Not so long ago it would have made her heart flutter. Now all she felt was a slow, burning tension forming between her shoulder blades.

"I know," he said. It sounded compulsory, not understanding. "But things are different now. This is something greater than ourselves, Milani. This is our chance to kill the Company." He gestured around them at the walls, the deck. "This is how we win."

She looked at him and saw a bright blindness in his eyes. A willful devotion to a version of reality she still couldn't understand and wasn't sure she wanted to. The look reminded her of how she'd found Kwazi in the engine room when this ship had been called the *Pax Corporatum*, almost lifeless and nested in his own filth—divorced from the real world, lost in a deadly dream.

"How is the..." She was afraid to finish it. Afraid of him getting angry with her for asking, maybe? Or afraid of the answer. Maybe both.

"What?" he prompted.

"Dreamscape." Milani held her breath.

Kwazi released his own. "It's fine," he said tightly. "I realize—I mean, I have Amy there, and we talk and we ... I have Amy there. But there's something else I can do to honor her, and that's what I'm doing now, Milani. That's what *we're* doing."

The way he emphasized *we're* gave her pause. Did he mean the two of them, or did he mean him and Amy?

"We're changing things," he continued. "For the better."

"Rebranding Tony Taulke's starship something hopeful doesn't change things," she said. "Not really."

Kwazi squeezed her shoulder. He was trying hard. Trying hard for her, she realized.

"But it's a start," he said. "The ship's a symbol of freedom now, literally. Of liberation."

She nodded, accepting his acceptance of that belief. Kwazi smiled. Was he assuming she agreed with him?

"Rabh's regency is on its last legs now," he said, encouraged. "Valhalla Station is boiling, ready to blow the lid off."

"What do you mean?" Milani asked. "What's happening?"

"You don't know?"

She shook her head. The first thing Helena had done was to disconnect her sceye to make sure the only reality Milani knew was the world Helena created for her. A world of isolation and pain and persuasion.

"Earth is in turmoil. Mars is a Company fortress, but it'll be broken soon. The outer colonies like Valhalla Station—their lifeline to food has been cut off." He raised his hands. "The hydroponics and grain stores here will sustain the station for a while, but they're not enough. You should see the vid protests on *The Real Story*. There aren't enough SynCorp soldiers or marshals to contain it. This is what happens when the people rise up, Milani. This is how tyranny dies."

The stars were in Kwazi's eyes again. The fervent fire of a believer who's absolutely sure he knows what heaven looks like.

"Here," he said, excited, "let me show you."

Kwazi pulled up CorpNet. *The Real Story* presented, in rapid succession, short videos from around the system. Five- and ten-second snapcasts showed the faces of men and women who mined Jupiter's atmosphere despite the dangers. The miners on Callisto fancied themselves the modern descendants of Vikings, rugged and fearless, but the people in the snapcasts seemed anything but. Men, women, the occasional child—they looked frightened. Headlines praising the SSR scrolled across the bottom of the screen. A breaking news banner claimed the hydroponics dome on Callisto had been seized, followed by Cassandra's promises that food distribution would begin soon. Was that doubt she saw in the eyes of the Callistans who'd heard?

"See? This is happening all over the system," Kwazi said.

"They look scared, Kwazi. The people in the vids."

"Well," he said, gesturing at the screen, "they probably are. I mean, I don't blame them. A lot has happened in a short time."

A mother's face, dirty and stretched by fear, flashed on the screen. A little girl, her daughter maybe, had her arms around the woman's waist. There was no audio, but a spokesman interpreted the woman's moving mouth as thanking Cassandra and the SSR for her deliverance. The woman was so happy she was crying, he noted.

"People are scared," Milani said again. "Afraid their children won't eat tomorrow."

Kwazi sighed beside her. "Why do you only see the negative?"

The negative? Kwazi, for God's sake—

"Change is hard," he said, his tone that of a placating parent. "There's always turmoil. There's always strife. But tomorrow will be better." It sounded like a prepared speech.

The woman's face had vanished, replaced by a man in a white tunic. Milani recognized him, one of the doctors in the station's infirmary. He looked exhausted. The clinic behind him was jammed with patients. A headline ran at the bottom, praising the professionals of Valhalla Station for their dedication to duty.

"Okay," Milani said, accepting for now at least that Kwazi would see what he wanted to see. "Okay."

"Come on, we have to go." Kwazi stood up and held out a hand. The smile on his face seemed forced. "We have our own vid to make."

Feeling she had little choice, Milani followed him out of her quarters. A last glance at the image of her parents standing in the ancient Martian riverbed felt like saying goodbye to a previous life.

When the doors opened onto the bridge of the *Freedom's Herald*, the busy noise of people talking over one another spilled out. SSR-uniformed personnel stood over the starship's corporate crew, drawn weapons enforcing orders. The white-hot light of spot welders flashed near the forward viewscreen. A large man, his face cast in a perpetual scowl, turned in the captain's chair to look her over critically. Then he glanced to Kwazi.

"Well, she's in better shape than the last time I saw her," he said.

"Yes," Kwazi said, urging Milani forward to the center of the bridge. She could smell the sweat on the man in the captain's chair. "Dr. Stuart's much better today. I think she's ready."

"She better be."

On the forward screen, Callisto's orbital ring stretched over the corona of the pockmarked moon. There was no activity, no docking shuttles full of tired miners coming off shift or gashaulers full of hypercompressed helium-3 or deuterium departing for the inner system. All commercial activity from Callisto had ceased.

No wonder those people are so frightened, Milani thought. *It's not just the food. It's the not having something to do. It's the idle minds turning to fear to keep themselves occupied.*

Milani understood that need for diversion. She felt that absence in herself even now, that hole where purpose had been before. She was a doctor. She should be helping people. Not watching them descend into ... whatever this was.

The doors behind her opened again. Soldiers dragged Helena Telemachus onto the bridge, her arms secured at her sides. Her hair was tangled, her eyelids heavy. Helena had been having a hard time of it.

Payback's a bitch, bitch.

"And now, our guest of honor," the man in the captain's chair said. He stood formally. "Helena Telemachus, welcome to the bridge of the *Freedom's Herald*. I'm Captain Braxton."

Telemachus jerked her arms, trying to free them. At a nod from Braxton, the guards on either side released her. Helena drew herself up, and her green eyes blazed. Her elfin ears, an affectation of body morphing from her youth, recalled a sad memory of the pride of self-worth they'd once represented.

"On behalf of the Syndicate Corporation, I'm willing to offer you clemency," Helena said. "But only if you release me and surrender to Company authorities. *Immediately.*"

Milani could hear the SynCorp spokesperson behind the words, a ghost of the irrefutable power her pronouncements had once carried. Now the sound was hollow, a flaccid echo of its past authority.

"I'll have to decline," Braxton said, nodding at the comms station. The image of Callisto's docking ring disappeared, replaced by the rigid expression of Adriana Rabh. "Regent. So glad you could make the time."

"Go fuck yourself," Rabh said. The background behind her was plain and unadorned. "Surrender that starship and yourself to corporate authorities. I give you my word—your summary execution will only hurt for a second or two."

The personnel on the bridge, whether they be Company prisoner or SSR trooper, stopped what they were doing. Rabh's reaction, the steel in it, had surprised everyone. Its solid, palpable strength was a stark contrast to Helena's earlier, empty threat.

Braxton laughed and turned to Telemachus.

"It's like you have a script, you two," he said. Then, to the screen, "Adriana Rabh, you are judged an enemy of the people. For too long, you and your fellow faction leaders have built your empire of riches on the backs of the citizen-workers of Sol. Retribution is at hand. Deliverance of justice is at hand. The end of the Syndicate Corporation is at hand."

"Pretty speech," Rabh said without hesitation. "Type it up, print it out, roll it tight, and shove it up your rebel ass."

Braxton opened his hands, as if he'd done all he could do. "We'll begin with Ms. Telemachus's trial. Very public. Very lethal. It won't take long. Then we're coming for you, you old bitch. Victory is assured."

Adriana Rabh lifted a carefully sculpted eyebrow. "Assured? Is that why you're hiding in orbit on the far side of Callisto in Tony Taulke's silver space yacht? If your victory is so assured, why are Callistans rising up against you?"

Braxton effected a look of confusion. "Perhaps you didn't notice the object of their anger—they're rising up against *you*, Regent."

"Keep telling yourself that," Rabh said. Her eyes tracked beyond Braxton. "Helena, this is an unfortunate situation. And that's a goddamned understatement."

Helena swallowed. "We swear our loyalty," Telemachus said. Her throat had sounded wounded and raw. Milani noticed Helena's hands trembling at her sides. Was it possible she was starting to feel sympathy for the woman who'd tortured her without mercy? Who'd murdered Kwazi's loved ones for the sake of a lie? "We do our duty."

Braxton's gaze swung between the two women. "Corporate catchphrases at the hour of your death? Now that's true dedication."

"Last chance," Rabh said, regaining his attention. "Surrender now or—"

Braxton made a slicing motion with his thumb. The forward screen went dark.

"Take her back to the brig," he said.

"Wait!" Kwazi said. "There was to be a trial. She's to be executed!" He sounded childlike in his frustration.

Braxton stepped down from the center of the bridge and into Kwazi's space. "We have a new priority. That bitch in the station. That attitude gets out over the 'net, and our lives get harder. We can kill Telemachus anytime."

"But you said—"

"Jabari! That's enough!" The captain turned to the guards: "Back to the brig!"

They moved, jerking Helena along with them. The door closed behind them. Braxton leaned over Kwazi and Milani again.

"Never ... ever ... question me publicly again. Or, by Cassandra, I'll end you."

Kwazi said nothing, but his eyes held Braxton's.

Milani felt the air rush from her lungs as the captain resumed his seat. And all around her, from Soldier and SynCorp loyalist alike, she heard the same.

15

RUBEN QINLAO • DARKSIDE, THE MOON

The wee hours in Darkside were pretty much like everywhere else Ruben had ever experienced them: a collection of random, subtle sounds that marked time's passing.

The beeping of Brackin's medical equipment monitoring Tony's vitals. The doctor's own slow, rhythmic breathing, while Ruben took the watch. The random disturbances outside the clinic, which often involved someone screaming at someone else down the narrow street, usually about money. For Ruben, they'd melded into a comfortable white noise, a companionable non-silence.

To avoid falling asleep, he stood up from the ratty chair and took in what passed for the defrocked physician's office. A couple of straight-backed chairs stood near the door for patients. Behind him, a converted breakfast nook served as an exam area. A white privacy curtain sectioned it off. Tony lay in Brackin's one and only treatment bed, that rhythmic beeping softly testifying to his tentative hold on life. The equipment was old, of course, thrown away from somewhere like everything else in the clinic. But it still functioned.

Ruben continued to marvel at the role obsolete technology played in the story of their survival.

A wallscreen near the front door offered up *The Real Story* on a constant feed. Brackin had turned down the volume so he could sleep, but the images onscreen told Ruben everything he needed to know. The viewer-driven content was obsessed with the manhunt for him and Tony. Snapcasts from all over Darkside showed bumpy footage of SSR teams knocking on doors. Personal, probing interviews with ragged, frightened residents. Ruben had watched the loop of breaking news from Point Bravo until he couldn't watch it anymore—the blowing of the outer hatch, the "battle against half a dozen Company loyalists," the dramatic escape of SynCorp's CEO...

He wondered how Richard Strunk would feel being described as "half a dozen Company loyalists." Probably insulted.

"I'm worth more than half a dozen," he heard Strunk grumble in his head. "Twice that, even."

Really, their escape had been simple and straightforward. Brackin had guided their slow-moving scooter through the tunnels beneath Darkside. From LUNa City's earliest days, they'd connected an underground network of black marketeers skimming UN goods for sale. The United Nations was long gone, but the black market still existed. Whenever they'd run across shadowy types, it was Isaac Brackin's reputation and con man's wit that got them through. He might be a doctor stripped of his license, but in Darkside Isaac Brackin was everyone's friend.

Ruben turned his back on the hype playing out for the hundredth time on the wallscreen. At the front door, he slid aside the small viewing window and took in the dark, narrow street beyond. More invisible voices, echoing in their disagreement somewhere distant. Someone demanding something. Someone else, upset at being rousted from bed.

"I don't think he's coming back."

Brackin's voice startled him. Ruben almost cursed out loud. He was tired of reacting to every little thing.

"I know," Ruben said, hoping that would end the discussion.

"He's one tough sonofabitch," Brackin continued, swinging his legs off the couch. Ruben slid the tiny window shut. "But that strike team had nearly a dozen Soldiers. And all Strunk had was a couple of pistols and—"

"Yeah," Ruben said, his tone testy. He didn't need Brackin to remind him Strunk was either dead or in custody and likely being tortured. That particular diagnosis didn't require a medical degree.

Tony murmured from the other side of the room, dreaming aloud again. Brackin's eyelids flickered lazily, but he hauled himself to his feet. Before he'd crossed the short space to the bed, Tony was thrashing, pulling at the plastic tube feeding into his arm.

"Help me here," Brackin hissed, steadying the IV bag before it smashed to the floor.

Ruben crossed the distance quickly.

"What do you want me to do?"

"Hold his arms down," Brackin said, "before he rips the IV out."

"What are you doing here, Pop?" Tony demanded, looking upside down at Ruben. Sweat covered his sour skin. "You're supposed to be dead! I killed you!"

Ruben leaned in with his full weight, holding Tony's arms against the bed frame.

"Delusions," Brackin reported, preparing a hypodermic needle.

"Right," Ruben said, though he knew differently. Tony wasn't acting out the feverish visions of an addled mind. He'd risen to power the old-fashioned way—by filling the vacuum he'd created through patricide. The memory seemed to fuel Tony's struggles, and Ruben had to fight to hold the older man down.

"You're not going to fuck up the business anymore!" Tony yelled.

"If we don't shut him up..." Brackin grabbed a small towel and stuffed it in Tony's mouth. He injected the IV line as Tony's struggles grew more frenzied and he shouted incoherent obscenities through the towel.

"You'll suffocate him!" Ruben said.

Tony's eyes fluttered, his limbs went limp. With a sigh, he became unconscious again.

"If only it were that easy," Brackin groused. "It'd be no more than he deserves."

"What did you give him?" Ruben demanded, removing the towel. "Sedatives never work that fast in real life."

"A propofol-diazepam cocktail works that fast in real life. I had to stop his yelling."

Brackin became pensive as the room calmed down.

"What is it?" Ruben asked.

The doctor's eyes flashed uncertainty. "I'm just not sure about the diagnosis. I thought sepsis, but..."

"But?"

"His recovery should be further along," Brackin said. "It could be encephalopathy."

The way he said it made Ruben loath to ask his next question. "What does that mean?"

"Much more serious. Much longer recovery time." Ruben could see the checklist ticking off in Brackin's head. "Could explain the delusions though. But so could sepsis—"

More shouting came from the street outside. Only this wasn't a dispute over money. Holding a finger to his lips Ruben quick-stepped to the front door and its tiny window... He stopped short, doing a double take as he passed the wallscreen.

"I know her," Brackin said, coming up beside him.

"I do, too."

Just up the street, Ionia was trading insults with a woman leading an SSR tactical team trying to gain entry into Eros Erotics. How long would it be until she mentioned the strange man in the hood who'd asked after Brackin's practice?

The leader of the TAC team turned to give one of her troopers an order. *The Real Story* camerabot floating nearby showed her in profile.

"And I know *her*," Ruben said. "Elissa Kisaan." The second of Elise Kisaan's knife-wielding clone-assassins he'd fought in hand-to-hand combat, this one while fleeing SynCorp HQ. She was the reason they were hiding on the Moon. And the lead dog in the hunt to track them down, apparently.

"Jesus, I recognize her too. Goddamn, they're almost on top of us, Qinlao. You guys have gotten me so deep in shit—"

"Shut up!" Ruben said. "Let me think."

"Think?" Brackin paced nervously. "What's there to think about? They're a few doors down from—"

"Shut up! Go check on Tony. I'll think of something."

The voices outside drew nearer. A rapping came from the neighbor's apartment.

Brackin moved deeper into the room. Ruben could practically hear the con man in him rehearsing excuses: *I hate Tony Taulke. He took my license! They said they'd kill me if I didn't help...*

But Brackin was right. They were trapped. They couldn't run, not with Tony in his current condition. And Kisaan and her TAC team were coming.

Ruben grabbed his cloak.

"What are you doing?" Brackin asked. "Where are you going?"

"Leading them away from here," Ruben said. He had the katara, but he needed something with longer range. Something louder. "Got any projectile weapons?"

"What? No, of course not!" A short debate broiled behind Brackin's eyes. "Well..." He opened a drawer and withdrew a handgun.

More old-fashioned tech to the rescue. Ruben almost laughed out loud.

"I thought so. Burner bands?"

Brackin gave him another knee-jerk defensive look, then, grumbling, pulled a syncer from a drawer full of them. "This has a thousand SCDs on it."

"Untraceable?" Ruben asked.

"What do you think?"

"Okay. A thousand should be enough." Brackin's black-market syncer should be just the thing to divert the dogs.

There was more pounding, more yelling from the next-door neighbor.

"Take it." Brackin handed him the illegal syncer. "If you make it back, I might have something else for you. But it needs repair. If they don't arrest me," he said with sarcasm, "I'll try and get it working."

"Okay." Ruben snapped the syncer around his wrist. "Suggestions for how to get out of here?"

Brackin jerked his head. "Go out the back. Make three right turns in the alleys and you'll end up across from Ionia's place. You can hit them from there."

Ruben took the 11-millimeter pistol. He ejected the clip, found it full, and snapped it back in.

"Thanks."

"Just get the fuck gone," Brackin said.

Ruben opened the back door to the clinic, surveying the alley beyond. He might be signing Tony's death warrant by leaving. Brackin was an opportunist, especially when it came to saving his own hide—a motivation Ruben understood all too well in that moment.

But he'd have to trust Brackin. This was their only play.

He slipped into the alleyway, leaving his doubts and Tony Taulke behind him.

Three right turns. Brackin had been straight about that, at least.

Elissa Kisaan's TAC team had finished with the neighbor. Turned the small apartment upside down, Ruben assumed, given the man's animated attitude. He aimed the pistol at Kisaan from the dark alleyway, bracing the butt in his left palm. The shot was at least two hundred feet.

Ruben thumbed the hammer back. His sister Ming had always emphasized hand-to-hand combat when training young Ruben to defend himself. Shooting had never been his talent.

One of Kisaan's Soldiers made for Brackin's door, pointing at the upside-down caduceus and laughing.

Ruben fired.

A sharp *crack* was followed by a spark, shattering the relative quiet of the Darkside street.

Kisaan dropped to the ground, but the ricochet told Ruben he'd missed. The Soldiers spun toward the alleyway, seeking a target. Infrared beams painted the wet stone near him. Ruben fired twice more, and one of the Soldiers went down.

Someone screamed.

"There!" a woman cried, pointing in his direction. "It came from there!"

Ruben ran.

Boots slipping on the floor of the alley, Ruben rounded a corner and halted. He couldn't outdistance the pursuit. Not if he was to lead them away from Tony.

Two Soldiers appeared at the far end of the alley, silhouetted by the painted neon of Eros Erotics. One of them bent over and picked up a shell casing. Ruben cupped the pistol again, aiming carefully.

Crack!

The casing dropped to the alley floor, followed by the Soldier who'd picked it up.

The second Soldier fired. Stunner tech. He'd missed because Ruben was still alive. Without MESH clothing, one hit by a stunner set to kill would electrocute him with his own EM field.

He darted down the corridor and came out in the grand expanse of the barrio. The massive, multistoried ring of tenements was quiet, its residents sleeping. The refuse pile that was Challenger Park flickered in shadow. Sprinting for the skyway, Ruben noticed a second TAC team enter the barrio from the other side.

He felt the target painting his back and dived into the massive refuse pile that had once been the green grass of picnic grounds. The hooded cloak made the shoulder roll awkward, but he found his balance and regained his feet. Red targeting beams scoured the garbage below from the apex of the skyway overhead.

Ruben exited the dump, kept moving. A jaunt down a long, poorly lit corridor delivered him to Darkside's busiest red-light district.

Oh, you lovely, flesh-packed Fleshway.

The doublewide corridor was thicker with people than it had been during the day. Martian bars and brothels closed in the middle of the night by law. Not so in Darkside.

Ruben put the gun in his belt and thrust his wrist wearing the burner band into his pocket to avoid the sticky hands of thieves—he'd learned that lesson—and waded into the crowd. It parted and filled in around him. The combined sounds and smells and flashing lights dazed his exhausted senses. With any luck, they'd have a similar effect on his pursuers.

Ruben pressed through the throng, stepping over the hackheads and drunks lying along the gutter, ignoring the insults and challenges of passersby. Behind him, voices rose in protest. He didn't dare look back. In his mind's eye he pictured Kisaan and her teams searching frantically for the man in the hooded cloak.

"How much for a hopper?" he asked, pressing into a booth. Over it, the sign *Shuttles Los!* blazed in sunburnt orange.

The vendor didn't glance up as *The Real Story*'s theme music died down, allowing a commentator's voice to rise. Ruben leaned in to listen, prompting a grunt of displeasure from the vendor. Had Brackin sold them out after all?

"—in pursuit of one of them now," the reporter reported. "His capture is imminent. Stay tuned!"

Ruben relaxed. Testing the limits of his own willpower, he resisted looking over his shoulder.

"Mind the personal space, buddy," the vendor said.

"Sorry. How much for a one-way to Earth? Next available. Priority."

Smirking, the man said, "For you? Five hundred."

Ruben didn't argue and offered the burner band on his wrist for scanning. "Ticket's e-tagged to your syncer, bub. Happy trails." The man resumed his fascination with *The Real Story*.

Returning to the crowd of the Fleshway, Ruben spotted a drunk lying unconscious along one wall. The vomit around him acted like a shield, keeping the teeming crowd at bay. A quick glance over his shoulder found Kisaan's TAC teams spreading out among the vendor booths.

Ruben removed his cloak. Kneeling down, he draped it around the sleeper's shoulders. The man grunted, rousing a little when Ruben snapped the illegal syncer to his wrist.

His sister Ming had once told him she was placing the Qinlao Faction into his hands because Ruben, she said, was a moral man—not the heartless battle-queen she'd become to win their family's place in SynCorp's hierarchy. His moral leadership was what the Company needed now, she'd said—a preserver, not a builder.

Scenting the dogs onto a helpless drunk didn't feel like the actions of a moral man.

He stood and edged away, averting his face from the crowd. Ruben watched from a distance as the Soldiers methodically worked their way along the Fleshway. When they reached Shuttles Los!, the vendor would tell them of a cloaked man who'd bought a ticket to Earth and wanted to get out of Darkside fast. He'd hand over the syncer ID without a second thought. It was supposed to be untraceable, but Ruben suspected Cassandra's people would easily pierce that veil. It would lead them right to the drunkard.

They'll let him go, Ruben, the practical man, told himself. *I didn't even plant the gun on him. They'll let him go.*

Sure they will, Ruben, the moral man, responded. *Sure they will.*

16

REBEKAH FRANKLIN • MASADA STATION, ORBITING TITAN

"It's 'round the clock now," Carrin Bohannon reported.

She glanced from one to the other of Masada Station's skeleton crew. They were in the War Room, what they'd come to call the station's nerve center. Bekah's tech team was taking shifts monitoring Cassandra's constant, relentless cyberattacks against Titan. Only four—Bekah, Carrin, Daniel, and Maya Breides—were awake. Aisha Alvi and Noa Comar were asleep in their quarters.

"They're actually tightbeaming worms over CorpNet," Carrin said, her voice open with admiration. "They're propagating across the Labyrinth... I mean, I can't even keep up."

She also sounded frightened.

The corner of Bekah's mouth ticked up anyway. Every time she heard the name of Titan's decoy database—Gregor Erkennen's morbid sense of humor at work—it made her want to laugh: the Labyrinth! Opa Simon would have approved. A callback to Greek mythology and the maze built by King Minos to trap the Minotaur in a perpetual loop of confusing pathways. *Loops and pathways*, she thought, smiling at how appropriate those terms were for the cyber snipe hunt they'd set Cassandra on. Billions of worms tunneling through the Labyrinth, delivering their exfiltration payloads and snatching yottabytes of corporate data. Information gold, mined from the veins of the Erkennen Faction's genius.

"But all they're getting is pyrite," Bekah said out loud.

"Say again?"

Eugene Fischer sat at an empty workstation, hands behind his head, feet on the console. Simon Franklin would have admonished him to put his feet down, to show a little respect as a guest. But she wasn't her opa. And Fischer wasn't someone she was comfortable being around, much less giving an etiquette lesson to. For hours she'd sat here with her shift mates and Fischer, observing the attacks on the Labyrinth and marveling at the tag-team defenders of Erkennen and Zafar and the other defenders at Prometheus Colony. Sometimes they were able to fend off the attacks; sometimes they weren't. But every seeming victory for Cassandra was an actual victory for SynCorp. Every prize the attacks took was no prize at all. Just a collection of empty code, false test results, and flawed schematics.

"Nothing," she said.

"No, you said something," Fischer said, curious. His feet came down as he sat forward. In her mind, Bekah nodded to her grandfather's spirit, as if invoking his memory had somehow influenced the old man to demonstrate some couth. "Something about pirates?"

Bekah's grin came spiced with indulgence. "*Pyrite*. As in iron pyrite. Fool's gold. It's what—"

"I know what it is," Fischer said. "I was making a joke."

"Okay."

"Seriously, Bekah, I don't know how Rahim is doing it," Carrin said. "The SSR worms have zombied the whole system, or damn near all of it. I don't see how he's walling off his own response code."

"Zombied?" Fischer asked.

Bekah's tight expression returned. "It's when—"

"Never mind," he said, waving a hand. "I don't need to understand."

"He's not in the system."

Everyone turned to look at Daniel Tripp.

"Rahim's not in the system," Daniel continued. "He can't be. Cassandra's AI reaction response is too fast for any human to keep up with."

"Go team," Fischer said flatly.

"What I mean is," Daniel said, throwing a nervous glance the enforcer's way, "Rahim and I discussed the defense strategy before he left. The algorithms he and the regent programmed set up millions of fake techs, right? The castles with the Holy Grails in them. Only, instead of spikes in the moat to impale attackers who fall in, there are code bombs hidden to blow up infiltrator worms."

Fischer yawned.

Bekah gave him a look. "Go on, Daniel."

"Any time a data exfiltration request hits one of the bombs, it puts up the most vigorous defense it can against the breach attempt. Never good enough, of course, in the long run. Cassandra can outthink it. But that takes time, and there are millions of those defenses that have to be overcome."

"But eventually those will run out, right?" Fischer said.

"No," Carrin said. Daniel had been about to answer, but she put up a hand. "This is how I'd do it. I'd use a botnet that only connects to the Labyrinth at random times and downloads no data, not a single packet—it only uploads random algorithms to generate new castles around new fake tech grails. And I'd use—"

"—adaptive heuristics to keep Cassandra on her toes," Daniel finished. He turned to Bekah with an I-told-you-so look on his face. "That's exactly what he's doing."

"Wow," Fischer said. "How do you people ever get laid?"

Bekah turned to him. "Mr. Fischer, what Rahim is doing on Titan is protecting the entire Company by protecting Masada's mainframe from attack. You realize that, right?"

Fischer's eyebrows went up. "More or less," he said, holding her gaze.

The data readout on Carrin's screen chittered, monitoring the SSR cyberattacks. When no one else spoke, she cleared her throat. "Well, it seems to be working." The Erkennen Faction's expert had transferred her admiration from the enemy to Rahim for his stalwart cyberdefense.

Bekah's face flattened and she rubbed her eyes. "You guys got this? I'm tired. I need some sleep."

"Sure," Maya Breides said. "You and Daniel were here all night. Carrin and I have this."

Carrin offered a thumbs-up of confirmation, then turned back to her screen.

Daniel got to his feet. "I think I'll hit the gym."

Fischer stood when Bekah stood. "I'll escort you to your quarters," he said. "I'm due a little shut-eye myself."

"That isn't necessary."

"Sure, except that it is," Fischer said. "I'm your shadow. Regent's orders."

Bekah's face flashed an expression that was too tired to argue. "Sure. Okay." She led the way from the War Room.

"I'll send Richter to stand watch with you guys," Fischer said over his shoulder.

Carrin gave another distracted thumbs up. Had Maya winced at the sound of Richter's name? Bekah couldn't blame her. Even more than Fischer, Richter tickled her creepy bone.

"I get the sense you don't care much for me," Fischer said.

How perceptive, Bekah thought. What she said was: "Whatever gave you that idea?"

Their footsteps bounced off the walls of the empty corridor. The lights were set to fifty percent brilliance. Anyone looking in from the outside would think the station empty, part of a narrative Gregor Erkennen had leaked through semi-secure channels he knew were being tapped. The Erkennen Faction and all its secrets were turtled up in Prometheus Colony, the story went. Not easily defended, to all appearances, Masada Station had been abandoned. Move along, Cassandra. Nothing to see here.

"I study people for a living," Fischer answered. "Especially people I'm contracted to protect."

Bekah nodded. He'd reminded her of something it was easy to forget under the abrasion of Fischer's personality. He was here at her regent's request. She didn't have to like him. She just had to tolerate him.

"Coffee?" she said. The cafeteria was just ahead. She could use the diversion. A twelve-hour shift in the War Room made you long for walls that looked like anywhere else.

Fischer cocked an eyebrow. "I thought you were looking for shut-eye."

"I was looking to get out of there. Watching the attacks on the Labyrinth, even knowing that's exactly what we want to be happening ... every time I see code turn red, my anxiety spikes. I need to rest. My brain more than my body."

Fischer nodded. "Coffee's good."

The cafeteria was dark. All lights defaulted to *off* except in occupied areas, and those were set to the fifty percent luminescent threshold. Windows facing outward to space were set to maximum opacity, effectively blacking them out. All external comms traffic was forbidden, including calls to Titan—to prevent accidentally opening a back door to the station for Cassandra, Bekah told Fischer when he asked for an explanation. Internal comms were allowed only on a local network with a range that stopped at the station's walls.

Bekah stepped the cafeteria. The motion sensors switched on the lights to half brightness. Vacant but for the two of them, the hall designed to accommodate fifty or more personnel felt cavernous and cold. Its white walls and chrome fixtures and tables and chairs shone with their own emptiness.

After programming the coffeemaker, Bekah joined Fischer at his table. The sound of heating water *shushed* behind her.

"It's not that I don't like you." Bekah felt inexplicably guilty that Fischer had pegged her feelings so accurately. It made her feel like an open book exposed to his flat, probing eyes. "You seem like a dark man to me," she said with a sudden need to be authentic. "It makes me uncomfortable."

"Never heard it put quite that way before, but that's pretty spot-on." Fischer took off his hat and set it on the table. "I'm in a dark business. It's not for sunny people."

That truth was so on-the-nose, it made her smile. Like everything else, Bekah had heard stories of SynCorp's seedier side. Seen the vids on *The Real Story*, had wondered about them. She'd known the factions employed fixers, enforcers, assassins—whatever you wanted to call them—to see that the business necessary for making the Company was done. Meeting Bruno Richter upon her arrival at Prometheus Colony had been a singular moment of revelation for her. It wasn't pretty, but it was necessary—that's what her Opa Simon had once explained. A strange rationalization coming from such a deep-thinking man, she now thought.

"It's just that..." Bekah began, not quite sure how to put it. "I lost my grandfather recently."

Fischer cleared his throat. "I heard. My condolences."

"Thanks," she said, meaning it. There was something about this man, an odor of personality. It came on strong at first, smelled offensive because it was refreshingly honest, if dark—not hidden by social niceties or a cordial veneer cloaking some personal political agenda. Fischer seemed a simple man of obvious intent. Sarcastic and bold and enviable in his transparency. But, Bekah was coming to realize, Fischer was really a multilayered, complex man wearing a mask that hid the hard heart of a brutal killer. Yet, even that seemed too simple an answer for the Fischer equation. In a way, he reminded her of her opa, and that thought almost made Bekah laugh.

The coffeemaker beeped once.

"Hypnos's bane," Fischer said.

"What?" Bekah asked, rising. She grabbed two insulated cups and drew the coffee.

"The Greek god of sleep, Hypnos. I'm guessing he hated coffee."

Bekah handed him a cup and sat. With Fischer's explanation, the reference came back to her. Part of her classical training, Opa Simon's influence. *An assassin familiar with obscure Greek deities?* Like her grandfather, indeed. Simon Franklin, master of philosophy and archaic trivia. Apologist for the Syndicate Corporation.

"I think you and my grandfather would've gotten along," she said. "You're both fans of long and winding conversations."

"Those can be the best kind."

"That's what he'd say!" Bekah allowed with light laughter. "He'd say we don't learn if we don't explore."

Fischer offered a supportive nod. "True enough, I guess. Sometimes you find the good by exploring." He took a swig of coffee and grimaced. "Sometimes you don't." The way he said it got her attention.

"Why did you go into ... the line of work you do?" she asked. Voicing the question embarrassed her. She hardly knew Fischer. She couldn't even tell him to take his feet off a computer console. She wasn't sure how much better she wanted to know him.

He took another sip of coffee, then appeared to make a decision.

"The Weather War was tough on everyone," Fischer said. "And before that, when whole populations were migrating inward from the coasts, away from submerging cities... I'm talking about Earth now—long time before you were born, kid. People wanted to live where the food was and the floods weren't. Insurance companies went under because claims outdistanced premiums. Governments tried to take up the slack, but their coffers ran dry too. When the world's power grid and transportation system started to fail, the global economy went to shit. Tens of thousands moved to government poorhouses."

Fischer looked at Bekah, and there was a weariness behind his eyes. "We'd lived in luxury for so long, we forgot what it was built on. But we found out, boy-o. Mother Universe reminded us." He took a long swig from his cup.

Bekah listened, drinking her coffee while Fischer spoke. She knew the history, and what Opa Simon had told her fit what Fischer said. No wonder mankind had stepped into space. Desperate people take desperate chances. Sometimes, you decided to hell with the devil you knew.

"You didn't answer my question," she said. "About why you got into the ... business you're in."

"Yeah," Fischer said. "I didn't." He brushed a finger toward her cup. "Take that to go? I'll see you safely to your quarters. And I need to roust Richter out for his shift guarding the geek squad."

Bekah knew the end of a conversation when she heard one. She refreshed her coffee, and they left the cafeteria. The motion sensors cut the lights behind them as they stepped into the corridor. The lift took them up to the vacant eeriness of the habitat level. The dim half-light snapped on as they stepped onto Level Three of the station. Unlike earlier, Bekah found herself glad to have Fischer walking beside her. She keyed in the lock code to her quarters while he waited like an awkward date.

Swish.

"Lock the door behind you," he said.

"Okay," she said. "Hey, Fischer—Stacks—we're safe here, right? Gregor camouflaged us well. You're here. Bruno's here."

He held her gaze a moment.

"Sure," Fischer said. "Like I said, lock the door."

17

STACKS FISCHER • MASADA STATION, ORBITING TITAN

I left Erkennen's protégé, but not until I'd heard that lock cycle. Bekah Franklin was a living, breathing dead man's switch. If she died, so went the Company.

That weighed on my mind a bit, so I took a walk. I do some of my best thinking when my feet are moving and my mouth isn't. I didn't really have anyone 'cept my contract to talk to, and she'd be counting sheep soon. My only other options were a handful of geeks who spoke English but in a different language, and Bruno Richter, who preferred one-word grunts from Hunland to real conversation.

Well, that was just fine with me. Maybe it was professional competition or maybe it was his killing style—indirect, with poison—but every time Bruno Richter breathed, he rubbed me the wrong way.

I walked and thought and found myself comparing Richter to Daisy Brace. He came up short in every way. I chalked that up to my reaction to his reaction to my being on his turf. Defensive, offended, jealous. *Something.* But if Gregor Erkennen thought Richter could handle the job of keeping Franklin safe, he'd never have brought me here, right? I was playing nursemaid to his Number One Man. That had to curdle the milk in Bruno's cornflakes. The looks he gave me were one trigger finger short of homicide.

I took my time, my steps clicking and clacking along Level 3's lifeless corridor. They were the only sound around. I cocked an ear at the tiny apartments the crew would have occupied were they still in residence. Every single one was silent as the grave. Hell, the doors, labeled for their occupants who'd moved moonside, even reminded me of tombstones.

My joints had begun to ache, the left knee particularly. The air felt heavy in my lungs, like the cold of space was seeping through the walls. So the heat, like the lights, had been set to minimal function, part of Gregor's distraction strategy. Plenty warm to ward off a need for a winter coat, but not warm enough for my old bones. If we'd been back on Earth, I could pretty much guarantee a thunderstorm was coming.

I favored the knee a bit as I slow-walked the habitat level. The light in the section I'd just left blinked out. The one in front flickered alive. Masada Station was big. Not as big as Adriana Rabh's ornamented headquarters belt-buckling Callisto's ring, mind you, but it felt bigger—the absence of the living will do that to a place. I'd counted thirty or so doors since I'd left Rebekah Franklin. Thirty or so vacant quarters, half the station's complement.

Masada Station was more rigid in its design than Rabh's HQ too, more clinical, which made sense given the tech-types that built it. I literally doffed my hat to Erkennen as I walked. He'd achieved something by dressing up Prometheus Colony as the actual prize. He'd managed to fool Cassie Kisaan sitting in her iron throne on Earth. Imagine how much data he'd had to fake to do that. Apartment assignments. Food shipment deliveries going back years. The absence records for staff kiddos, sick from school on a given day. And all just to make it seem like the brain trust's heavy lifting happened on the moon below instead of this li'l ole asteroid outpost.

Ah, here we were: my destination. I pushed the door chime. The beepity-beep of an unlock code answered a second later, and the door slid open. Richter's bony frame looked bonier in a wife-beater T-shirt and gray trousers, suspenders hanging around his legs. His face was impassive and ice cold. Looking at it made my knee flare up.

"Ja?"

"Your shift to watch over the Geek Patrol, Bruno," I said. I tried to sound friendly, though not too hard. We all have our pride.

"Where is Bekah?" he asked, each syllable like a jackboot on a street.

"In her quarters. Locked up tight."

"*Gut*," he said in glottal-stop German, beckoning with his hand. "I'm getting dressed. Come in, Fischer."

Richter backed away. I stepped into the doorway so it wouldn't close, but I didn't go in. Always get the lay of the land before you offer your back to it. There was a light on in the small bathroom. He headed for it.

His quarters were dimly lit like the rest of the station, but I got the impression they were that way all the time. A window looked out to the stars, or would have if it hadn't been blacked out by Erkennen's camouflage protocol. Otherwise, Richter's quarters were about what you'd expect. Clueless bachelor styling—and if you don't know any clueless bachelors, that means no style at all. A well-stocked liquor cabinet. The handful of mid-sized glass cases across the small apartment caught my eye. Bruno had a hobby.

I stepped in. The door closed behind me.

A faint, musty, musky odor crawled up my nose. It seemed to leave a slick backtrail in my olfactory factory the more I breathed it. It was an earthy scent. More like Earthy—I hadn't smelled anything like it since I'd been on Ye Olde Home World. It smelled like wild fur that hadn't been dunked in a river in a while.

"Want a drink?" Bruno called from the bathroom.

"I'm good," I said.

I could see his face in the mirror, his eyes cocked at me on the angle. His face was wet, but he was shaving without cream. It's what men who have something to prove to themselves do instead of the smart thing—namely, using cream. There was a dragging scrape as the old straight razor decapitated the hairs from his jawline. I began cataloging potential weapons in the apartment as I stepped closer to the glass cases, my curiosity getting the better of me. Close up I saw they were actually aquariums. Empty of water, but the bottoms lined with rocks. Fake flora under solar lamplights. In one corner of each there was a box up top with a fat, hollow tube hanging into the tank.

I peered closely. There was a small, rolling thump inside. Something squeaked.

"Say, what's in here anyway? Pet rocks?"

Hungry pet rocks? A mouse emerged from the tube, dropping from the small box up top. Its nose twitched left and right. Its tiny, black eyes opened wide. I don't think dropping into an aquarium full of rocks had been on its tiny to-do list today.

Something moved under the rocks. I took a half step back and bumped into Richter. He's quiet, he is, when he isn't shaving.

"Like them?" he asked.

I put a little distance between me and Richter's pal-o'-mine smile. He held the razor in his right hand. Half his face was smooth as a baby's bottom. So, the razor was plenty sharp then. Good to know.

"What, the rocks? Or the mouse?"

I bent my right hand about thirty degrees, out of his eye line. Instinct on my part. Just verifying my springblade was tucked tight where it ought to be, in its launcher under my wrist.

Bruno held his smile and brushed past me. He lifted the aquarium's lid, reached in, and picked up the mouse by its tail. It squirmed and squeaked.

"Nein, neither," he said, dangling the mouse above the rocks. They shifted again, and a scaly head emerged. Grayish-brown, a body followed the tail, uncoiling. It kept coming, shedding the rocks like a second skin. It must have been two feet long, though most of it stayed hidden beneath the rocks. The snake's eyes didn't leave the mouse. The little bugger's struggles became frantic. Bruno dangled it like a hypnotist's watch.

"Black mamba," he said, dropping the mouse. "Very dangerous."

Bleating its terror, the mouse ran for the tube. The snake was faster. It struck, vise-gripping its jaws around its prey. The mouse's feet pumped, hoping for purchase. The mamba dropped it, and the mouse scrambled for the tube again. Watching it was like watching gravity being turned up in the tank. The closer the mouse got to the tube, the slower its movements became. The snake struck again. This time, the mouse froze. After the mamba dropped it, the mouse twitched on the rocks, the snake's venom flooding its system.

"Beautiful, isn't she? A perfect killing machine," Bruno explained, not looking at me. It was a good show in the tank. "She will not eat until the prey is fully paralyzed."

"You can't be too careful."

The mouse had quit struggling. Its whiskers stopped twitching.

"That is true." Abruptly, Bruno stood up and offered me his hand. He'd moved the razor first, I noticed. "I owe you an apology, Fischer."

"Okay." My hand came up on its own and accepted the handshake. I set my body weight on my back foot as we shook, ready for him to pull me in and start slicing with the razor. Old trick.

But that didn't happen.

"Gregor brought you here," he said, pumping my hand. "I took it personally. But he's the boss, yes? And what, eh, the Geek Patrol as you call them—what they're doing is too important to risk. I get that now. We work together, yes? We keep Bekah Franklin and the others safe."

"Okay," I said amiably. What I was thinking was how Bruno Richter would make a first-class undertaker with that thin, ghoulish grin of his. For a man who hardly used words, Richter had just unpacked a suitcase full. "I appreciate that."

Maybe it was the snake beginning to devour the mouse, or maybe it was that, when Bruno dropped my hand, he left his sweaty DNA mixing with mine. But something about the thin man's little speech sounded rehearsed. Maybe he'd wanted to make a good impression and actually *had* rehearsed it. And if he'd wanted to kill me, he'd had ample opportunity and a sharp straight razor to do it. Yet, here I stood, unmolested save for a slightly sweaty palm.

"I will finish getting dressed," he said. He patted the tank on his way to finishing his shave. The front half of the mouse was on its way to an acid bath in the black mamba's gut. The smug-looking snake was enjoying its dinner.

"All right," I said. "I think I'll walk around the station a bit more."

Fuck you, screaming knee.

"Sounds gut."

One last look at the show in the tank. Only the hind end of the mouse was visible now. Its tail lay limp while the mamba gulped another gullet full. I wondered what it felt like to be eaten alive, paralyzed and aware.

Does the stomach acid burn when you get there? How long could you live while the enzymes broke you down? Would you feel your skin as it disintegrated? Or would you hopefully, mercifully suffocate first?

Richter's eyes found mine in the mirror's angle again. As he brought the razor up to finish guillotining, he jerked his head up in a manly, half salute between colleagues. Then flashed his toothy, mortician's smile.

Made me wonder if *his* victims died paralyzed and aware too.

With Richter's penchant for murder by poison still on my mind, I took the lift to the station's second level. That's where all the fun stuff is. A promenade of small shops, shuttered and deserted, of course. A bar patterned after a German bierhaus, likely my new best friend's second home. Then there was the fitness section. Jesus, they even had an Olympic-sized swimming pool! Gregor took care of his people, made sure they had the good life. I knew without looking too closely there'd also be an upscale brothel or two somewhere on the promenade. Gregor knew how to keep his geeks happy and loyal.

Grunting—a loud sound of human effort in the otherwise silence.

Someone was working hard at something next door to the pool. I walked along and found a small sign that read *Gymnasium*. Inside, the guy named Tripp sat at a machine trying to add more muscle to his girlish figure. I'd noticed him arguing with Franklin on more than one occasion. He seemed harmless, but so do rocks until a snake crawls out from under them.

I walked up behind him, quiet as a mouse.

"How's it going?" I said.

The weights dropped with a loud, metallic *clang*. It boomed around the deserted gym.

"Oh, hey," he said, like his mom had just walked in and the bedcovers weren't high enough to hide the sin. There was a sign on the wall telling weightlifters to be careful with the equipment. Maybe that was the source of his sheepish look. Tripp hopped off the machine and grabbed a towel to wipe his face. His hair was plastered down. He'd been there a while.

"Nervous about something?" I said. He looked it.

"What? No. You just surprised me is all." He must have really wanted to clean up, cuz his towel got a lot wetter pretty fast. He mopped his arm pits. It took a few passes to do the job. I'd gotten close enough to smell the sharp, sour scent of sweat coming off him. Tripp smelled like fear.

"It's okay if you're nervous," I said, and meant it. "Times are sketchy. Nervous is fear's way of keeping you on your toes."

He nodded. "Yeah, I guess."

"Figured you were headed for bed when we all left the War Room."

Tripp walked to a rack and stretched the towel over it to dry. He made sure its two halves hung symmetrically over the metal bar, each side the length of the other.

Geeks are like that. Meticulous. Anal.

"I always work out before bedtime," he said as he eyed the towel. He sounded more impressed with his efforts than I was. A hot, sharp sting of pain arced randomly across my knee. I told it to fuck off again.

"That's a healthy thing," I said. "I guess."

"Yeah."

"Think I'm gonna turn in myself," I said. "Long night."

"Yeah, okay." Tripp walked past me. "This whole thing—it's just one long night, isn't it?"

Since it sounded rhetorical, I let the question go. We took the lift together back up to the Habitat Level. The towel absorbed Tripp's sweat but left that sour scent, wafting up from his underarms. It reminded me of the feral smell in Richter's quarters.

Tripp tossed me a goodnight as he unlocked his quarters. I went to my own, hoping for a decent night's rest for a change.

Snakes and pits. Somehow I knew that's what would fill my dreams tonight, boy-o.

Snakes and pits.

18

KWAZI JABARI • ABOARD THE FREEDOM'S HERALD

Carl Braxton had failed to keep his promise.

Fulfilling it now hinged on taking Rabh Regency Station, he'd said. Once that was done, Braxton pledged—for whatever that was worth—then and only then Kwazi could execute Telemachus live on *The Real Story*.

"It'll play great with the masses," Braxton assured him. "The Hero of Mars exacting justice on the puppet master who once pulled his strings, who murdered those closest to him. It'll be the most popular vid of the revolution."

And yet, still they waited—for someone Cassandra was dispatching from the inner system. A leader to take the conn of the *Freedom's Herald* and prosecute the assault on the station for the camerabots. To Kwazi, it was just one more delay on the way to obtaining justice for Amy. And Aika and Beren.

"Hey, Jabari, did you hear me?"

Braxton's curtness brought Kwazi back to the briefing. The captain had been especially touchy since he'd endured Adriana Rabh's tongue lashing on the bridge. The SSR had managed to keep her from broadcasting her defiance beyond the Jovian system, but it'd taken a while to cut the feed locally. Braxton's humiliation had played dozens of times over the local network. The Callistans, it seemed, took their Viking virtue of loyalty damned seriously. *The Real Story* had lit up with pro-Rabh, pro-Company sentiment. Braxton's inability to quash the playback and control the narrative had convinced Cassandra that someone else needed to bring the Regent of Callisto to heel. A general had already been on the way—all the way from Mars, in fact—to take charge of the situation. Now, they'd learned since the PR debacle, she was to lead the assault on Rabh Regency Station in Braxton's place.

"Jabari!"

Kwazi forced himself to pay attention. Others were looking at him.

"Sorry," Kwazi said. He wasn't, not really. He was glad to see Braxton humbled, especially after his failure to keep his promise. "Could you please repeat that?"

"I asked if you had any questions about the assault plan," Braxton said. Each word was grudgingly given, a babysitter's frustration with a problem child. Kwazi was becoming aware that that's how his recruiter to the cause saw him—as a burden to bear. Braxton held up a hand. "But now that you're paying attention, I'll repeat. Just ... *once*. For everyone's benefit."

Braxton reset the 3D model on display in the middle of the room. Callisto hung in the center, its orbital ring circling from top to bottom. On one side of the moon hung the *Freedom's Herald*. On the other, separated and in orbit of Callisto, was Rabh Regency Station, no longer a part of the ring itself.

"It was clever, making the station detachable," Braxton said with frank respect. "A safety measure, no doubt, in case something devastating ever happened to the ring. But their thrusters are for shit. They can keep themselves in orbit and conduct minor positional adjustments, but that's about it. That station's made to sit and wait for rescue. No Frater Drive for interplanetary travel. We can fly rings around them in the *Herald*."

Braxton was rewarded with a titter of appreciation for the pun.

"Her point defense cannons," he continued, "that's another story, now. They can shred small ships before they get close enough to do any damage. They'd heavily damage the *Herald* too before we could board. So that's why we're sending in the shuttles. The one we crashed into the ring a few weeks ago? Testing the concept. Now we're gonna fly every shuttle in the barn into Rabh's station. Even the ones the PDCs shred—some of them anyway—

their momentum will carry them through. They'll slam into that hull, create breaches—a mass-scale version of what happened with the ring. Our strike teams will aim for Engineering, Rabh's safe room in the penthouse, and Environmental Control, in that priority."

He paused. A hand went up.

"Yes?"

"How will we hold the station after the attack?" a woman asked. "Won't the structural integrity be so compromised that—"

"We're not going to hold the station," Braxton said. "That's not the point. The point is to kill Adriana Rabh. And capture us doing it on camera. Then, blow up the station. And capture us doing that, too."

A muttering of approval and some trepidation passed around the team leaders. Braxton let it die a natural death. He returned his gaze to Kwazi.

"Any questions?"

"No, Captain," Kwazi answered, his words as Spartan in emotion as Braxton's own had been. "I have no questions."

"Attention on deck!"

Someone blew a bosun's whistle, an old naval tradition calling the crew to attention when a ship's captain entered. Kwazi and the others sitting down stood up quickly. Everyone in the room snapped to attention.

A woman who resembled Cassandra to a remarkable degree strode in, flanked by two guards. Her dark hair was tied in a tight knot behind her head. Sheathed on each hip was a dagger, their silver blades gleaming against her black SSR uniform. She walked calmly to the front of the room without a single acknowledgment of the Soldiers she passed. Her stride projected authority; her demeanor, command.

"And there she is," Braxton mumbled under his breath. "Mother's little helper."

Kwazi liked her already.

"My name is Elinda Kisaan," she said, clasping her hands behind her back and facing the assembled SSR troops. "I am Cassandra's hand for this operation." She turned to Braxton. "Your captain is to be commended for securing this ship with relatively little bloodshed. We must remember— most of those we fight are held in bondage by the Syndicate Corporation.

They are our brothers and sisters awaiting liberation. Loss of life must be kept to a minimum. When possible."

Sidling a glance at Braxton, Kwazi heard him release a breath. Kisaan's public praise had let him save face with his men. That was something, at least.

"We launch our attack in an hour," Kisaan finished. "Be ready." She walked toward the door as briskly as she'd entered. The team leaders snapped to attention again as she passed. "Captain Braxton," she called over her shoulder, "accompany me."

Kwazi watched them go. "I have an hour," he said as Braxton picked up his briefing PADD. "I'd like to see Amy."

The captain stared after Kisaan. His eyes were hard. His cheek, rippling.

"Tell the bitch hello for me," he said before following their new commander.

Kwazi leaned against the wall of his tight quarters. He was tired. Physically, emotionally. Spiritually, if that was even a thing.

Seeing Milani again, and knowing what Helena Telemachus had done to her... He should go see her, he thought. Milani must be afraid to be caught in the middle of all this. Terrified. He should go see her and prove to her that the SSR wasn't the enemy, that SynCorp needed to pass into history. The Company used people like a natural resource. Mined the sweat from their bodies. Extracted their talents like precious metals and profited from them. Raised crops of workers for Earth's farming communes and the asteroid platforms in the Belt that supplied the inner system's insatiable need for raw materials.

He shook his head, tired of the heavy thoughts inside it. Kwazi wanted Dreamscape. He wanted Amy. He had less than an hour until the attack on Adriana Rabh's stronghold. Not enough time. Never enough time. But it was all the time he had.

He opened his sceye, but before he could engage the program, an incoming call flashed red on his retina. Braxton, probably. Another fucking briefing?

Kwazi ignored it and pressed the capital-D on the display to launch Dreamscape.

Nothing happened.

His sceye flashed red.

Malfunction, he thought. He tried to activate it again with his gaze, but the program refused to start.

What the fuck?

His sceye flashed red.

"All right, all right!" he said, anxious to get off the call and find a tech to fix his sceye. No, he needed to see her. Get whatever this was over with, so he could get back to Amy.

"Hello, Kwazi."

He blinked, Dreamscape all but forgotten.

"H—hello."

Cassandra stared back at him from her office atop the former UN building. It was the same angle as always from the camera. A long shot, with her mother's head on its pike next to Cassandra's throne. Gravity and time, the two universal constants, had been unkind to Elise Kisaan. Her tongue was black, bloating from a slack jaw. The whites of her eyes were rheumy, surrounding vacant pupils. Rats could have nested in her hair.

Mercifully, the camerabot zoomed in on Cassandra. Her face was beautiful in its symmetrical reflection of her mother's. Her golden eyes sparkled. Her thick, black hair fell around her shoulders like the mane of a lioness. Like the lustrous crown of a conqueror.

"I know the operation is happening soon. I won't keep you."

It was somehow ludicrous that the most powerful woman in the solar system valued his time. It made Kwazi uncomfortable.

"Elinda has arrived, yes?" she said.

He had the feeling she was filling out the conversation. Laying the convivial groundwork for something else.

"Yes," he said. "We attack the station shortly."

Cassandra acknowledged the information. Kwazi was quite certain it was an operational detail she'd already known.

"Your help in taking the ... in securing the *Freedom's Herald* was essential," she said. Again, that feeling she was reading a social script crept up on him. "When you and the others burst into that room and took Helena Telemachus hostage ... well, it's *still* the most popular thing on *The Real Story*. If you don't count the manhunt on the Moon."

"About her—" he began.

"Yes, I know," Cassandra said, raising a hand. "By your hand, when the time comes."

"When the time comes," he repeated, his tenor deepening. This was Cassandra he was talking to, not Braxton, but the burning anger inside him was the same. A universe waited to find its balance again by levying justice. Waited impatiently.

"By your hand, I promise it, Kwazi. But first, I need you to do something for me."

Ah, there it was, he thought. The polite portion of the conversation was over.

"Yes?"

She leaned forward into the shot. "You're in Braxton's squad again, as you were when liberating the *Herald*. And for the same reason."

Kwazi pursed his lips, sensing the trap in front of him.

"What does that mean, exactly?"

"It means," Cassandra began, a smile forming, "that you're a natural on camera. You represent everything we're doing, Kwazi. You're a moral man who's been forced to endure immorality at the hands of Tony Taulke and the Qinlao Faction and Helena Telemachus, most of all. You're the Everyman of the billions of citizen-workers across the system. You're the face of our cause."

"The face of your cause," he repeated.

"*Our* cause." Her smile dimmed a fraction with the reminder.

"Of course. But ... I have a question."

"Yes?"

"Why don't you just use my autobiographer?"

Cassandra turned her head. She had the detached look of a computer attempting to compute. Then, "The video avatar?"

"Yeah. Him."

She stared at Kwazi from a projection onto his own retina. It was a strange feeling, having her literally inside his head.

"He was ... adequate for the purposes of the vid," she said. "You have no idea how many refinement algorithms we had to go through to perfect your human affectations."

"*My* human affectations," he repeated. Saying it made Kwazi proud for some reason.

Cassandra's smile bloomed again. "Nothing beats the real thing," she said. "We're working on it, though. It won't be long till your avatar can do the hard work. No public appearances, of course. We still need you for that."

She seemed taken with her own sense of humor. And the way she said *we still need you for that* made his skin crawl.

"Will you be the face of our cause, Kwazi? Will you inspire the billions who, just like you, have lived in servitude to SynCorp all their lives?"

Go be an icon, Mr. Jabari. Go be a fucking Viking hero.

Adriana Rabh's words stepped forward from the dark corner of his memory.

"I get to kill Telemachus," he said. There was a hissing sound to his voice. A hunger in it. "You promise."

Cassandra waved a finger. The camerabot moved back. The sagging, sallow skin of her mother's head reappeared.

"You have my word," she said.

Kwazi nodded. "Then sure. I'll be your trademark."

I'll be you're fucking Viking hero.

Cassandra's eyes narrowed briefly, but she took the win.

"Excellent. Take the time you have left before the assault, Mr. Jabari. Enjoy yourself."

Her image faded.

Kwazi's eye scanned to the capital-D in the lower-right quadrant of his sceye, but he paused before attempting to launch the program again. He was now quite sure Dreamscape would work. He was also quite sure it had been Cassandra who'd prevented it working before.

And he knew something else, too. A grim certainty delivered from the back-channel of his brain. He'd only ever been a patsy for Braxton. The SSR had accepted Kwazi so easily, with a modicum of questioning to make it look good, because there was no risk in taking him into their confidence. They would use him until they didn't need him anymore.

When would that be? Once his avatar had been perfected, maybe?

Until then, he'd be the symbol of the Soldiers of the Solar Revolution. Their icon on camera reassuring all those frightened citizen-workers in the system that the change that was coming was change they could embrace. *Should* embrace.

Then, from somewhere that wasn't quite memory and wasn't quite conscience, a deep, tinny sound emerged, as if marching toward him from far away. It became throaty as it came nearer, then took on the tenor of a cackling, madwoman witch. Kwazi recognized the timber of her voice, full of irony and self-satisfaction. He recognized the pure, joyous laughter of Helena Telemachus.

"Two hull breaches, sir!" said the shuttle pilot.

"Acknowledged." Braxton's voice crackled through Kwazi's helmet comms.

An hour earlier, the first assault shuttle had delivered troops to the Engineering Level of Rabh Regency Station, where resistance was reported as fierce. The second breach by a sacrificial ramming shuttle was the signal for a second shuttle full of SSR troops to launch from the *Freedom's Herald*, its mission to secure Adriana Rabh's offices. Elinda Kisaan herself led that boarding action. Securing and then publicly executing Rabh to demoralize the enemy was her primary mission.

The troops on Kwazi's shuttle were nicknamed the glamor squad. Armed and able to fight, but with the sole mission of protecting Kwazi while camerabots shot the taking of Rabh Regency Station for *The Real Story*. A victory on video, Kisaan had called it. The real fighting would be elsewhere, but the citizen-workers of Sol wouldn't know that. An SSR victory here, Kisaan said, would inspire uprisings all over the system.

"Spinning up the drive," the pilot said.

"Hold your water," Braxton told her. "We're not there yet."

The pilot's enthusiasm was infectious. Kwazi's heart hammered in his chest. The heat and smell of sweat inside his vac-suit made it difficult to breathe. He watched the monitor as the SSR threw mining shuttle after mining shuttle at Rabh's stronghold. They'd adapted the *Herald*'s own to ferry troops to the station, but those luxury craft weren't armed. They'd been designed to carry dignitaries to Tony Taulke's flagship in comfort, not land assault troops on a space station.

"That was genius," Marcus Beecham said. He stood beside Kwazi, fascinated by the fireworks display on the monitor. The station's point defense cannons sprayed tracer slugs in a lightning arc. Another ramming shuttle exploded into flames, short lived in the vacuum of space.

"What was?" Kwazi asked. He was getting irritated with Monk Beecham, his squad buddy and personal protector—irritated with Beecham's physical closeness in the tight quarters of their shuttle, and with his constant need to talk over the squad channel. Kwazi's sole focus was taking Adriana Rabh's station, a required precursor to meting out justice on Helena Telemachus's bodymorphed head. Beecham's jabbering was an unwelcome distraction.

"Weaponizing Rabh's mining shuttle fleet and using it against the old bitch," the man said. Then, despite his bulky vac-suit, Beecham jumped, jostling Kwazi. "Yes!"

Similar celebrations overwhelmed comms. Another mining shuttle had slipped past the station's point-defense cannons and rammed full speed into the loading bay. The station seemed to shudder in its position-holding orbit over Callisto. Atmosphere blew outward from the point of impact, feeding the combustion of fuel reserves from the shuttle. The resulting expulsion of burning O_2 appeared, if only for a moment, like dragon fire erupting into space. Then the bulkheads closed, sealing off the inner station, and the fire began to sputter and die out. In the last of the orange light, Kwazi could see tiny figures spinning away from the station.

Bodies, he thought. *Those are bodies.*

19

REBEKAH FRANKLIN • MASADA STATION, ORBITING TITAN

Despite her fatigue, it hadn't been easy for Bekah to find sleep. The relentless cyberattacks on the Labyrinth had unnerved her, despite their being key to the success of Gregor Erkennen's plan. Her conversation over coffee with Fischer had grounded her some, but sleep had still proven coy and flirty, disappearing around corners whenever it seemed close enough to touch.

For a long time she floated in a twilight state of semi-awareness, knowing she was prisoner in a waking dream she couldn't control. A glass of water sat on a table in the gym after a shift. Bekah would pick it up and chug it, her goal to empty the glass for some unknown reason, though the water would always refill. She was starting to feel waterlogged in her own dream. The semi-aware part of her worried she'd wake up soaking in her own urine.

Empty of other people, the gym was semi-lit by Gregor's camouflage protocol, casting the far corners of the room in angular darkness. An icy kind of aloneness prickled her skin. Not loneliness exactly, but a sense of being alone, on her own in the universe. Bekah's only companion was the magically refilling water glass and her own, driven desire to see it empty.

Clunk!

A heavy, thudding sound when she set the glass down. Then the hollow

sound transforming into a spine-cringing crash of metal on metal. It reverberated around the gym, and before the echo of it died, there was another.

Clunk!

And another.

Clunk!

Dream-Bekah turned to find a man working the overhead press. His
back was to her. He'd push up the machine's handlebars, then let the
weights crash down.

Clunk!

It took a moment for her to realize he was seated, naked, at the
machine.

"Stop that," she said, emotionless. "You'll damage the weights." Didn't
he see the sign on the wall?

The man pushed the handlebars up again, then released them to fall.

Clunk!

"I said, stop that! Stop it!"

The man released the handlebars. He stood up and turned around. It
was Daniel Tripp. Why hadn't she recognized him from the bald spot on
the back of his head?

Daniel advanced across the gym. He was smiling. Bekah kept her eyes
up, on his, red embarrassment at his nudity creeping up her neck. There
was something strange about his eyes. They were almost radiant.

"Could you maybe put on a towel?" she said, trying to make it a joke.
They'd worked together a long time. They were family. But some family
you should never see naked.

He continued walking casually toward her. He didn't seem to care about
his state of undress. Bekah's heart beat with a distinct, deliberate rhythm.
Not excited. Plodding, in fact.

"No, really," Bekah said. Curiosity won out, and her eyes darted down,
then back up. "Please, Daniel—a towel. *Something.*"

His eyes shone, though not the normal brown of Daniel Tripp's irises.
They were golden. Like Cassandra's eyes.

"I'm the future," Daniel said, advancing across the gym. "Embrace me."

Bekah attempted to rise from the table, to get away. Her dream-body
betrayed her. She sat paralyzed, unable to move. The full glass in front of

her demanded she drain it dry. It was all she could do not to pick it up again.

"I'm the future," Daniel repeated, arms spread wide as he drew closer. "Embrace me."

The weights were dropping again, making the ringing sound. The press lifted and dropped on its own. Like it was haunted. Or afflicted by a poltergeist.

Clunk!

Daniel stood over her, arms still open. She somehow knew he planned to absorb her wholly, physically, into his own body. His eyes shifted from golden to red.

Clunk!

Dream-Bekah stood suddenly, the steely screech of her chair scoring the floor. The version of herself watching from twilight consciousness shouted a warning. Unable or unwilling to hear, her dream-self opened her arms to receive Daniel.

Clunk!

"I'm the future," he said. His lips parted in a smile. Her feet edged forward, anxious to partake in what felt like victory, even if it was someone else's—Daniel's victory, or Cassandra's. His red eyes flared. "Embrace me."

Bekah bolted upright in her pitch black quarters. The chilled air blowing from the ventilation system teased the sheen of sweat on her skin, drawing a shiver through her like an electric current.

The station alarm. Her ears identified the plodding, metrical noise. The reason for the alarm finally registered. Something had tripped the security protocol she'd set to monitor communications. Someone must have opened a comm port from the station.

"Shit! Lights!"

Bekah jumped out of bed to her computer console and ran a quick report from the alarm log. The message had been short. Only three picoseconds. Long enough to compromise the camouflage of Masada

Station, if anyone was listening. Long enough to open a back door, if anyone was trying.

"Shit, shit, shit."

First things first—Bekah verified that the port used to send the message had already been buttoned up behind the station's firewall again. It'd been opened, the message sent, and the port closed again. Three picoseconds. A lifetime to a programmer. A canyon of opportunity that could allow an army of bad actor code access to the mainframe. She ran a second diagnostic on all traffic since the breach. There was no evidence of incoming data packets being received. In theory, that meant no virus had been inserted into the local network.

Unless the delivery payload wiped the log as part of its programming.

Bekah ran a second security program that she and Carrin Bohannon had just perfected together. It reviewed all incoming data through a strainer algorithm to compare random pieces of extant programming in the mainframe to ferret out aberrant code.

The program finished. No anomalies found.

Bekah hailed the War Room.

"Richter."

Bekah opened her mouth, then closed it again.

"Where's Carrin?" she asked.

"Bohannon is busy," Richter answered in his clipped German accent.

"Okay," she said. "Put Maya on, then."

Richter cleared his throat. "She is busy too," he said. Then, "Is something wrong, Ms. Franklin?"

"No, it's just … well, yes," Bekah said. "Someone opened a potential security breach a few minutes ago. I ran a check and I don't think there's any damage, but I want to talk to one of my team down there. I want to know exactly who it was and ream them a new … wait, what do you mean *busy*?"

There was a pause from Richter. "Something about an increase in cyberattacks against the Labyrinth?" He laughed in a way that sounded rehearsed. "Too much tech talk for me."

The attacks on the Labyrinth had increased? At the same time there'd been a security breach on Masada Station?

"I'm coming down there," Bekah said. "And as soon as one of them comes up for air, I want a full report on—"

"No, you stay there," Richter said. She could hear him moving. "I'll come to you. You shouldn't be walking around the station alone."

"I can call Fischer," she said, grabbing her personal access data device. Her jumpsuit felt glued to her skin. She hadn't changed since the previous shift. Oily fingerprints dotted her PADD's display. She wondered if she smelled.

No time for a shower.

"No, it's *my* shift," Richter said. "Let the old man sleep. I'll come up and escort you down. Stay where you are." He switched off the comms.

Her mouth was open to answer, but Bekah closed it again. Something was happening. She tried to calm her hitching, anxious breathing. But she couldn't just sit here, waiting for Richter. She needed to be doing something.

Bekah re-opened the channel to the War Room.

"Richter?"

There was only silence.

"Hey, anyone? Can someone get a message to Bruno Richter for me? Trying to save him a trip. Hello?" She checked the channel. It seemed to be open.

What the hell? Bekah was ready to kick some serious team ass...

Bekah grabbed her PADD. When she slid into the corridor, the half lighting snapped on. She headed for the vator, then pulled up short. The nearest lift was near the gym. She knew Daniel worked out before going to bed, and her sceye showed only a couple of hours had passed since they'd parted company. If Daniel was as restless as she'd been, she might run into him.

The thought made her blush.

Don't be an idiot. It was only a dream.

Sure, yeah. That's all it was. Still...

Turning and retracing her steps, Bekah opted for a slightly longer, less direct way to reach the War Room. She quickened her steps, like that would make up for the decision, the corridor lights blinking on and off as she passed between sections. Distracted while reviewing data on the

PADD, she almost flattened her nose when the southside vator's doors failed to open.

"What the hell? Is everything fucking broken on this station now?"

The control panel was dark. Inactive.

Maybe the breach had done damage after all. Maybe there was a worm in the system their cleaner code hadn't caught.

The mainframe. A chill bloomed behind her breastbone.

At least the mainframe was on a separate, isolated network. The only way Masada's mainframe could be compromised was if—

—someone opened a port directly to it.

Three picoseconds would do it.

The corridor went dark, and Bekah stood for a moment in the blackness. First the vator control, now the lights?

"Lights," she said, deliberately calm. The blackness remained. And the air—was it starting to get cooler? Maybe the worm that shut down the lifts and lights had also compromised life support...

"Shit!"

Bekah tried to clear her head and think. There was a maintenance tube around here somewhere, near the vator shaft. Feeling along the chilly wall, she quickly found the raised wrench-inside-a-triangle icon identifying maintenance access. The tube had a ladder allowing repairs between station levels. She'd have to be careful in the dark, but she could feel her way down. The War Room was only two levels below.

Part of her regretted not waiting for Richter.

"Ms. Franklin?"

As if summoned, Richter's voice came alive in the darkness, amplified by Masada's public address system. *"I asked you to wait for me, Ms. Franklin."* The glottal, German consonants sounded harsher in the dark. They carried an odd, eager quality. *"You should have waited for me."*

There was a sense of the predator about them.

Oh, no.

She removed the panel and reached in to grasp the cold rung of the ladder. Either the heat or all of life support was off, Bekah was relatively sure of that now. A hint of ozone, sharp and itchy, wafted up from the shaft below. Was the power grid totally fried?

She opened a new message in her sceye.

"Fischer, come on, come on," she muttered. It buzzed in vain. She couldn't even find him in the registry. Then she remembered: Fischer didn't have an implant. "Damn it!..."

"*Ms. Franklin.*" Richter's voice again, station-wide. "*Where are you, Ms. Franklin? Just hand me the Hammer. Then this will all be over.*"

He was coming. She would have run right into him if she hadn't been worried about meeting Daniel.

Daniel. Carrin and the others.

Richter had been in the War Room when she called ... fear gripped Bekah's heart. Her team hadn't been too busy to answer her call. They'd been unable. She knew it like she knew the station's systems had been compromised ... from the inside. And what had happened to Fischer?

Oh, no, no, God...

She stepped into the tube. Halfway to the second level, she spied the blinking emergency light of a maintenance comms panel. Like the mainframe, maintenance was on a dedicated power circuit in case of emergencies. She engaged the panel and released a breath when it lit up. Bekah dialed the code for Fischer's cabin. He might not have a sceye, but his quarters had wall comms.

In the dark corridor above, she heard footsteps. Glancing upward, she saw the roaming glare of a handheld light.

"*Ms. Franklin, really, none of this is necessary.*"

Richter's voice, salivating. And echoing eerily, so close above and also, a half second later, coming over the station's PA system.

Bekah held her PADD against her side and swiped the volume on the panel down with a finger. She felt a cramp threatening her other hand as she clutched at the cold rung of the ladder. She tried to relax her grip without losing it.

"Fischer, please..." she whispered. "Please, please pick up..."

His cabin comms chimed again and again, barely audible in the tight space of the tube.

Goddamnit, Fischer! I need your help!

The footsteps stopped.

"Is that where you are?"

His voice wasn't amplified now. It was normal, if a little distant. Somewhere just above her.

The access panel. She hadn't replaced it! How stupid could she—

A light shone down from above. "Hello, Ms. Franklin." Behind its sudden brilliance, the face of Bruno Richter, gaunt and sharpened by the shadows, cracked wide in a broad smile. "I'm going to need that key hanging around your pretty neck."

The hand that had been desperately trying to raise Fischer reflexively went to the key resting cold against her skin.

Viking warriors wore a hammer around their necks as a holy symbol. They touched it before battle, asking Thor to protect them.

Her grip on the ladder spasmed, the cramp taking hold. Bekah dropped the PADD, and it careened off the ladder below. She fumbled to regain her grip and missed the cold metal.

And she fell.

20

STACKS FISCHER • MASADA STATION, ORBITING TITAN

The goddamned beeping wouldn't stop. I'd been conked out like a hackhead living the high life in Dreamland until the *beep-Beep-BEEP ... beep-Beep-BEEP* popped my sleep balloon.

I was half awake and still cursing the noise. It'd been the best rest I'd had in a long time. I love the Hearse, but she's a small ship that loves to cuddle. Sometimes I just like my space, you know? Pun intended.

That's when I felt it. Still half asleep, sorta drifting in a demi-dream. I was at Minnie the Mouth's place in Darkside. I did side jobs for Minnie on occasion, like making sure a john paid the full fee for services rendered. You might say I was on retainer. In the dream, Minnie was paying me back in full, her light-fingered caress trailing up the inside of my leg. The beep had finally stopped beeping. I was ready to lie back and enjoy the fruits of my fancy's labor.

"Ms. Franklin, really, none of this is necessary."

Richter's voice over the PA system. The last thing I wanted was Bruno Richter in my fantasy. My brain elbowed my libido aside and rebooted itself. The image of Minnie's teasing fingers disappeared. The sensation didn't.

Two and two made a baby named four. Richter's voice. It'd sounded wet and hopeful. And it didn't take a genius to figure out what was crawling up my leg.

Sonofabitch, I thought. I'd sensed the ferret's betrayal coming somehow, but I hadn't really acknowledged it. And now he was after the kid.

But I didn't move, not an inch. My instincts at work again, with a little help from the obvious.

"Sonofabitch."

The snake slithered against my skin.

It scales were cold, rough.

I shivered.

"Lights," I whispered. Then, assuming the system hadn't heard me, I tried again: "Lights!"

Nothing.

Well, shit. I guess I should've seen that coming. So to speak.

Apparently enjoying the experience, the snake kept climbing Mount Stacks. It slid along my belly, slow and easy as you please.

Not moving a single muscle I didn't have to, I pulled my hand holding my knife from under the pillow. Wearing blades to bed is a good way to wake up with something you highly value cut off. But there's careful and there's suicidal.

It was hard to keep my mind on task, especially when the mamba settled its weight into the nest of my chest. It hadn't even sunk its pointy pearlies into me yet, and I was already paralyzed. I could see Richter strangling Rebekah while I lay there afraid to move. With my free hand—slowly, so slowly—I lifted the sheet.

In the pitch black of my quarters, I couldn't see a thing. But I could hear it. That lisping, dinner-bell sound serpents make. That come-into-my-parlor sound. It was the only sound in the room. The only one that mattered, anyway.

I wasn't sure what to do with the knife. If I got stabby, I'd more than likely injure myself first, then the pissed-off mamba would finish the job. Lying there till it decided to move off wasn't an option. That image of Richter giving Rebekah Franklin a throat-wide under-smile plagued me. But if I moved...

I lowered the sheet, and the snake lisped its disapproval. I could feel its scaly chill setting up permanent occupancy in my chest hair.

Inspiration struck.

I hovered my hand over the sheet where I thought its head was. I had one chance to get this right or I was going to be one, long smorgasbord to swallow. The mamba moved, then relaxed again into its nest of salt-and-pepper curlies. I hesitated, but then Rebekah appeared in my mind's eye, bleeding out from the neck like a stuck pig. Waiting wasn't an option.

I dropped my hand and clamped it around the snake's head, hoping the sheet would protect me. I yelled curses like a sailor at a spelling bee, or maybe I screamed like a little girl. The mamba thrashed. It slipped and twisted in my grip. I jerked myself out of bed in one fuck-you-knee motion, and the cold air hit my skin. My skin pimpled with gooseflesh as its fangs worked at the sheet. I threw the shrouded snake onto the mattress and brought the knife up and down, over and over. The whole thing was a three-second eternity of shouting and slashing and hoping my adrenaline wasn't so high I'd missed myself getting bit.

The emergency lights came up. In the red glow, it was hard to tell blood from sweat in the sheets. I ripped back the snake's shroud and hopped away like the deck was hot coals. The bed was saturated. I'd sliced and diced the damned thing. Twitchy segments, separated, still moved on the bed.

I remembered that breathing was a thing I should do.

The blinking light on the wall comms caught my eye. It was Rebekah's missed call that had chased me away from Minnie's lustful attentions. I owed the kid my life.

I'd never run a marathon, but my heaving lungs showed me what it might be like. My brain started to focus, get past the threat that lay in bloody pieces in my bed, still not quite aware they were dead. But enough of that.

Richter was after Rebekah. I'd gotten that much from the PA system. She'd likely be terrified. She'd have to stay terrified a little bit longer. I could let her know I was coming, but then Richter would know too. He'd set the mamba on me and gone about his business. My state of undeath was my one hole card.

I threw on clothes, trying to reason out where she'd go to ground.

Maybe she'd head for the War Room. Strength in numbers with her colleagues. That seemed as good a place as any to start.

Cleaning the snake's blood off my knife, I reset the blade in my wrist spring. I strapped my .38 to my ankle. I stashed my stunner in the holster under my arm.

Time to get to work.

Rebekah Franklin • Masada Station, Orbiting Titan

She'd managed to break her fall, but the impact had twisted her ankle. Gritting her teeth, Bekah stood at the bottom of the maintenance tube and unsnapped the access panel from the inside. Richter's light danced two levels up, searching.

She loped onto the Lab Level, wincing whenever she put wait on the ankle. She had to get to the War Room. That breach had been Richter inviting the wolf inside the house.

Masada Station's backups kicked in, and the emergency lighting came on. Well, that was something.

"Rebekah, just give me the Hammer. I'll let you live."

Richter was back on the station's public address system. Her stomach flip-flopped every time she heard his voice now. She staggered into the War Room, gazing first to the large screens monitoring the cyberattacks. Bekah stopped short. They were activated but blank, devoid of data. Cassandra's attacks on the Labyrinth had stopped.

"Carrin?" she called. "Anyone?"

"Rebekahhh..."

The familiar fear uncoiled inside her again, but she locked it away, contained it behind a stony resolve to complete the mission assigned to her by Gregor Erkennen. Then, she spied Carrin Bohannon bent over her console.

Oh, no.

Bekah rushed to her friend's side. She slipped as she neared the body, had to catch herself. Carrin's death hadn't been a clean one. Her eyes were open. Blood still oozed from the half-moon wound midway down her neck. It dripped from the cold console to pool on the deck.

She was part of my team. I should've protected her.

An alarm next to Carrin's bloody right hand went off. Its strident grating made Bekah jump.

"Oh, God."

Data began flooding Carrin's screen.

Cassandra was assaulting Masada's mainframe.

A low chuckle sounded from the public channel.

"Soon this will be all over," Richter said. *"Let's complete our business, you and I."*

Setting aside her guilt, Bekah took the seat next to Carrin's. Her job was to protect Masada as long as she could. A quick assessment showed that Carrin had been working on a series of floating protocols based on a self-replicating, machine-learning algorithm Daniel created. In theory, it would delay Cassandra's penetration of the firewall for a while. At least until she figured out how to bypass it.

It looked like Carrin had been seconds away from finishing it before—

The door to the War Room opened behind her.

"Alone at last."

Richter's voice was smaller without the walls of the deserted station to amplify it. He walked slowly forward, almost leisurely, an odd reflection of the nude Daniel from her dream. Richter moved patiently. Despite his earlier rush to find her, he now seemed to relish their time together.

The thought made her ill.

With willpower, Bekah turned away from his hungry gaze and keyed in a sequence, completing Carrin's work. She sent a silent thank-you to her murdered friend through the twilight void now separating them. Then she stood up and backed away from Richter's advance.

"Cassandra's not getting in anytime soon," she said.

"Only a matter of time," Richter answered as he came nearer. His narrow face leered at her. "Only a matter of time."

Stacks Fischer • Masada Station, Orbiting Titan

The emergency lighting made everything red. The artificial gravity was working, but life support still seemed to be off. Or set to minimum, anyway. My achy knee barked about the cold. There was the sharp, pungent scent of chlorine in the air, like the pool had drained into the station. My brain reshuffled that data point; it wasn't chlorine, it was ozone. Like after a thunderstorm, when lightning strikes. Maybe the primary electrical grid was offline too.

I spied a heap near the vator. I knew what it was before I even got close. One of the geeks, a young woman. Asia something, I think. Aisha something. I knelt down to confirm the kill. That red under-smile I'd seen splitting Rebekah's face in my mind's eye? It wasn't a dark fantasy anymore. Richter's razor at work. Staring at that murdered waif of a woman, I wondered why he hadn't simply killed me in his quarters? It felt sloppy to me.

"Rebekahhh..."

Then, the way Richter drew out her name, I understood. It was like he was playing hide-and-seek with Bekah Franklin—ratcheting up the fear to the uninitiated. So I'd answered my own question, then. Richter hadn't killed me outright because where's the fun in that?

He enjoyed the game of hunting, of killing. He enjoyed the smell of fear in a victim's sweat. He must've gotten tired of killing by poison. He'd chosen a very personal way to murder Aisha. Brandishing that razor around me in his quarters had been a private little joke for him. Showing the black mamba off to me and how the mouse suffered—he'd planned for me to think about that while I lay in bed, suffocating, while snake juices shut me down, one involuntary system at a time.

I could see him standing over Aisha on the floor while her panic set in. Watching her eyes as she realized she was going to die, and nothing and no one could stop it. I could see Richter smiling down at her terror, drinking it in like a vampire sucks blood.

That ferret-faced fuck was one sick bastard.

But not for much longer.

The moment he stopped taunting Bekah Franklin—that's when I needed to worry. So far, she'd outwitted him, a professional killer, and that confirmed the kid was clever. I finally got why Erkennen had entrusted the Company's future to her.

Another alarm began to howl.

"Soon this will be all over," Richter said. *"Let's complete our business, you and I."*

You said it, asshole. Be patient. And keep letting me know she's still alive.

I stood up and keyed the vator. Part of me—the male part, the dumb part, the lizard-brain part that doesn't think about strategy—wanted him to hear it. Wanted him to see me coming for him over the security feed.

I stepped aboard the lift and pushed the button for the ground level. The hydraulics whined as I descended the two stories. It felt like I was moving in slow motion.

I pulled my stunner before the vator opened. No Richter. Part of me was disappointed. A few quick steps later and the War Room doors swept aside.

"...a matter of time." Richter's words were sautéed with honey and vinegar both.

"Well if it ain't Mr. Big Mouth," I said, overly loud. I leveled my artillery at him. First order of business—get attention off the kid.

Richter whirled. "Fischer?"

There was a body laid over a computer console. My heart did a two-step, then I realized from the hair color it wasn't Bekah Franklin's. My angle brought her into my eye line, and my ticker settled down.

"Yeah," I said, affecting nonchalance and walking into the room. "Your perfect killing machine made for the perfect kill. Mice everywhere: rejoice!"

Richter's anger drove him a step or two forward. Then he noticed the barrel pointing his way. I pulled the trigger.

Punk!

Richter bounced back a step, then smiled. He was wearing MESH clothing like me. It'd deflected the stunner fire.

"Stay right there," I said, crouching to grab my .38.

Richter ran.

Aiming carefully takes time, and when the target's running, sometimes you don't have that much of it. I threw a couple of shots his way, but they ricocheted off the fancy walls. He'd moved quickly, expertly, then dived through the other door to the War Room. It closed after him.

Bekah moved quickly to the comms panel.

"Noa?" she said. Her voice sounded scared of itself. "Maya? Aisha? Daniel!"

Not a single member of her team answered.

"Hey kid," I said, not knowing how to give her the bad news. When Bekah looked at me, it was like she knew what I was about to say. "I found Aisha upstairs. She was…"

She closed her eyes tight. "What about the others? Have you seen anyone else—"

"No, but … what are you doing?"

Bekah hopped to another panel and called up a list of data records. "Their implants. We can at least see…" Then her words stopped. She'd pulled up three data sets. Two were flatlined. They were labeled Noa Comar and Maya Breides. "All of them? How can … no, Daniel! Daniel's alive."

I hated to rush her. But I didn't have time for nice.

"Can you lock down the War Room? Keep Richter out if he doubles back?"

Bekah stared at me, shock frozen on her face. She was still processing that most of her team was dead—murdered—and how close she'd come to their fate, I imagine.

"Rebekah!"

"Yes," she whispered. Then, more aware: "Yes!"

"Then do it." She worked buttons on the console in front of the bloody corpse. The cybersecurity expert, Bohannon.

"We have a bigger problem than him," Bekah said. "Cassandra's attacking Masada's mainframe. She's found the real prize, thanks to Richter." She spat his name out, but outlining the threat was helping her mind to focus. "She's already breached one of the seven security levels protecting the system."

"That was fast," I grunted. "And not something I can do anything about."

Bekah gave me a look that told me she'd wrestled her grief to the mat. "I can. Maybe."

"All righty, then. You protect the tech stuff. I'll take care of Richter."

"Wait, Stacks ... do you think they suffered?" she asked. "Do you think—"

"I think it came quickly for all of them," I lied, trying not to remember the look on the face of that young woman sprawled next to the station lift. She and the others; they'd all been mice to Richter. Terrified mice with death overtaking them, one hitching, shallow breath at a time until the air wouldn't come anymore.

"That's something, anyway," Bekah said.

It wasn't anything, not really. It was nothing. My lie was cold comfort at best. But I left Bekah with it because it was all she had left. And I needed her thinking and functional.

"And Daniel's still alive, somewhere."

"And so is Richter."

"I'll lock out his biometrics from accessing the War Room," she said. "He won't be able to get back in here."

I made for the door, and it slid aside.

"Stacks!"

"Yeah?"

"Please be careful."

I winked her way, hoping it gave her confidence. "Stay snug in here," I said. "And can you get the lights back on? I can't see a damned thing."

"Sure," she said. "I'll—"

The door to the War Room closed behind me.

Time to beat the brush and scare out a snake wrangler named Richter.

21

KWAZI JABARI • ABOARD THE FREEDOM'S HERALD

"Three breaches now," Monk Beecham said. "We should be about ready to—"

"Assault shuttle three: launch."

Elinda Kisaan's order was tinny and loud through Kwazi's headset. The oversized platoon of twenty Soldiers, tightly packed aboard, raised another cheer. Kwazi's palms were wet and cold, and when he glanced at Braxton, he found the thick man clearly irritated. Probably from hearing Kisaan's voice give the launch order. This was supposed to be *his* show.

"I'm honored to be your wingman," Beecham said. "Or battle buddy, or whatever we're supposed to call ourselves." The rest of their squad chuckled over comms. Most were green recruits, pressed into service like the luxury shuttle about to carry them into combat.

One trooper smiled over her shoulder at Kwazi, giving them both a thumbs-up. "It's a big honor, protecting the face of the revolution!"

Kwazi worked to keep his face neutral.

"Snag your straps!" Braxton growled. "Launching in ten ... nine ... eight...!"

Everyone grabbed the nylon straps hanging from the hastily installed metal runners along the shuttle's roof. The thrusters fired, and they lifted off. The starship's bay doors parted, an infinity of starlight shining beyond.

"Here we go!" The excited pilot sounded downright giddy.

The shuttle swung quickly around the *Herald*'s port quarter. A wing of ten Rabh mining shuttles flew ahead of them, bait for the station's point defense cannons. Ten kamikaze pilots on ten suicide missions.

"I feel sorry for those guys," Beecham said.

"Don't," the woman ahead of them replied, her tone corrective but reverent. "They're martyrs for Cassandra. We'll reap what they sow here today." Over comms, the rest of the squad *oo-rahed*.

She'd sounded proud, but what struck Kwazi was her lack of empathy. There'd been no concern at all for the pilots' sacrifice.

"Five seconds to PDC green zone," the pilot said. "Five..."

The shuttle bucked, steering away from incoming fire. Two sacrificial craft erupted to starboard. Kwazi grabbed his strap with both hands. He could hear the blood pounding in his ears. Adrenaline made his senses sing —colors were crisper and smells were sharper, even in the vac-suit. He heard the rapid breathing of his comrades over the open channel and the shuttle's engines straining to get them past the kill zone.

"We're clear!" the pilot reported. Another cheer went up. It reminded Kwazi of sports fans watching their favorite team score a goal.

Rabh Regency Station loomed ahead. Three dark, sputtering patches of mangled metal stood out like massive bruises along its superstructure. The pilot powered back to control entry as the shuttle flew through the breach and into the station's loading bay.

The doors parted before they'd even settled on the deck. Braxton was the first out, his step steady as he adapted to the station's gravity. Beecham and Kwazi were the last to exit per protocol. The assault squad broke in two, each team with its own mission.

"Get that barrier up!" Braxton ordered Alpha Team, pointing at the breach. Turning to the station's interior and the second team, he said, "Don't open that door until it is."

The bay was tall and expansive. Autoloaders were maglocked along one wall. The shuttle that had opened the breach in the station's hull was a mangled mass against the bay's interior wall. No one would be coming out of there.

Alpha Team worked to erect a hermetic barricade over the shuttle-sized hole in the station they'd just passed through. If the breach wasn't sealed, the minute Bravo Team cracked open the bulkhead door to the interior, they'd all be blown into space.

After a few moments of cursing effort, Alpha's sergeant reported in. "Barrier in place. Seal nominal."

"Open that door!" Braxton shouted to Bravo Team.

A screeching like talons on metal filled their comms. Several troopers doubled over, gripping their helmets. Kwazi managed to keep his feet.

"They're jamming comms!" someone shouted. But that didn't make sense. If comms were jammed, Kwazi wouldn't have heard the trooper announce that fact.

There was movement along the gantries above. The shadows became solid. Large shipping containers, just like the ones Kwazi had used to practice variable gravity maneuvers, began dropping to the deck. One crushed a trooper beneath its massive weight.

"Shoot those fuckers!" Braxton called over comms.

Their job done sealing the breach, Alpha Team moved toward the middle of the bay, rifles at the ready, as more containers hit the deck from above. No one fired.

"What the hell is wrong with you people?" Braxton demanded. "Shoot, shoot!"

Sporadic rifle fire cracked from Alpha's weapons. Personnel in vac-suits leapt over the railings from the gantries above, dropping behind the containers for cover. One attacker went down. The screaming came again through their headsets, and Kwazi realized that's exactly what it was —*screaming*. The high-pitched ululation of warriors challenging their enemy with bloody murder.

A man in a worn, orange vac-suit landed next to Kwazi. He carried a long-handled tool with a metal hook at one end. "Hirst!" he shouted, swiping at Kwazi, who just dodged away in time.

"Kwazi!"

Beecham sprinted forward, raising his rifle, and the attacker turned to meet him. Beecham fired twice, and two dark holes appeared in the man's chest. He fell to the deck.

"You all right?" Beecham asked.

"Yeah," Kwazi said, staring at the unmoving body. The man had been a miner. Kwazi recognized Valhalla Station's red-eyed Jupiter patch on the arm of the vac-suit. Why were miners defending Rabh Regency Station?

"Hirst ... Hirst ... Hirst!"

The enemy had somehow hacked their comms channel, and a score of voices shouted their challenge. Kwazi could hear the rapid breathing of the untried troopers around him. The glamor squad, called to action.

"What is that?" he asked as the enemy got louder.

"Probably some goddamned Viking death chant," Beecham said.

Alpha Team had reached Braxton, Kwazi, and the others, surrounding them like wagons attacked by Indians, facing outward toward the scattered shipping containers hiding the miners. A rifle appeared around a crate and fired, and one of the troopers went down.

"Attack, goddamn it!" Braxton shouted. "This is what you trained for!"

But the miners moved first. They appeared from cover on all sides, some armed with projectile weapons like the shooter had, but most holding tools from the colony on Callisto—tethering hooks, heavy chain-hoses for securing scoopships in the Jovian atmosphere, farming tools from hydroponics.

"Hirst! Hirst! Hirst!"

They came on quickly, drawing a noose of deadly intent around the SSR troopers.

"Open that goddamned door!" Braxton yelled at Bravo Team.

With a single, screaming shout of "Valhalla!" the miners charged.

A trooper pulled his trigger, and the flood of fire began. Vac-suits were no match for bullets, and the first rank of attackers went down. Kwazi brought his rifle up but couldn't bring himself to pull the trigger. A miner moved against him, brandishing a heavy piece of plastisteel pipe over her head and shrieking the warrior's cry. Then holes opened in her vac-suit, and she collapsed with a shriek.

"You need to pull that fucking trigger," Beecham said. He shucked his empty magazine and loaded another.

Dismayed at their casualties, the miners fell back to their shipping crates.

"Engineering's taken!" Braxton announced.

But there were no high-fives or *oo-rahs* as there had been earlier. Half of Alpha Team was dead or dying on the deck. Fearless of death, the miners were regrouping, preparing to charge again.

"Hirst! Hirst! Hirst!"

Kwazi heard in that cry a furious, unified purpose. The few of the enemy armed with rifles fired, and two more SSR troopers went down. One, then another of those still standing edged a foot backward toward the shuttle. They were here to shoot video with Kwazi as the star, not face an angry mob of Callistan defenders. He could see more troopers shifting their bodyweight backward.

Another wave of miners appeared along the gantries circling the bay's second level, prepared to leap into the fight below.

"Fall back!" Kwazi heard himself saying. "Fall back to the shuttle!"

Several troopers from Alpha Team didn't wait for a second order. They turned and fled, firing blindly behind them. A shot felled one of their own with friendly fire.

Braxton whirled on Kwazi, face full of rage. Before he could countermand the order to retreat, the bulkhead door disappeared into the wall. Atmosphere flooded the bay, and everyone in it staggered under the sudden pressure.

More miners poured through the open door. The first few died quickly at point-blank range, but bolstered by reinforcements from above, their comrades in the bay charged again. The few SSR recruits still standing their ground panicked, turning to follow those who'd already fled.

"Hold your ground!" Braxton cried. "Kill these bastards!"

This isn't how it was supposed to be, Kwazi thought. They were losing and vastly outnumbered. The heavy fighting was supposed to be in Engineering and Rabh's penthouse, not here at the photo-op site.

The bulkhead door continued hemorrhaging miners shouting for Valhalla, cursing with their battle cry of "Hirst! Hirst! Hirst!"

In the middle of the chaos, Braxton stood straight as a statue, his hand to the side of his helmet. It was almost comical, Kwazi thought, with all that death and disorder around him. Alpha Team fought its way toward the shuttle, while pressed by the sheer weight of the enemy coming from inside the station, Bravo Team fell back toward the middle of the bay, pumping bullets into miners assaulting from the station's interior.

The tide of fighting had shifted away from Kwazi, and for a moment, he found his own eye of calm in the storm. Braxton faced him and hefted his rifle. Kwazi could still hear shouting. Another Soldiers went down ... miners were being shot and falling around him. But his vision tunneled to the black mouth of Braxton's barrel pointed at him. Braxton set the rifle tight against his shoulder.

A shot and a blur, and Monk Beecham hit the deck hard at Kwazi's feet. Stunned motionless for a moment, Kwazi dropped to his side on the deck, gathering the rough material of Beecham's vac-suit in both hands.

"Rabh's HQ has fallen!"

The ecstatic voice dominated the general comms channel, even drowning out the miners' battle cry.

"The station is taken!"

Alpha Team's survivors had almost reached the shuttle. But hearing the news, they'd stopped and turned back to the battle. The miners still standing ceased their advance. Their warrior's cry faded.

"The station is taken!" someone shouted again.

Kwazi looked up to find Braxton still standing on his island of calm. Their eyes locked together, and the captain lowered his rifle.

Holding Braxton's gaze, Kwazi keyed the medical channel on his mic. "Soldier Beecham needs emergency evac!"

After a moment's unblinking hesitation, Braxton nodded and moved toward them.

Beecham reached up to grasp Kwazi's hand. "A martyr for the cause," he said, a bloody smile streaking his face.

"You shouldn't have done that," Kwazi said. His brain was buzzing. His skin felt hot. Around him, miners were dropping their weapons.

Gasping, Beecham motioned, wanting his helmet removed. Kwazi unsnapped the locks of his own first and set it on the deck, then removed Beecham's.

"You're more important than me," Beecham said. "You're the promise of the revolution."

I'm nothing, Kwazi thought. *I'm just a Martian miner.*

"He's the Hero of Mars."

Kwazi's head snapped up to find Braxton standing over them, his rifle slung. Alpha Team's remaining troopers began taking Rabh's miners roughly into custody.

"Yeah," Beecham said proudly. "I saved the Hero of Mars."

Kwazi watched the light leave Monk Beecham's eyes.

Behind him, Braxton sighed. "Poor bastard. If he just hadn't gotten in the way."

Kwazi stared at him from the corner of his eye. "If he just hadn't gotten in the way ... what?" He heard the challenge in his own voice. The steel in it.

Braxton held Kwazi's gaze. "If he just hadn't gotten in the way," he said, nodding in the direction of the prisoners, "we'd have one less miner to guard. The one that was about to put one of those long hook-things into your spine. I guess you didn't see him, huh?"

"No," Kwazi said, his tone flat. "No, I didn't see him." If there'd been a miner about to skewer Kwazi and Beecham took the bullet meant to end that threat, why was Kwazi still alive? Beecham had been shot *in front of* Kwazi. Not behind him.

"Huh. Damnedest thing." Braxton's head turned sideways. "I don't know what Beecham was thinking. Damned shame. He was a good man."

"And what of Adriana Rabh?" Cassandra asked via subspace.

Braxton cleared his throat but didn't speak. Kwazi eyed him from behind. That would become a new and necessary habit, he thought, still trying to make sense of what had happened during the battle. Braxton was undoubtedly waiting for Elinda Kisaan to answer Cassandra's question. The victory was hers, after all. And so was the failure wrapped inside it.

"She's avoided capture," Kisaan said directly. She had courage, a core of confidence Braxton lacked for all his bulk and bluster. "We're scouring the colony. Looking in every nook and cranny of the station."

Cassandra's silent, appraising glare spoke volumes. Not only had Adriana Rabh managed to effect her escape, but the willingness of the

miners to sacrifice themselves on her behalf had shocked everyone, especially the raw recruits assigned to Kwazi's glamor squad. The average
citizen was expected to welcome Cassandra and the SSR—why were they
fighting to the death for the old regime instead?

"She's a sly one," Kisaan said in a voice that sounded like it needed an
excuse. "And Kwazi's ... cowardice..."

"I..." He wasn't sure how to respond. Braxton turned his head, regarding
him with flinty eyes. "I've never fought in a battle before," Kwazi said.

"That's not true," Braxton said. "You helped take this ship."

"That was different." *The killing was less. The killing was at a distance. And
I didn't have to do any of it.* "People were dying on both sides. I..."

"Yes?" Cassandra prompted with impatience.

"I didn't see the point," Kwazi finished.

Braxton grunted but said nothing.

"The *point*," Kisaan said, "was to liberate Callisto from the Rabh
Faction's oppression."

Kwazi was silent. In his head, though: *We liberated a lot of them with
death, then.*

"His battle buddy died in the firefight," Braxton suggested. "Beecham
was a friend."

No, he wasn't, Kwazi wanted to say. *I hardly knew him. He annoyed the crap
out of me.*

The hole in his gut—the one first opened when he'd learned Amy and
his mining family had died, then been ripped wider when he'd learned
Telemachus had murdered them—that hole bled anew inside him now.
He'd barely known Monk Beecham, it was true. Or more to the point,
Monk Beecham had barely known him. And yet, he'd sacrificed himself to
save Kwazi's life.

"War is hell," Kisaan said to the expression on his face.

"Don't quote platitudes to me," Kwazi replied without thinking. He
heard the disrespect in his voice, the potential for violence. He wondered if
Braxton would try to kill him again for saying it.

Try to kill him *again*? Was that what had happened?

"You're right," Cassandra said quietly. "But war does require sacrifice.
Our Soldiers, even the civilians we're trying to free from the Company's

enslavement—every revolution has casualties, a price that must be paid for the greater good."

The greater good, Kwazi thought. *Maybe that's what Helena Telemachus said to herself when she ordered the executions of Amy and Beren and Aika.*

"Elinda, find someone you trust and leave them with a garrison to secure Valhalla Station," Cassandra said. "They're to maintain order and find Adriana Rabh. You, however, have a new mission."

"What mission?" Braxton asked.

A smile bloomed on Cassandra's face. She was a she-wolf scenting the next kill on the wind.

"You're going to Titan."

22

RUBEN QINLAO • DARKSIDE, THE MOON

The camoshades Brackin had given Ruben were killing him. The technology was old, a prototype that had never been commercialized because of the side effects—excruciating headaches for the wearer. The shades reshaped facial features temporarily, molding the wearer's own skin and enhancing the alteration with 3D projection. The constant flow of that much frequency spectrum so close to the human brain and the resulting headaches had proven an insurmountable problem to solve, even for the Erkennen Faction's brilliant inventors.

Ruben Qinlao had the pulsing cranial blood vessels to prove it. But whatever the downside of wearing the glasses, it beat getting recognized. He'd left the hooded cloak on the drunkard, and Elissa Kisaan knew that man wasn't who'd fired at her. She'd resumed the search, drawing in the local marshals.

At least Tony was improving, thanks to Brackin's new bacterial therapy. He was still unconscious, but he no longer suffered from hallucinations, and the doctor's prognosis for him had improved. But the two days' grace they'd gained by leading Kisaan astray wouldn't hold. Nobody was that lucky. So Brackin had dispatched him to pick up a piece of proto-tech on the black market. It would supposedly kick Tony's healing into overdrive. And then they could see about getting out of Darkside and off the Moon.

"Hey, you here to buy? Or just scabbing for the marshals?"

Ruben regarded the man. Young, broad, a bouncer type.

"I'm looking for meds."

The man grunted. "Third stall. Myerson. Don't dawdle."

He moved off.

Probably paid by the merchants who'd set up shop here to move along the riffraff. And make sure no one was working for the law or, if they were, cared too much about enforcing it.

Ruben surveyed the booth the bouncer had pointed out. Brackin had explained the way this would work. The floating caravan of black-market vendors calling itself the Darklight Bazaar would spring up from time to time at a random location in the tunnels below Darkside. The word went out on a private network, and buyers descended from up top. Then the caravan would evaporate into the Darkside underworld again before the Company or the marshals or, now, Cassandra's Soldiers showed up.

This time the caravan had set up where four underground tunnels converged. The bazaar was busy but oddly quiet as buyers and sellers haggled in murmured voices. The lighting was dim and schizophrenic. The price for the item he'd come to purchase would be outrageous, Brackin said, so he'd given Ruben six more of the preloaded burner bands to trade for it.

The bouncer glanced his way with another get-about-your-business look. More attention Ruben didn't need.

He approached the stall, and an older man dressed in worn wraps of gray and black sidled up to the tabletop displaying his wares. His smile was broken and greasy. He looked Ruben over warily, like an expert appraising what was likely fake jewelry. Ruben's headache flared again.

"Do fer ya?" the man asked.

"You Myerson?"

"Sure, we can agree on that. Good start, eh?" A chuckle came through the broken teeth. It sounded almost genuine. It smelled moldy.

"I'm looking for a Novy autoimmune stimulator."

Myerson's smile dipped a little. "Those are highly illegal."

"That's why I came to the black market."

"I mean, *controlled* illegal. Erkennen Patent Enforcement illegal. Hey, you need something for that headache?"

Ruben forced his eyes open. Myerson was a rough portrait outlined in red.

"No, it's fine. Look, I don't know if you've noticed, but Gregor Erkennen isn't in much of a position to enforce anything these days."

"These days, yeah. Things change. Then they change back."

Ruben cleared his throat and leaned over. "Brackin sent me."

"Isaac Brackin?" At Ruben's nod, Myerson's cheek twitched. "Should've said so in the first place."

"My bad."

"Yeah." The black marketeer glanced around the Darklight Bazaar. "Novys don't come cheap," he said.

Ruben pulled out the handful of syncers from his pocket and placed them on the booth's smooth surface. He didn't remove his hand.

"Half a dozen of these," he said. "Each holds a thousand."

Myerson blew out a breath. "Are you kidding? For a Novy?"

Leaning in again, Ruben said, "Watch your volume, old man."

"Right, right."

"This is what I've got. Brackin said it would be enough."

"He's wrong. Price went up."

"When?"

"Now."

"Why?"

"Cuz you seem desperate," Myerson said. His smile was natural enough now. "Also, the way things are these days? Everything I got's going up in price, damned near by the hour. The banker-in-chief, Rabh, herself just got ousted. How the hell do I even know a SynCorp dollar is worth, well, a SynCorp dollar?"

Ruben gasped. His head felt like a boiler about to explode. "I need that stimulator."

"We all need something. Life's full of disappointments."

Ruben was tempted to reach across, pull the asshole off his feet, and demand he hand over the damned stimulator. The pain in his head urged him to it. But the bouncer was nearby, and a public brawl would just draw more unwanted attention.

"It's all I've goddamned got. Brackin said—"

"I don't like repeating myself. Dig deeper or get gone. The caravan's moving on and ... what the hell?"

Ruben had doubled over, the heels of his hands pressed to both temples. The pain had redoubled. Unable to stand it any longer, he ripped the shades off.

Myerson had reached out to steady him. "Look, bub, I don't need no medical emergencies. I'll get..." He stopped talking, and Ruben looked up to find the red haze surrounding the man dimming to an angry pink. "Holy shit, you're him. You're him!"

"*Volume,*" Ruben warned. He could feel the bouncer's eyes on the back of his neck. Words were hard to form. "Hear me out. Still want to turn me in after, it's your call."

Myerson licked his lips. There was a serious discussion happening inside his head.

"Yeah, I'm him," Ruben said. "And I need your help."

Laughing, Myerson stuck his thumbs in his too-wide belt. "You've got to be fucking kidding me. The Regent of Mars, with half a million SCD bounty on his head? What could you possibly have to offer me that I can't buy with half a million SCDs?"

"How do you even know the reward's actually worth that?" Ruben asked slyly. His ability to think was coming back. The agony in his temple had begun to lift.

"I see what you did there," Myerson said, clearly intrigued against his better judgment. "Keep talking. But hurry up before someone else recognizes ... say, what was..." His eyes lit up, darting to Ruben's hand. "Are those what I think they are?"

In his peripheral vision, Ruben could see the bouncer sidling over. Myerson waved him off.

"Camoshades," Ruben said.

Myerson clucked his tongue and reached out, drawing Ruben closer. "Volume, Qinlao, volume."

Ruben had a hard time keeping his smile inside. "Worth something, I see."

"Are you kidding?" Myerson glanced around them, keeping his voice soft. "There were only a dozen prototypes ever made, and most of those were confiscated by SynCorp. The rest just disappeared—probably thrown away by people who didn't realize the fucking mint they had. I've only seen one other pair and—" Ruben could almost see the saliva pooling in Myerson's mouth. "—they didn't work."

Ruben turned them over in his hand. "These do," he said, wiping one of the lenses with his shirtfront. "Very well."

"So I saw." Myerson chuckled again, clearly enjoying his own joke.

"I'll make you a deal," Ruben said. "The syncers and the camoshades for the stimulator."

Myerson's shrewd salesman replaced the geek with a tech fetish.

"Maybe I'll just sing out to Meskal over there and take them and the half-million dollars the Soldiers are offering."

Ruben's expression was musing. "You could do that. But before he'd get to me, I'd—oops!" He dropped the shades on the tunnel floor, then made grinding noises with his boot.

Myerson practically leapt across the flat tabletop. "You didn't—"

"I didn't," Ruben said. "Yet. And think of the future, friend. Who knows who's in charge tomorrow?"

"I know who's in charge today."

Myerson's meaning was plain and menacing and on the cusp of a decision.

"Today, yeah," Ruben said. He shrugged. "Things change. Then they change back."

The exasperation on Myerson's face resembled a roadmap of bad life decisions. "Pick them up. I want to see them work again."

Ruben squatted without taking his eyes off the vendor. He wiped the shades off and replaced them on his forehead. He hoped Brackin's patch job to make them functional again had survived a three-foot drop to a lunar rock floor. The headache began to come back immediately. They were still working, all right.

"Yeah, okay," Myerson said, then wiped his forehead. "Things were so much simpler when Zeke ran things around here. Money and goods. Goods and money."

"Who?" Ruben removed the glasses. Once again, instant relief.

"Never mind. Hand them over. *And* the syncers."

"Here are the syncers. You get the shades when I have the stimulator."

Myerson swiped the half a dozen burner bands into a basket Ruben couldn't see. From a box he pulled out what appeared to be an oversized hypo and laid it on the tabletop. Ruben was almost disappointed in how simple the device appeared.

"Shades," Myerson whispered.

Ruben put one hand on the stimulator and slid the other with the shades to Myerson. They took their trades at the same time.

"Thanks," Ruben said. "How do I know you won't turn me in the moment I leave here?"

"You don't," Myerson said. "But your point about who's in charge tomorrow ... if it's you, I'll come calling, and I'll expect a grand reception. I've always wanted to see Mars. And here..." He reached to the display behind him and handed Ruben a hat. The logo on the front showed Earth and Mars connected by an oval ring. "I don't want anyone tracing you back to me."

"Me either. You sure this is enough?" Ruben asked, putting the cap on his head and pulling it down as far as he could.

"It'll do," Myerson answered, a critical eye roaming over him. "No one looks anyone in the eyes here. Now, get gone."

And Ruben did.

Whenever he made a run for supplies, Ruben always reconnoitered the clinic from the alleyway across from Eros Erotics. It had given him a clear firing angle at Elissa Kisaan, and now it offered a broad, hidden view of the street. The caution had proven its worth.

Far down the narrow street, SSR troopers marched out of the alleyway near Brackin's clinic. They were headed straight for it.

Myerson.

The sonofabitch had turned him in anyway...

Or maybe not. How many members of Brackin's black-market network had seen him in the last week? The doctor had assured him the marketeers were tight. No one ratted on anyone, or all the rats on the ship would drown, Brackin explained. And yet, here they were, the SSR surrounding his front door, and not an hour after Ruben had left the bazaar.

Elissa Kisaan appeared while a Soldier pounded on Brackin's door. Ruben could imagine the doctor's terror. He fingered the gun in the right hip pocket of his workman's overalls. He had half a clip left from the fox hunt before. Enough to make noise, maybe even enough to put an extra hole or two in Kisaan, if he was luckier this time.

Brackin opened the door. Ruben could see him attempting polite conversation. The Soldiers pushed past his protests and into the clinic while Kisaan waited outside. She looked around. Could she feel his eyes on her? Her gaze lingered on his hiding place, and Ruben backed further into the shadows. Her eyes moved on.

The ruckus drew curious bystanders from their homes and businesses. Ionia appeared in the doorway of Eros Erotics, a smile spreading across her face. She leaned against the window frame in her looking-for-business pose, then lit a cigarette. She was waiting for the show to start.

A thin, elongated vehicle appeared at the far end of the alley, tailor-made for Darkside's narrow streets. Two marshals stepped out. One was a short, unimposing woman with apparent attitude in her body language. Her male companion just looked nervous.

Ruben pulled the pistol from his pocket. It felt heavy in his hand.

Two troopers brought out Brackin, his wrists in gravity cuffs behind him. He was still making his case to an unsympathetic jury. The male marshal put his palm on Brackin's head and ushered him into the back of the vehicle.

Next came Tony. Two Soldiers escorted his medical bed, while a third brought along the IV. A fourth trooper bent his mouth to Kisaan's ear. She nodded and surveyed the area again. And again her eyes focused on the shadows around Ruben, sending a shiver up his spine.

This was it. It was all or nothing. Blaze of glory or whimpering in a prison cell? He knew what his sister Ming would want him to do.

Ruben edged backward so he could extend his arm and aim without being seen. He bumped against something that wouldn't move. Bracing his back against it, Ruben steadied the pistol with his left palm.

"Not yet," said a deep, weak voice behind him. It sounded familiar and foreign at the same time. A hand came down on his shoulder. "Lower the peashooter."

The hand was heavy. Massive.

"Strunk?"

He turned around expecting to see the mountain of a man he'd known before, returned from the dead. Instead Ruben found what more resembled the battered slope of a rocky hill after a fierce storm. Strunk's left shoulder drooped, and there was a makeshift bandage protecting one eye.

"Yeah, Boss Man," Strunk said, his voice sounding like a bellows full of holes. "If we're gonna break Tony out, we've got planning to do." He paused to refill the bellows. "And there's someone you need to meet."

23

STACKS FISCHER • MASADA STATION, ORBITING TITAN

I didn't like leaving Bekah alone, but her tech talk reassured me. If she could keep Richter out of the War Room by screening his bio-code, it was hard to beat that for security. And she'd already switched off the emergency lighting protocol. Erkennen's camouflage program was back in place, running the utilities in the place. Minimal heat. Ahead of me, dark. Behind me, dark. And me lit up in half-light in the corridor I was in. I felt like a target in a shooter simulation set on *easy*.

Where would Richter go? Masada Station's ground floor contained a series of labs dedicated to technology development. The hidey-holes he might be in were too many to count. I could spend hours on Level One alone and still never find the bastard.

I reasoned it out. He'd never go to his quarters because he'd assume that's the first place I'd look. Then he'd think about that and decide I'd never go there looking for him. So that's where he'd go. That made as much sense as anything, so I headed to the lift.

Lying next to the lift doors was the access panel Bekah kicked out running from Richter. My knee said, *Don't get any ideas*, but I got one anyway. Taking the lift like an old man was a good way to get myself ambushed. All Richter had to do was listen for the hydraulics and shoot me when the door opened. The rest of my body overruled my knee.

I climbed into the small maintenance tube wondering how the hell anyone could work in such a tight space. I stared into the shadows above. Was Richter looking down? Doubtful or I'd be dead by now—so Plan B was working so far. I put my .38 in my coat pocket and grabbed two handfuls of ladder. My knee voiced its minority protest all the way up, so I had to go slow.

But that gave me time to think. No matter how Cassandra's crazy coup turned out, Bruno Richter was out of a Company job—permanently. The trust between an enforcer and his boss is sacrosanct. It's stronger than man and wife. It's stronger than man and God. When a faction leader hands someone like me or Richter or Daisy Brace the job of guarding their life, it comes with a nice compensation package—and the ironclad understanding that anything done against the leader's interests kills the deal. Then, you. Richter had sold out Gregor Erkennen, Tony Taulke, and the whole goddamned Company. And for what? Some vague promises of riches and power from the lead snake in a snake cult? He should know better. Or maybe, once I knew Richter's fondness for snakes, I should've seen it coming.

And that's a little payback I owe him, too. Oh, I was gonna enjoy killing Bruno Richter for all sorts of reasons.

I'd reached Level Two, and my left leg demanded a rest.

Richter had about twenty years on me. He'd run like a rabbit from the War Room. I hadn't sprinted like that since ... a long time ago. My arms and good leg lodged a class-action complaint demanding to know why Left Knee could get away with shirking like that. I gritted my teeth and climbed.

Something activated the corridor lights above me. I froze and pulled my .38 and waited for Ferret Face to sight down his barrel at me.

Nothing.

I resumed my climb, begrudging every sound. When I reached the top, the corridor was empty. And completely lit. Either Bekah had overridden that part of Erkennen's program, or someone had just walked through there.

I pulled myself from the maintenance tube and willed blood back into my extremities. The station was still as cold as hell. I surely wished Bekah would fix that heat.

Richter's quarters weren't far.

I took a step and stumbled. My knee, taking its revenge for ladder servitude. Once you pass a certain age, the things you took for granted—taking a reliable step, let's say—have a way of humbling you by their absence. A few seconds of willpower, and I was limping toward Richter's apartment. I passed the skeleton coder Erkennen had given me over the lock, and the door slid aside. I ducked in quickly.

Nada. Nothing. Zilch.

"Lights."

The place lit up with emptiness. The aquariums were there, and the rest of his stuff. But no Richter. There were a thousand other places on the station he could be, I reminded myself.

Maybe I'd outthought myself after all.

A sound came from his bedroom.

Or maybe I hadn't.

I grabbed a pillow from the couch and moved swiftly across the room. My knee played ball for once. It knew if I died, it wouldn't have anybody to bitch to anymore. The bedroom had gone silent. A glance inside made it look deserted. My ears knew better.

"Out, Richter," I said. "Let's wrap this two-man play up right now."

Richter was smarter than he looked. I moved in. When I rounded the bed where the little prick was hiding, I'd shoot first. None of those so-this-is-how-it-ends speeches.

Just one dead traitor.

"Don't shoot! It's just me!"

The geek who loved to argue with Bekah crouched on his knees beside Richter's bed, a pair of very shaky hands over his head. Could his eyes bulge any bigger?

"Tripp? What the hell are you doing here?" I asked, holding my gun on him. It was a damned good question. Richter wasn't the sharpest tool in the shed. Maybe Daniel Tripp had helped Ole Bruno compromise the station.

"What's it look like?" he squeaked, squirming out of his hiding place.

I stepped back. "Getting ready to die, maybe."

"No, please," he said, "you can't."

"Wanna bet? Hard to miss at this range."

Backing away, Tripp bumped into the wall. "No, you don't understand. You kill me, you kill the Company."

My brain took a second to process that. My knee started to whine again. Hold, please. There's a customer in front of you named Curiosity.

I turned and tossed a command behind me. "Engage lock." The door to Richter's bedroom slipped shut. Then, "Explain what you just said."

He winced. "I—it's a secret."

I wagged my head. "Okay, then." My pistol firmed up its argument. "You and your secret can hug each other in the grave."

"Wait! Okay, okay!" Tripp deflated a little, like a burden had been lifted off his shoulders. "I guess it doesn't matter now anyway."

"Clock's ticking," I said. Whatever this was, it needed to be over. Richter needed killing.

"I'm working on a secret project for Regent Erkennen. A way to stop Cassandra."

I blinked. That's how you know I'm thinking. When I'd arrived at Masada Station, I remembered Erkennen mentioning something about "curing Cassandra." A tech miracle that would give SynCorp the edge.

Okay. Attention gotten.

"You're Gregor Erkennen's secret weapon?" I said. "He left you here to work on the Cassandra killer?"

Tripp nodded like his neck was a spring.

But it seemed too thin by half. Tripp, squatting in Richter's quarters? And why would Erkennen leave his secret project up here, so exposed?

"I don't believe you," I said, taking a step forward. "You argue with Bekah Franklin all the time."

"Sure!" he said, his hands coming up like they were bulletproof. "That's to make it look good! Besides, she doesn't appreciate my specialty, not really." When Tripp said that, a little professional pride crept in. Ego trumping fear.

"And that is?"

"Machine learning. Specifically, the heuristics that define how programming can become sentient. How we bridge the gap between if/then binary thinking and the infinite possibilities of human decision-making."

I regarded him a moment. "In English."

Tripp rolled his eyes, and I almost shot him on principle. "I'm figuring out what makes Cassandra tick," he said.

"Okay. But do you know what makes her stop ticking?"

Tripp drew himself up, his ego inflating again. "As a matter of fact, I do."

I lowered my gun a whit. If that were true, Daniel Tripp could be the key to popping the mainspring on Cassie Kisaan's clock. *If* it were true. For all I knew, this Yahoo was in it to win it with Richter—a butcher with a blade and a techspert. Brawn and brains, the classic combination. But my conversation with Erkennen lent enough truth to his testimony that I elected to let Tripp keep breathing. For now.

"Okay, then. You're with me."

"What do you mean?" he said. Worry lines furrowed his forehead.

"I can't leave you here."

"He'll never come here," Tripp said, reading my mind. "That's why I hid here."

"And it was smart. But..."

Tripp waited for my counterargument.

"Tripp ... don't move."

"What? Why—"

Then he heard what I'd seen. The slithering hiss from the vent overhead. One of Richter's pets, its black tongue flicking, tasting Tripp's heat.

"Stand very still."

"You're goddamned right I will..." His eyes tried hard to see through the top of his skull. He didn't dare turn his head up to look.

The mamba extended unnaturally longer. I brought my revolver up and braced it with my off hand. I warned Left Knee to stand fast.

Tripp's eyes widened. "Now, what a second—"

Crack!

The snake dropped straight onto his head.

Tripp screamed, arms flailing.

The door slid open behind me.

"That's the last fucking one you kill, Fischer!"

Richter charged into the bedroom.

I started to turn. Two quick pops from the ferret's stunner bounced off the midsection of my coat.

Punk! Punk!

I fell backward, firing in Richter's direction.

Crack! Crack!

The shots went high. The bitter smell of gunpowder filled the air.

The ferret barreled into me, and we both went down. Tripp's screaming bounced off the walls. He was still struggling with the snake.

Richter brought his stunner up again. In that half second, I could feel the cold of its barrel mouth tattooing the underside of my chin. I batted it away with my gun hand, and his shot went wild.

Punk!

I brought my .38 up into his gut, but Richter countered, hitting a pressure point on my wrist. The revolver flew out of my hand.

His face hovered close to mine.

"Thanks for leading me right to him, dumbass," he said. Richter's spit speckled my face. His stunner came around again. I sprung my blade from under my wrist, blocking him like he'd blocked me. The knife sliced deep into his forearm.

"Fuck!"

He dropped his stunner and rolled away from me. Away from Tripp, who was screaming about blood. I was too busy to tell him it was all from the snake. Its headless body kept jerking.

Richter found a knife of his own somewhere. I had the quick-witted concern that it might be coated with venom.

He spider-crawled toward me, faster than I expected. I couldn't risk retreating or he'd be in striking distance of Tripp.

I'd barely rolled onto all fours when Richter diverted, springing to his feet and onto the bed. His crawling charge had been a feint. He was flanking me, going for Tripp.

I dropped the knife, grabbed the bedcovers with both hands, and yanked as hard as I could. Richter lost his balance and fell onto the mattress, cursing. Tripp realized the danger and backed against the wall, as far as possible from Richter.

"Enough of this shit," Richter said. He rolled off the bed and stood on his feet. "You first, Fischer. Then him."

I grabbed up my knife again and rose to meet him, my breathing hard and ragged. I tried like hell to inhale big gulps of air. My muscles needed the fuel. My knee didn't say a fucking word.

I showed Richter my teeth. "Bring it, Ferret Face."

Richter snatched a pillow from the bed and backhanded it at me. I deflected, but he was on me then, sliding the knife into my right side before I could counter. The wound missed the vitals, but if it was poisoned... Richter tensed to rip it upward and through my innards. I thrust my own blade forward, but he blocked me. The effort pushed me away from him, and his knife slid out, leaving a wildfire of pain behind. Blood flowed, red and slick.

I pulled back, trying to get my feet under me, a fighter needing recovery from a bell-ringing blow. My vision clouded with three Richters, then reduced to two, then became the real one again. My free hand went under my coat, but I'd no sooner pulled my stunner than he'd advanced, fast as a serpent himself, and batted it away. It disappeared under the bed.

"Let's do this old school," Richter hissed.

His knife came up, and I countered too slow again. But I'd jogged left, and it found my thigh instead of my belly. It slid into me like my flesh was warm butter. This time the pain didn't wait so long. My vision fogged over with it. Everything around me swam in red seas.

Richter's other fist came up, then down, cracking my left eye. My head swiveled under the blow, and I fell to my bad knee. He yanked the blade out to stick it somewhere deadlier. I countered without thinking, without seeing really. My instinct was true.

My knife gored his solar plexus.

Richter grunted surprise.

A rage bloomed spotty and red on his face. I jerked the knife up and left, gutting him.

Richter screamed in pain.

Tripp screamed in fear.

I howled like a caveman getting over on a sabretooth.

Richter grabbed my knife hand and pulled me in. His blade thrust out so fast, I felt it in my chest before I saw it move. Now it was me screaming, three wounds bleeding. He faltered, letting go of his knife, and I twisted my blade still opening his intestines. Crying out, Richter brought his bony fist down once, twice, cracking my skull again and again.

My knife hand came to the rescue, twisting my spring blade and ripping a new angle upward.

When Richter screamed his holy ghost wail, my hair stood on end.

Then Tripp was there. He wrapped a belt around the ferret's neck and pulled up and backward. Richter's free hand clawed weakly at the belt. Tripp twisted it tighter. I fell away, leaving my knife at the center of a blooming, purple-red gore welling out of Richter's center. I'd opened his intestines, and it smelled like death from downwind. The whole scene wavered, out of focus and awash in a crimson haze. Richter's struggles loosened as life and lunch bled out of his belly. Before I blacked out, I realized Tripp hadn't used a belt at all to kill that traitorous sonofabitch.

He'd used the still-twitching carcass of Richter's own snake.

24

REBEKAH FRANKLIN • MASADA STATION, ORBITING TITAN

At least she'd managed to get the lights back on for Fischer. That had been a considerably less overwhelming problem to solve than what was in front of her. Cassandra's cyberattacks were overwhelming her. The fifth security gate had just fallen, setting off an automated alarm. Only two security gates remained to protect Masada's mainframe.

If only Bekah had still had Carrin Bohannon to help her. But she didn't. And she refused to look at Carrin's body. That would only distract her. She didn't have time for that. Not now.

"Sound off," Bekah said. The audible alarm ceased, leaving only a flashing red light to mark the threat.

She rotated the model she'd been studying. The 3D image hovered over the biggest smart desktop in the War Room, helping her to visualize Cassandra's progress in wearing down their defenses. At the center, resembling a small planetoid, was Masada's computer core. The two remaining firewalls surrounded the core like dermal layers. Thousands of tiny dots constantly assaulted the outermost wall, and it reminded Bekah of an image from a long-ago biology class showing thousands of sperm attempting to fertilize a human egg. A more striking metaphor came to mind—the dots resembled piranha eating their way past the muscle and sinew of security protecting the Company's secrets.

She grabbed the outer security layer surrounding Masada's core from the air and threw it to the main screen. The spheroid shield morphed into thousands of lines of nested security code. Most of the lines still appeared green, indicating they were uncompromised. An entire section suddenly turned yellow, showing a threat. In places, the yellow had become red.

Bekah touched the Hammer around her neck. She'd never quite believed she'd need to use it but now ... after watching five gates eaten away by Cassandra's piranha code, Gregor's nuclear option seemed inevitable.

But it wasn't necessary yet. She targeted her diagnostic algorithm on the red bits of code. The cleaning program constantly trolled the code underlying the mainframe's security to identify weakness. It monitored, evaluated, and diagnosed how the assaulting code acted, then targeted that same friendly code for rewrite. Using the algorithm, Bekah could update, test, and shore up code on the fly like a medieval defender bracing the castle gate against an enemy's battering ram.

Each time she revised the security protocols—the mortar between the layers of Masada's virtual walls—Cassandra's piranha code adapted to attack another, weaker spot. Carrin had been right, Bekah thought, grief at her friend's loss returning. This time, she couldn't avoid a glance at Carrin, a kind of acknowledgment of the dead woman's wisdom. Not all the collective brain power of the entire human species could best Cassandra's ability to process trillions of decisions per second. Humans grow tired. Humans make mistakes. Cassandra's layered, constant assault was too sophisticated, too relentless.

Break it down, Bekkalleh.

Opa Simon's wisdom came on its own.

Complex problems often have the simplest solutions. Hearing his voice in her head calmed Bekah's racing heartbeat. *Don't let the drama distract. Find stillness, find the answer.*

The red, blinking code had multiplied tenfold. It must have made up a quarter of the code onscreen now. Already, Bekah could see the metaphorical mortar crumbling faster than her algorithms could plug the gaps.

The Hammer hanging around her neck felt heavier. Her mind playing tricks on her.

Simplify, Opa Simon said. *Solve the problem.*

"In the beginning..." she said. The phrase her grandfather had always used to help Bekah clear her mind and focus on the fundamentals.

What was computer code? A mathematical language used to generate predictable outputs via executed operations. And like all language, a way to communicate. And communication requires—

"Connection," Bekah said aloud.

She stood up so fast from her console, her chair toppled over behind her. She turned and was stopped hard by the sight of Carrin's corpse.

No, she thought, shaking her head. *That comes later.*

Masada's second to last security gate had fallen.

The console alarm began barking again.

A glance at the model showed the piranha code already gnawing at the thick, green code-skin of the last wall protecting SynCorp from extinction.

Bekah yanked the Hammer from around her neck, the gold chain snapping in two, and inserted it into the mainframe's quantum port. One turn, that's all it would take. One turn to wipe away all those secrets. They'd exist only in the engrams of the Hammer itself, waiting for Gregor's magic ingredient of human DNA to return them to life as human knowledge.

She glanced up at the 3D model. The last wall still stood strong. For now.

"Sound off," Bekah said. The barking alarm disappeared again. Stabbing herself with *Stupid, stupid, stupid, stupid!* she moved quickly to the communications station. She didn't need to use the Hammer, not yet. The answer was the simplest solution to every computer problem that had ever existed.

Pull the goddamned plug!

Bekah called up the station's communications array. Onscreen, the large dishes on the roof of the station appeared, a pale line of eight battleship-gray sentries arranged in a horseshoe, pointing at deep space. Saturn hung behind them, a curtain of orange and white.

She'd tried closing the infiltration point Richter's betrayal had created, giving Cassandra access. But Cassandra's worm merely adapted, hopping to a new port channel and reopening access to continue the attack. But there was something Bekah *could* do—she could simply turn off the array. Cut off all connection to the universe outside Masada Station and, with it, Cassandra's ability to reach the mainframe at all.

Bekah brought up the array's controls, her fingertips dancing a happy ballet over them, powering down the eight dishes, one at a time. She watched with exhausted glee as the power indicators dropped to zero.

So simple, she thought, turning her attention to her 3D model. *So simple it was hard to think of.*

The final wall guarding Masada's mainframe stood strong, its perimeter a thick, healthy green. The thousands of viral attackers had vanished. Cassandra was cut off.

"Take that, bitch!"

Bekah took a moment to enjoy the sound of her own voice in her moment of victory. Human ingenuity—perhaps a bit late in the game, but better late than never—had triumphed over the shock and awe of artificial intelligence. She couldn't wait to tell Daniel Tripp all about her solution.

Closing her eyes, Bekah conjured the image of her opa's smiling face. He would be proud, she thought. A complex problem solved with the simplest solution imaginable.

The alarm barked again.

The red light blinked again.

"Oh, please," Bekah said. "What now?"

She turned to find the visual model over the smartdesk alive with activity. Cassandra's piranha code was pounding on the final gate again.

"That's not possible."

In sections, the defense code had already begun turning a bloody red.

She glanced down at the array's controls. The power levels on two dishes were at eighty percent. The other six were returning to life too.

"That's not possible!"

From the back of her brain, something teased at her memory, something Rahim had said in the department head meeting.

Cassandra might already have viruses trolling Masada...

"No, no, no, no," Bekah exclaimed, punching keys on the console. The commands were nonresponsive.

Cassandra had outthought them—a backup program was powering up the array, had locked Bekah out. Cassandra must have inserted similar programs around SynCorp facilities all over the solar system. Infiltrator code waiting to be activated whenever she needed it.

"Think, think, think!" Bekah shouted. In the 3D model, green lines became yellow, vulnerable code. Yellow surrendered to red as the code was compromised.

She stared at the Hammer loaded in the quantum port of the main-frame. One twist, and all this would be over. One turn of that platinum key would deny Cassandra victory... But what if Gregor's magic process for rebuilding the knowledge base failed? What if Cassandra had anticipated the Hammer as she'd clearly anticipated the strategy to shut down the array? What if she was just waiting to trigger a counter-program?

The alarm's volume rose as the defending code crumbled beneath the piranhas' assault. It was like a dull metal rod dragged across the naked vertebrae of Bekah's spine.

"Sound off, goddamn it!"

Bekah reached out, taking the Hammer between thumb and index finger.

She should turn it. Play it safe. Gregor's tech almost never failed. She should trust in that.

"What do I do?" Bekah demanded of the universe. "*What do I do?*"

Simon Franklin appeared in her mind's eye. He was smiling.

Simplify. Solve the problem.

In that instant, she understood. She had the answer.

"If I can't turn it off," Bekah whispered, cautious of the new hope rising inside her, "I'll overload it." How that would work appeared in her head like a gift. She pictured it with absolute clarity.

"I'll overload it!"

Releasing the Hammer, she pulled up the array's positioning program. Quickly scanning the code, Bekah searched for the command language that would—and there it was. Part of the program's function was to prevent exactly what she was attempting to do.

Piranha code ripped at the final gate. Red lines of code dissolved like flesh submerged in acid. It would be close. Very, very close.

Bekah overrode the parameters prescribing how the dishes faced outward to deep space. Dishes eight and one began to rotate, as did three and six. Each pair of dishes angled to face its opposite in the horseshoe. No receiver, no way to accept the signal. Even Cassandra obeyed the laws of physics.

A glance at the 3D model confirmed it.

Crimson reflections from the flashing red code lit up the War Room, but there were fewer piranha already. Repositioning the array, interrupting the signal, was cutting them off. They winked out of existence by the dozens, the score, the hundreds.

But there was only one way to ensure the signal was cut for good: short out the entire array. Overload it with a broadcast so powerful, so broad across the frequency spectrum that it would take weeks of replacing burned-out components to bring it back online.

Bekah turned her eyes to Carrin Bohannon's body. She still had time. Her responder code was shoring up the final gate, gaining ground, driving the piranha back. She still had time!

The corners of Bekah's mouth ticked upward. Carrin had loved Richard Wagner's epic *Der Ring des Nibelungen* and how it dramatized Norse mythology. She'd play it over and over again whenever she encountered a stubborn programming problem. It inspired her to think bigger, Carrin said. Now it was Carrin who inspired Bekah.

She called up the music library, searched for Wagner's Ring Cycle, and programmed her selection to blast from Masada's eight dishes at maximum power across all frequencies. Carrin had sacrificed everything protecting Masada. It would be her honor in death to save it.

"Thanks for the inspiration," Bekah said to her friend. She patched the sound through to the War Room, so she could listen too. It wasn't necessary. But it was something she needed to do.

Bekah called up the music selection. Strings swept upward, followed by flutes hovering like hummingbirds, holding the strings aloft in the air. Then the woodwinds churned like horses' hooves cantering, preparing for a grand charge. The flutes and strings became eagles' wings beating hard as they carried their riders high into a blood-red sky. Then a battle line of brass marched forward, calling the charge, and "Ride of the Valkyries" reached every corner of the War Room.

Bekah watched the overload warnings flash on the comms panel. Her tears made it difficult to see them. At last, a moment to pause, to grieve for Carrin and the rest of her team. In the model, the piranha swarming Masada's final gate were fewer. Dishes four and five went first, followed quickly by each of the other facing pairs. In less than a minute, Masada Station had dropped completely off the grid of the subspace network, the circuitry of its array burned to cinders.

Bekah turned her blurring vision to Carrin.

Sleep, Valkyrie of Masada Station.

Then the emotion came, not tears alone but sobs that racked her chest, a self-exorcism of guilt for their having died at Richter's hands. Bekah let Wagner's music sweep her upward with its emotion, her screams of sorrow rivaling its thundering crescendos.

The War Room was quiet, now. The Valkyries had carried Carrin to Valhalla a while ago.

"Daniel? Are you there?"

Bekah tried again to raise Daniel Tripp on his sceye. And, once again, she received no answer. Where was he? Why wasn't he answering?

She returned to her ministrations, dipping the napkin lightly in the glass of water. She drew it slowly across Carrin's forehead, washing the skin that was already beginning to cool.

Bekah had lowered the gravity and laid Carrin on the small meeting table. She'd buttoned her uniform formally, flattening the fabric with her palms. She'd considered removing Carrin's clothes and performing the same death ritual she'd performed for her grandfather. Except Carrin wasn't Jewish, and she hadn't really been family—except, of course, that she had been. But the most intimacy Bekah had ever shared with her had been to hold Carrin's head over the porcelain god after a night of too much drinking. So she'd settled for perfectly arranging Carrin's uniform and washing her friend's exposed skin as a sign of love and respect, of appreciation for Carrin Bohannon's life and too-soon sacrifice.

We're put here to do good, Bekkalleh. That's really what loving God boils down to. Anything else is just Man placing himself at the center of the universe.

Bekah dipped a handful of fresh napkins into the water and resumed her task. The crusted blood rehydrated. She was doing good for Carrin. She thought her opa would be pleasantly surprised.

Maybe I'm a bit pleasantly surprised myself.

Carrin Bohannon's ritual was, in one way, more personal than Simon Franklin's had been. Certainly, it was more horrific. Bruno Richter had sawed through Carrin's neck, half decapitating her. The violation of Carrin's flesh gaped at Bekah, a ragged jack-o'-lantern scream. Maybe Bekah couldn't save Carrin from what was already done. But she could offer her a final act of kindness.

In a little while, the wound grew clean.

No less horrific. No less unnatural in its barbarism. But clean.

And Carrin, Bekah hoped, was at peace.

The comms pinged, startling her. Was it Fischer or Daniel or...

She touched the panel.

"Franklin here," she said in little more than a whisper. "Stacks, is that—"

"Bekah! Thank God."

"Daniel! Are you okay? Richter's out there! You've got to—"

"Richter's dead."

Those two simple words lifted a burden from Bekah's shoulders she hadn't realized was on them.

"What's the status of the mainframe?" Daniel pressed.

"It's ... I fried the array. We're cut off."

"Excellent!" he said, taking a moment to breathe. "Listen, I need you to get down to the infirmary—"

"Wait," Bekah said, "Richter's dead?"

"Bekah, I need your hands! Fischer's in bad shape. Come to the infirmary now!"

She blinked once. A need to move injected adrenaline into her bloodstream. Death wasn't taking someone else from her—not today. Bekah snatched the Hammer from the quantum port and slipped it into a pocket.

"On my way!"

25

KWAZI JABARI • ABOARD THE FREEDOM'S HERALD, APPROACHING SATURN

They were nearly there.

Kwazi didn't understand the specifics, but he knew they were headed to Titan so Elinda Kisaan could hand Cassandra a clean victory. The battle over Callisto had certainly not been that. Adriana Rabh was still at large. She seemed to have disappeared into the ether of space itself. And Valhalla Station was already pushing back against SSR occupation, though the colony wasn't yet in a state of open rebellion.

As they neared Saturn, Kwazi wondered if that cycle would start all over again. They'd liberate Masada Station and Prometheus Colony as they had Rabh's headquarters and Callisto ... with smiles and assurances of new liberties and an acceptable casualty ratio. But might not the citizen-workers under Gregor Erkennen's rule simply follow the example set by their Callistan cousins?

Kwazi didn't understand their resistance. Didn't they know what SynCorp was? Didn't they care about living a life in freedom?

He'd hardly been able to sleep since they'd departed Callisto. His mind kept racing, infected with a kind of self-imposed, impotent responsibility for managing events beyond his control. And even when Kwazi found snippets of sleep, he'd awake in a cold sweat, the same image branded on his brain: Carl Braxton, sighting down his rifle barrel at Kwazi on Rabh Regency Station.

He needed a distraction, if only for a little while. He needed the blanket of serenity Kwazi felt laid over him that was spending time with Amy.

He engaged Dreamscape, and Olympus Mons unfurled in front of him, a painting in dusty reds stretching across the canvas of Kwazi's mind. Just viewing it calmed his breathing. Puzzle pieces of the idyllic view fell soothingly into place. The bluish horizon of the Martian sunset. Deimos, one of the two moons of Mars, sinking slowly in its orbit. And Amy sitting on the rocky outcropping they'd claimed for their own.

"Hi," he said, approaching her. Amy glanced over her shoulder and smiled. The light breeze teased a strand of her hair over her eyes. She brushed it away.

"Hi."

Kwazi sat down beside her, taking her hand. The thin powder of Martian sand felt gritty through the worker's coveralls he wore. It literally, he thought with a light laugh, made him feel grounded. Yes, this is where he needed to be. Where he wanted to be.

"It's weird, isn't it?" Amy said.

The sound of her voice was like cool water.

"What's weird?"

"The sunset." She pulled her hand away and gestured at the horizon. "It has that bluish tint. Kind of ironic for the Red Planet, don't you think?"

"It's the dust in the atmosphere," Kwazi said. "It's so fine, it allows blue light through but not colors with longer wavelengths."

Amy nodded. "It's just not what you'd expect, you know?"

"Yeah."

He edged closer to her on the lip of the overlook. Rather than take his hand again, as he hoped she would, Amy brought her knees up and wrapped her arms around them.

"How are you doing?" she asked.

Kwazi shrugged. "Fine."

"I mean, about the battle on the station. About what happened to Beecham and the others."

The wind blew cooler. It was almost chilly.

"I'm fine," he said again.

Amy turned to him with an unsatisfied expression.

"Well," Kwazi began, not wanting to get into it. He hadn't come here for this. He'd come here to get away from this. "I mean, I'm sad, of course."

"Sad?"

"I regret that Monk and the others—"

"You *regret*..." Amy sighed, laying her chin on her knees. Her gaze returned to the horizon. "You sound like you're reading a prepared statement."

Kwazi blinked once, twice, while staring at the side of her face. Her profile was beautiful, crafted with Dreamscape perfection. But the peace he'd sought in coming here seemed a distant, foreign thing now. Replaced with irritation and defensiveness.

"What do you mean?"

She didn't answer at first, squinting at something distant—the white and pinkish pitted surface of Deimos sinking lower in the sky, maybe.

"I just wonder sometimes what happened to the miner from Mars who was so afraid to ask me out," she said, turning to face him again. "You were happier then. You seem so different now. When did the Kwazi who loved it that I loved it when he spoke French become a sleepless soldier?"

He withdrew from her. The harsh Martian surface dug into his bony frame.

"When the Company murdered my family!"

Amy wiped dust from the side of her face, then reembraced her knees and returned her gaze to the darkening Martian desert. "Some of your family," she said.

"What?"

Her eyebrows arched curiously. "Helena Telemachus ordered my death. And Beren's and Aika's."

"Yes."

"But it was Cassandra who killed Max and Mikel in the mine, right?"

Kwazi thought he must have misheard. It was like the needle playing the thoughts in his brain had skipped out of its groove.

"And *almost* killed me and Beren and Aika, for that matter. In the mine." Again her eyes found his. "And you."

"I suppose," he said. What the hell was this? Kwazi was tempted to grab Amy by the shoulders and kiss her to force an end to the conversation.

"Why are you doing this?" he asked. "You've changed."

"*I've* changed?" Her response was nearly offended.

"Look, times are more complicated, I know." He wasn't sure where her attitude was coming from, but he wanted it to go back there. This was *his* fantasy, damn it. She was *his* Amy. Maybe if he reasoned with her, he could redirect the conversation. Bring her back to being the Amy he'd created in Dreamscape. "But it won't be like this always."

"Just a little death for a little while," she said in a way that seemed to be tasting the concept. "Then it will all be better."

"War requires sacrifice," he said. He could hear the testiness in his own voice. The anger at having to defend himself. And Cassandra.

"For the greater good."

"Yes! Exactly!"

Amy nodded. Deimos had almost disappeared entirely below the thin blue line of the planetary horizon.

"So, if you think about it," she said, "all those events—the sabotage of the mine, deposing Tony Taulke, killing those atmo-miners on the station —it's all part of a larger, necessary plan. The Greater Good Plan."

His brain was starting to throb. "I suppose," Kwazi said.

"Even me dying. When Cassandra bombed Facility Sixteen."

The anger built inside him, and Kwazi almost let it out. "No," he said at last, forcing himself to remain calm. "You died because Helena Telemachus—"

"—murdered me, yes. Just as Cassandra murdered Max and Mikel."

"Stop saying that!"

Kwazi put his hands against the gritty cliffside and pushed himself to his feet. The breeze and altitude made him feel lightheaded. His legs felt weak. His thoughts seemed half a step behind his emotions. Most of Mars had fallen into shadow. The stars shone in their thousands.

"Monk Beecham died for the greater good," Amy continued. "Maybe I did too."

"No!" He backed away. Amy was a shadowy form sitting on the precipice of Olympus Mons. "SynCorp murdered you!"

"As Cassandra murdered Max and—"

"Stop it!" Kwazi pressed the heels of his hands against his forehead. "Stop it!"

Amy rose to her feet, swaying in the wind on the edge of the cliff. She moved from darkening dusk toward him.

"Leave me alone!" he shouted.

"Kwazi, I just want you back," she said. Words recalling his own weeks before, when he'd been mourning the real Amy Topulos. The red dust crunched under her boots. "I just want us back the way we were."

Amy stepped toward him, one hand reaching. Her eyes shimmered in the fading light of Deimos. Only they weren't Amy's blue eyes ... they were a luminescent gold.

"Kwazi, I'm sorry," Amy said with Cassandra's eyes. "Don't listen to me, I'm just—"

"Quit program," Kwazi said, calling up his sceye. "Quit program!"

He sat up quickly. His quarters were the dark of shipboard night, but the red capital-D shone brightly on his sceye display. The side of his mouth was wet. He wiped the sleep drool away.

The door chime sounded again. It had been chiming for a while, Kwazi realized.

Sleep? Had he been sleeping or lost in Dreamscape? Had Amy—or her doppelgänger?—been real or just the fatigued fantasy of a weary mind?

In the darkness of his quarters, Kwazi had the sudden gut-memory of staring at a half-opened closet door as a child on Earth. He'd cried out, and his grandfather had come running with anxious questions. He'd sworn he could hear whispers or claws scratching. As he'd clung to the old man's arms, Young Kwazi had been certain that something waited inside the rest-less shadows of his closet. Something conjured by the fears of his imagina-tion, the darker Dreamscape of his childhood. Something that professed goodness behind a fake smile hiding evil intent.

The Amy in his dream ... or his fantasy ... the Amy he'd created. The words she'd spoken, the truths they'd contained that he'd never faced before. Cassandra's complicity in the deaths of his crew-family. They were his truths, yes? If he'd created Amy and she'd spoken them, the truths must be his truths too. But then she'd become...

...a fake smile hiding evil intent?

A fist pounded on the door to his quarters.

"Kwazi? Are you all right?" The door chime rang again. "Kwazi, answer me!"

"Open," he said. "Lights."

Milani Stuart stood framed in the doorway, her fist raised. Worry lines painted her face.

"I was stopping by to see how you were doing, and I heard you shouting," she said, entering his cabin. The door slipped shut behind her. She stood awkwardly for a moment, then walked to his bedside and knelt in front of him. "Are you okay?"

"Yeah," he said. When Milani took his hand, Kwazi almost pulled away. But he had a sudden craving for the contact.

"The dream again?" Milani asked. The weight of his disclosures to her since leaving Callisto—about Braxton and how Beecham had died—filled the spaces between her words. He could hear the probing concern of the counselor in them.

Kwazi considered telling her the truth about what had just happened. But did he even know himself? And if he'd actually been in Dreamscape instead of merely dreaming, he feared seeing disappointment in her eyes. The physician's judgment that a hackhead who'd had a bad trip got what he deserved. Lying was just easier.

"Yeah," he said. "The one where Braxton..."

Kwazi shifted on the bed as Milani moved to sit beside him. The dream-memory arose of sitting side by side with Amy on the Martian cliffside. Viciously, he pushed it away.

"You know, as your counselor, I'd probably suggest something like, those dreams represent your anxiety about what's happening," Milani said. Her voice was contemplative but caring. "But what you described on the station—Braxton turning on you, aiming his gun at you—"

"He said Beecham got in the way. That a miner was about to split my spine."

Why was he rationalizing for Braxton? He already knew the story was a lie.

"I know," Milani said. "But it feels right to me. Your impression that he might have been trying to kill you, I mean."

It does?

"I appreciate all you did—all the Soldiers did—to rescue me," Milani said. "Telemachus..." The doctor shuddered. "I still have nightmares myself."

Kwazi squeezed her hand, as much for himself as for her. Feeling the soft warmth of her skin against his was reassuring. Something real. And Milani's eyes were brown, he noticed for the first time. Not gold.

"But I feel like..." she began.

"Yes?"

"I feel like I'm in velvet shackles here." It was like Milani had lifted a flue, allowing a reservoir of secret thoughts to tumble out of her. "Like I'm supposedly free to do as I wish, but not really. Like Cassandra's promises are all crap covered in cake icing. But once you take a bite..."

Her words resonated like a bell ringing. They penetrated Kwazi's bones. First, he'd been the symbol for the Company. Then, Monk had called him the face of the revolution. Saying others' words for one side or the other, and all of it feeling false. Neither side more real nor more genuine than the other, so it seemed.

"I've always wondered why they accepted me so easily into the SSR," he said. "After only a few days. Now I think I know."

Milani squeezed his hand.

"I think, eventually, they meant to kill me all along," he said. *The way Telemachus killed...* he suddenly realized. "Dead or alive, I'm propaganda they can spread. And they've got that avatar now, the one in the video—it's not perfect, but ... will anyone know who doesn't know me?"

He looked to Milani and noticed her nearness. Her eyes were fearful and full of concern. "Would they even care if they did?" she whispered.

What was real? What was false? Amy had seemed real, so very real, but now...

"Part of me is asking," Milani said, "what's the real difference between the SSR and SynCorp? At least under the Company we had peace. And now the SSR and Cassandra's promises... I mean, who blew up the mine on Mars in the first place?"

It startled him, Milani asking the very question he'd pondered in his dream—or in Dreamscape through Amy? Milani's eyes searched his, looking a sympathetic soul maybe, or at least someone else who harbored doubts about Cassandra and her promises.

But Kwazi's brain was too tired to make sense of it. Reality, fantasy, truth, lies. It was all melting together, becoming muddled and monochromatic in his head, a white noise of confusion.

"Do you really want to kill Helena with your own hands?" Milani's gaze was piercing and fierce.

"Yes."

"Really?"

Here too, the doubts crept in.

You died because Helena Telemachus—

—murdered me, yes. Just as Cassandra murdered Max and Mikel.

"I—I thought I did. Now ... I'm not sure."

Her face offered him a small smile.

"You don't know how happy I am to hear you say that! Oh, Kwazi, I was so worried I'd lost you to—"

"General quarters." The red alert blasted from the speakers. *"All crew to general quarters. Fire teams prepare for station assault."*

Their eyes locked. Milani pulled him to her, their lips mashing together. Her arms hugged him hard against her. Kwazi melted into the kiss, surrendered to its human connection. And, more than that, to its connection with Milani Stuart.

26

REBEKAH FRANKLIN • MASADA STATION, ORBITING TITAN

She heard the beeping of the monitors before she walked into Fischer's room. The past twenty-four hours had seen a peaceful quiet descend over Masada Station. It was just as empty, but the atmosphere had cleared. It was like someone had refreshed the heavy winter air with a promise of spring sunshine.

Fischer lay in the med-bed, and for a moment she saw her opa in his thinness, his flattened posture. A glance at the monitors showed his vital signs continuing to improve. He was sleeping. Just a few days ago, she would have taken offense on her grandfather's behalf for having associated the two men in her thoughts. Now Bekah held an almost familial affection for Fischer she couldn't deny had she wanted to.

"You gonna hover all day?" Fischer asked.

"Oh. I thought you were asleep."

He opened his eyes and turned to face her. "Old survival strategy," he said. "Pretend you're sleeping till you know who's entered the room."

Bekah stared at him with a wicked glint of humor. "I guess you trust me, then. Telling me your survival strategies."

Fischer allowed a half smile.

"How are you feeling?" she asked.

"Fine. A few more holes than I woke up with yesterday, but they seem to be closing up nicely."

"You were lucky Daniel had field training in a former life."

"I'm lucky I got knifed on a station where experimental healing accelerants are available." Fischer rolled onto his left arm and pulled down the front of his hospital gown. The knife wound in his chest, still purple from internal bleeding, had almost completely healed over.

"I'm ready to get out of here," he said.

Concern clouded Bekah's face. "You sure?"

"Yeah," Fischer said, sweeping off the sheet. He levered around on the bed, dropping his legs over the side. The hospital gown, as they always seem to, gaped open in the back.

Bekah averted her eyes. "I'll just wait for you out here, then," she said, retreating to the hallway. After a few minutes punctuated by the occasional curse word, she saw his shadow cross the threshold of the doorway.

"Even my knee's complaining less," he reported, his voice somewhere between grateful and amazed. "Lead the way."

"Probably the steroids," Bekah said as she headed for the lift. She shortened her steps, hoping it wasn't obvious.

"What's the latest?" he asked. "Erkennen and his colony of eggheads back from Titan Amusement Park yet?"

"Not yet. They're prioritizing skeleton crew staff first. Still breaking down equipment, getting the shuttles ready. It'll be a day or so before the first wave starts returning."

"You fixed the heat," Fischer said admiringly.

"Yeah. I've taken Gregor's camouflage protocol offline. The station's systems are returning to operational norms. Hopefully, it'll feel like home when they get back."

They boarded the lift. Bekah pushed the Level One button.

"Where's Tripp?" Fischer asked.

"In the War Room," she said. "Still working on his project to stop Cassandra."

Fischer made a musing sound. "Glad I didn't kill him, then."

Bekah made a vague noise. It still stung that Gregor hadn't confided in her about Daniel's true mission. She would have spent a lot less angst on his attitude.

The braking hum of the vator vibrated through her feet.

"I haven't had a chance before now," she began.

"Unnecessary."

"No, but it is," Bekah said as the doors opened. "Thank you for protecting me. And Daniel," she added hurriedly. "I—"

"That's the job," Fischer said.

She exited the lift and Fischer followed. They were walking side by side now. Bekah was glad she didn't have to look him in the eye.

"You're not as hard as you make out," she said.

Fischer grunted. "Clearly." He rubbed his chest where the wound was still healing.

"You know what I mean," she said as they entered the War Room.

"—fucking piece of shit!" greeted them.

Daniel Tripp pounded his console.

Bekah exchanged a look with Fischer, who seemed amused.

"Problem?" Bekah asked.

"I can't get the goddamned sequencing right!" Daniel exclaimed. His face was flushed with frustration. "I ... every time I run the simulation, the algorithm breaks down before it's able to break down the hybrid genome's bridging base pair." He channeled his anger into a short, quick bout of pacing.

"That sounds downright terrible," Fischer said, earning himself a viper's look from Daniel.

"It means," Bekah explained, "we can deliver the viral payload into Cassandra's system, but not before her enhanced antibodies kill the genetic modification we're trying to effect."

Fischer looked from one to the other. "Oh, well ... now that you explain it, yeah, it's obvious."

Bekah ignored him. "Maybe you need some rest?"

"I can't rest," Daniel barked. Then his shoulders sagged. "I appreciate the suggestion, Bekah. I really do. But every time I lie down, my brain just keeps running. I need to work this out."

Bekah nodded understanding. Programmers were like preachers—

called to their service, not merely employed. It was easy to become so immersed in the work you couldn't eat or sleep until you'd solved the problem. Or saved the person.

"I need to call Gregor, get an update on the repatriation plan," she said.

"All right," Daniel acknowledged. "I'll continue working in the booth. So, y'know, I won't disturb you."

Bekah laughed a little as he signed out of the console and headed for the glass-enclosed station usually reserved for beta-testing new programs. Its soundproof walls helped the occupant focus. In Daniel's case, it would provide a judgment-free zone for any four-letter steam he might need to blow off.

"I thought communications were down," Fischer said, sitting down next to Bekah. "That's what Tripp told me."

"The station's are," she said, speaking while her fingers worked. "The Hearse's, though..." Bekah hesitated. "Uh, well—"

"Uh, well what?" Fischer said, giving her his full attention. "What'd you do to my girl?"

"Nothing," Bekah said. "Well not *nothing*. But nothing you'd disapprove of, I think."

"Try me."

"I hacked her security," Bekah said. Then, quickly, "With Daniel's help." Why did she feel the need to share the blame?

"You ... hacked—"

"Your ship has the only functioning interplanetary communications system on the station at the moment. I needed a way to talk to Gregor and the others."

Fischer absorbed that. "All right, then. Nothing permanently damaged?"

"Nothing damaged at all," Bekah reassured him. "Just, um ... hacked."

"I'm sure you'll put her to rights with a better security protocol when all this is said and done," Fischer said. It wasn't a question.

"Of course," Bekah said. "Masada Station to Prometheus Colony. Come in, please."

A sound of amusement came from Fischer.

"What?" Bekah asked.

"The colony. Named after the guy who stole fire from the gods."

"Oh, that. My Opa Simon named it. And this station."

Fischer drew a breath. "Your grandfather was a wise and cautious man."

Before Bekah could respond, the comms crackled to life.

"Prometheus Colony to Masada Station. Bekah, good to hear from you." Bekah had been listening to Gregor Erkennen's mild Russian accent since she was a child. It was like a security blanket woven from sound. Hearing it now felt like warm water running over tired muscles. "Fischer! I see you're up and about."

"More or less," Fischer said.

"I want to thank you for protecting Daniel and Bekah," Erkennen said. "Without you there, all our secrets would now be in the hands of the enemy. And Daniel..." He stopped, unwilling to continue on an open channel.

"Yeah, about that. If you suspected Richter was a traitor, you should've said so. I could've had a knife wound or two less."

"I didn't suspect a damned thing," Erkennen said. "Until he betrayed me, Bruno Richter never gave me cause to doubt his loyalty. I only wanted you up there to back him up. Turned out all right in the end, didn't it?"

Fischer cleared his throat. "I suppose."

"Bekah, your opa would be very proud of you," Erkennen said.

"He *is* proud of me," she replied, surprised that she'd said it out loud. They sounded egocentric to her, those words. They sounded prideful. But it was Gregor's verb tense she'd intended to correct. Though her opa had passed on, she still felt his very real presence in her life. Hadn't his wisdom saved Masada? No, Simon Franklin wasn't just a memory to his grand-daughter. He was a living force inside her heart.

"*Is* proud, yes," Erkennen said. "I couldn't agree more."

"When are the first teams coming back up?" Bekah asked in a hurry to change the subject.

"At lunar dawn. Essential personnel. We need to get that communica-tions array back up first thing. And yes, I know," Gregor held up a hand, "there's a lot of damage. But I think we can bypass and patch our way to functionality in short order. There's a lot happening in the system. Tony Taulke, captured. Callisto has fallen. Mars is a tug-of-war between Qinlao loyalists and workers swallowing SSR propaganda. And Earth—the rumors from Earth..."

"What rumors?" Fischer asked. "I thought Cassandra had her backyard locked down tight."

"Oh, she does." Gregor took a breath. "Maybe too tight. Feeders post snapcasts to CorpNet now and then. They're not there long, and it's very confused. But the story that's emerging if you stitch it together—Cassandra is murdering Earth's population. It sounds like mass genocide."

"But that doesn't make sense," Bekah said. "I thought she was 'freeing humanity?'"

"Maybe that's how she sees murdering them," Fischer said, his theory laced with cynicism. "Or maybe she's just a crazy machine with human skin stretched over for looks."

"That's one possibility," Gregor said. "How is Tripp coming along?"

Bekah glanced at the booth. If the fate of the Company—and maybe billions of citizens—hadn't rested on Daniel Tripp's shoulders, what she saw might almost be comical. His hair standing away from his head, his arms flailing.

"He's making progress," Bekah said. "But Project Jericho isn't ready yet."

Fischer turned to her. "Project Jericho?"

"I'll explain when we're not on a—"

The orbital proximity alarm blared in the War Room. Bekah hadn't heard it since the last time they'd had a drill, preparing them for the worst-case scenario of an interstellar body hurtling toward Masada Station.

"What the hell is that?" Fischer asked.

She ignored him, her eyes glued to the screen. Gregor was talking quickly with the techs behind him.

"Are you sure?" he asked. Then, turning back to the screen: "We've got company."

"What kind of company?" growled Fischer.

"Sensors show the *Pax Corporatum* has just entered the system," Erkennen said.

Beside Bekah, Fischer blew out a string of expletives. She knew why as she muted the Klaxon's sound.

"It's not Tony's ship anymore," Fischer announced too loudly.

"It's Cassandra's," Gregor confirmed.

"Why are they..." Then Bekah knew the answer before she'd finished the question. "Her cyberattacks failed. So they've come here to take the station."

"We've got nothing but unarmed shuttles here," Gregor said. "But I'll try and figure something out, get people up there. The three of you can't possibly defend Masada by ... selves." Gregor's image snowed, then re-formed. "They're jamming signals. Bekah, remem ... what I ... you! Don't hesitate ... use..."

Then his image was gone.

"Oh my God," Bekah said, the quiet, satisfied serenity of the last day now shattered. They were about to be overrun by the enemy. Gregor had had the right of it: there was no way the three of them could defend the station alone.

She looked to Daniel Tripp again. He'd stopped his raving and, like the rest of them, was staring at the main screen. On it, Tony Taulke's flagship bore down on Masada Station.

"We should wipe the mainframe, get aboard the Hearse, and get the hell outta dodge," Fischer said.

"No, I can't do that," Bekah said. "If it comes to it, trust me, I'll use the Hammer. But if we run now, we leave the colony open. If what they say about Earth is true ... the SSR won't hesitate to kill everyone in Prometheus Colony."

"But if we stay," Fischer said, connecting the dots of her logic, "we give them something else to aim at."

Bekah offered him a wan smile. "Right. At least ... at least for a little while."

The enforcer stood. "Can you lock them out of here? Protect yourself and Tripp?"

"On the station plans, this room is a waste reprocessing facility."

"It's a ... what?"

"It's where all the—"

Fischer held up a hand. "Another method of camouflage by Erkennen, in case the station was ever threatened?"

Bekah nodded.

"That brilliant sonofabitch," Fischer said. "What assaulting force would try to storm a latrine?"

"That was his thinking."

"Fucking brilliant." Fischer took inventory of his weapons and Bekah watched, fascinated. The stunner in his shoulder holster. The knife under his right wrist. He knelt, with difficulty, and pulled out his .38 from its ankle holster, spinning the chamber. Rising to his feet again, he said, "Looks like I'm back up to bat."

"You can't fight them by yourself," Bekah said. If Fischer faced the attackers alone, she knew that meant she was losing him—permanently. The odds were just too great. And she'd lost enough people close to her already.

"I don't suppose you got the internal security system back online, did you?" he asked.

"Not yet," Bekah said, abandoning any further attempt to dissuade him. "But I'm on it! Here, take this." Gingerly, she held out an earbud. "It used to be Carrin's. It's meant for data exchange, but I can repurpose the frequency for local, two-way communication. You really should get an implant, you know."

"So I've been told." Fischer set the bud in place and struck a pose. "Should I get one for everyday occasions?"

Bekah slowly shook her head.

"Yeah, doesn't go with the hat," he said.

"Put it on and keep it on," Bekah said. "I can help you from here."

Fischer nodded. "Keep a low profile, kid. And keep that key handy."

As he loped from the War Room, Bekah put her hand in the pocket where she'd put the Hammer after frying the comms array. Feeling it there produced a strange brew of hope and dread.

27

STACKS FISCHER • MASADA STATION, ORBITING TITAN

I left Bekah Franklin with a hell of a lot more concern than when I'd gone after Richter—a professional, sure, but at the end of the day, just one man. I had no idea how many of Cassandra's grunts would hit the station. But I was pretty sure it'd be more than one.

I moved pretty sprightly for an old ... a middle-aged man with three fresh knife wounds. When he'd brought me into the infirmary, Tripp juiced me with something Erkennen had been experimenting with. He used words like "inflammatory mediator" and "recombinant" something-or-other, so I stopped listening. But the upshot was that my natural healing had been accelerated by several orders of magnitude.

And a good thing too, given what was coming. Even my knee felt like I'd traded up for a newer model. I just hoped it wasn't a twenty-four-hour cure with the warranty about to run out.

I needed every edge I could get.

"Stacks, come in," Bekah's voice said in my ear.

"Yeah, I hear you," I whispered. I might as well practice that discretion. Pretty soon, I'd be my own worst enemy if I forgot the virtue of silence. I'd be embracing Mother Universe with both arms.

"Okay, I'll monitor you on open comms," she said.

"I thought they were jamming everything."

Her voice opened up with a sly tone. "I've managed to shield this frequency, make them think it's part of the station's maintenance program. Still working on the station's security system."

Oh, yeah, that's right. We had no automated station security to help us out. Well, add that to the list of negatives for the current situation. I made my way to Engineering and Systems Control, wracking my brain for what two geeks and a devilishly handsome but slightly past-his-prime enforcer could do to stop an assault by squads of troopers. Inspiration struck when the door to the ESC refused to open for me.

"Hey, Bekah, that thing you did with Richter—where you locked him out of the War Room. I got an idea for something like that for the ESC."

There was a pause while she thought about it. "I locked out his specific biometric signature, his DNA," Bekah said. "I have no idea who's about to come through the roof. So I can't prevent their entering—"

"Right," I said, standing in front of the ESC's double-hulled blast door, which was sealed up tight. A network of cruxes—a spider's web of six arms —secured the blast door to the surrounding walls. Heavy-duty, mechanical reinforcement in an age that relied largely on programmed protection. Even if the door had somehow been opened, the crux-web barred anything larger than a frou-frou dog from entering. A good example of why I preferred old tech to new. I still had Gregor Erkennen's skeleton coder in my pocket I could have used to gain entry, but I had another idea. "But can you reverse it? Code the lock to only open for a certain DNA reading? Like mine."

Sometimes new tech works, too. *Sometimes.*

"Sure, of course! I can lock out all biosignatures that aren't yours."

"Good. Add yours and Tripp's to that shortlist. Then lock out anyone who isn't one of us."

There was a series of beeps and pings, just like in the sci-fi vids. Bekah, working the keyboard like a Steinway.

"Done. But Stacks..."

"Yeah?"

"They have guns. Lots of guns." I could hear the fear in her voice. Bekah Franklin was a coder. A very gifted numbers-language expert, not a commando. "Lots of really big guns."

"Yeah, they'll pound their way through eventually," I said. For her benefit, I tried to sound like I did this every day and knew what I was doing. The reality was, I was making it up as I went along—not something enforcers excel at. Plans and practice—that's how we get the job done. "Engineering's always the best shielded unit on any station or ship. Got to protect the power systems first if the big asteroid hits, right? Lose that, lose everything. Your lockout will slow them down some. The double-thick walls, some more."

Honestly, that's about all the hope I had of doing anything anyway. Delaying them. For what, I had no idea—the faint hope that Erkennen and his faction flunkies would ride shuttles to the rescue from Prometheus Colony? Stopping the SSR by myself, though? That was a five-dollar fantasy on a cheap sex machine.

"Okay," she said. "Delay is the game, then."

"Speaking of which," I said, the irony of the idea that'd popped into my head making me smile, "unlock every other door on the station."

I could hear the mental health assessment through the silence in my earbud.

"Why?" Bekah asked, drawing it out.

"Because I want those troopers distracted. I want them stopping every time a door swipes open beside them. Green troops lack discipline. Some of these troopers coming will wonder what treasures Erkennen's people left behind in their quarters. Some will break ranks to dig around. Some won't. But every delay is another minute we haven't lost the station."

Another minute we were still alive.

"Okay. It's done. Oh, Jesus!"

"What?"

"They're landing. Stacks, they're landing! They're at the southwest airlock on Level Three, and Level Two's moon-side hatch. I wish you had an implant! I'd send you the locations."

"I know where they are," I said. I'd had lots of time for walkabouts. Lots of time to commit the station's floorplan to memory. And I trusted my memory over an implant any day of the week.

I touched the lock on the bulkhead to the ESC, and the six crux arms withdrew. The blast door opened. When I withdrew my hand, the door slammed shut, and the articulated arms of the crux webbed it to the wall again. "You and Tripp keep doing your thing. As long as they think the War Room is shit central, they'll leave you alone."

"That'll only work for so long," she said. "Eventually they'll..."

Bekah Franklin's voice shook. I took a minute before I answered, to make sure mine didn't. No sense spooking her more than she already was.

"Yeah, I know," I said. "Keep that key handy. First sign of a breach of the War Room, use it. Understand?"

There was a pause. Then, a simple "Yes."

"Good. Is Erkennen's camouflage program still functional? Can you turn it back on?"

"Sure. Why? I thought you liked the heat on."

I smiled. Bekah could still make a joke. That was a good sign of a level head.

"Yeah, it's not the heat I'm interested in. Can you activate it and tag it to my voice commands?"

"Um ... sure."

"Great." Like I said, making plans up on the fly isn't helpful to getting good results. I prefer stacking the deck in my favor, every time. But we'd been dealt the hand we had. Time to play it out. "Here's what I want you to do."

I knew something about military tactics from the early days of SynCorp. Back then, Tony and the other faction leaders still had to deal with pockets of UN resistance who weren't too keen about their hostile takeover, and occasionally I'd ride along as Tony's eyes on the ground.

From what I'd seen on *The Real Story*, the SSR's takeover of Callisto and Adriana Rabh's station had been semi-competent at best. Agitators playing at soldiery. They'd likely learned some lessons since then, but hardened veterans they weren't.

Through her commanders, Cassandra would urge them to be daring. She wanted Masada Station, and she had days of Bekah Franklin's brilliant cyber-defense fueling her hunger for a little revenge-victory. But if the troopers were as green as they seemed in the snapcasts, they'd be less gung-ho and more let's-be-sure. Having Bekah unlock every door to every apartment on the station would appeal to their natural reluctance about charging into danger. Also: human greed.

Delay, delay, delay.

My job was to cut the knees out from under their morale. The easiest way to make any soldier slow down and start looking backward is to make them think the enemy isn't in front of them, but behind. And fighting them from the front was suicide anyway. I wasn't that curious about what Mother Universe actually looked like up close.

I took the lift to Level Three and almost ran into a sweep team. I hopped into my old friend the maintenance tube and watched through the grate. They were moving in teams of two, typical, and the faces I saw reinforced my theory—the Soldiers were well-armed but young, their eyes wide open but lacking resolve. Lacking experience.

The first team passed me. I held my breath. If they'd had heat sensors, they'd have seen my rumpled form hanging in the wall lit up like a Christmas tree. But these guys were an ad-hoc army. Even their vac-suits looked like they were pulled from the surplus pile. They were barely space-worthy with minimal thruster packs. And sure enough, when that first apartment door slipped aside, the forward fire team nearly jumped through the opposite wall. Their comms channel was secured, but I could imagine the dialogue. In that moment, it was likely of the four-letter variety. Then, the first two-man team entered the quarters to check them out. The second team behind them continued up the corridor. When Team Two rounded the corner out of sight, I slipped out of the tube.

"Lights," I said.

The corridor blacked out. I pressed against the wall where the twosome had entered the cabin. I could hear the rustle of a vac-suit coming. I held my .38 in my left hand for backup and leveled my stunner at head height. The trooper walked through the doorway and turned toward the T-junction. Team Two was nowhere in sight.

I pulled the trigger and his body froze, then dropped to the deck.

So that proved another theory: their vac-suits weren't MESH woven. Mark one in the plus column for Team Masada.

I hop-stepped across the hall, and the door to the quarters opposite slipped aside. Marveling at my knee's willingness to cooperate, I knelt and waited. First rule of guerilla fighting. Never stay in one place. One location, one kill. Always moving. Makes one man seem like ten in the paranoid mind of a frightened enemy fighter.

The dead guy's teammate snapped a helmet light on and flashed it right and left till it found Bubba on the ground. I aimed calmly. He'd have called Team Two back by now, likely in a scared, squeaky voice. I was about to have more company.

Bubba Number Two looked up, his light flashing in my eyes, making me squint. His mouth cried out silently in his helmet. He brought his rifle up. I fired, blinded by the bright light. I was still standing. I'd gotten him first. Closer inspection showed him slumped over Bubba Number One.

I'd just ducked back into the tube and refitted the corridor panel when Team Two rounded the corner.

"Lights," I whispered. The corridor illuminated again. I wanted the returning team to see my handiwork in all its glory. They halted, brought their rifles up, and began to sweep back toward the airlock where they'd entered the station. One of them knelt to confirm his comrades' deaths. They were no doubt reporting deadly resistance on Level Three via that secure comms channel of theirs.

More troops were coming from the breached airlock, but two dead troopers should slow things down a bit.

Time to move.

Loud, concussive booms. I could feel them in Masada's walls.

"Bekah, talk to me," I whispered. "What's happening?"

"They're setting off charges on the ESC's main door," she said. Not unexpected. We'd planned for that. But her voice wasn't as confident as I would've expected. "They're smart. They're hitting the crosshatched cruxes securing the door, not the door itself."

Hmm. That *was* smart. Once the spider's web was disabled, it'd be a simple matter of bypassing the door's electronic security system. Looked like our delay was getting shortened.

"Security system?" I asked hopefully.

"I'm working on it!"

Okay, then.

Stay on target, Fischer.

I hung on the ladder in Level Two's maintenance tube. Three fire teams were there. One member from each team guarded the door to a different apartment. Their comrades must be inside, digging for treasure. Or, more likely, looting them. I'd surprised the team on Level Three. These guys would be on alert now. They didn't know where the next attack would come from.

I did.

"Lights."

Blackness, like space without the stars. I didn't bother with quiet. I kicked out the panel and stepped into the corridor. Helmet lights began to snap on and sweep the corridor. Thanks for that, dumbasses! Paint a target on yourself.

Punk-punk!

The first door guard went down. Bright lights swung toward the falling body, which happened to be my way. Rifles came up. I fired six inches below the brightness, then fell gut-flat against the deck.

Punk-punk!

Another body hit the floor. Or it could've been one of the smarter troopers going prone, like me.

I rolled across the narrow space, then low-crawled forward. One of the braver Soldiers ran forward. He was nearly on top of me when he realized I'd gone low. His helmet arced down, his rifle following. I thrust my stunner straight up and met the resistance of a vac-suit's crotch. I pulled the trigger half a second before he did.

Punk!

The shock of the shot jerked his arms up, and his rifle fired wide. He collapsed on top of me, and that probably saved my life.

His buddies exited each of the three apartments, almost at the same time. One brought her rifle up and aimed it at me. I pulled the dead trooper around me like a shield. Her bullets thumped into his corpse. From under his arm, I pointed my stunner and hesitated. I have a rule against killing women. It seemed stupid, silly even, to worry about that now. But my thumb still had its ethics straight and dialed down the stunner's force setting.

Punk!

She went down, unconscious but alive.

Her male comrades lost the faith. One backed up and took a knee, adopting a defensive firing position inside a doorway. The other turned and ran up the corridor, and I could almost hear his thoughts: *to hell with this!* Best to let him go. I needed him spreading the good word of fear-laden defeat. This station ain't the easy take they told you boys it was.

The man-boy in the doorway was scared. I could smell it. He hadn't fired his rifle once. Maybe he was superstitious and didn't want to hit his already-dead buddies. Or maybe he wasn't sure they were dead.

I hated to kill him. But I was one man against a boarding force. I didn't have the luxury of morality. Hesitation is suicide in combat.

He knelt there, his rifle aimed in my direction and not firing, his helmet light shining but diffused by distance. All he'd see was a fuzzy haze of blackness and the slightly reflective material of his dead buddies' vac-suits. But his head shone like a silver pumpkin inside the helmet. His mouth was open in an O-shape. His eyes were wide.

Punk!

I shut them for him.

Time to move.

28

KWAZI JABARI • MASADA STATION, ORBITING TITAN

"Hang back," Braxton said over comms. "We don't want your pretty face scratched."

Kwazi did as he was told. When he'd suited up to board Masada Station, he'd felt oddly dissociated from himself, swept up in events, with little control over the part he played in them. Just a few days earlier, everything had been crystal clear. His need for revenge on Helena Telemachus. His absolute hatred of the Syndicate Corporation. His unshakeable love for Amy Topulos. Today, he felt like an alien resident in his own life story.

Two demolitions experts from Alpha Squad were molding the C-4B explosives to the thick cruxes of the bulkhead door leading to Masada Station's engineering room. Once the massive door was blown, Kwazi and Braxton were to lead Alpha and Bravo Squads, camerabots following, in a triumphant takeover of the station's power center. Elinda Kisaan was prepared to broadcast it systemwide from the bridge of the *Freedom's Herald* —with a ten-second delay, in case something went wrong. They'd learned that lesson over Callisto.

The general comms channel erupted with chatter. The men sticking the primers in the explosives stopped to listen.

"Keep working!" Braxton ordered. He took off the helmet of his vac-suit, and Kwazi could see the sweat running down the back of his broad neck.

The captain pressed his receiver to his ear, trying to make sense of the conflicting, animated reports coming in. There was surprise, then panic in them.

"What's happening?" Kwazi asked.

"Shut up!"

There came the short, popping sound of stunner fire.

"This was supposed to be simple!" A Soldier's panicked voice. *"Cassandra promised us there was no one—!"*

The voice went away, replaced by hissing. The channel became snow.

"Captain," said a member of Alpha Squad, "we're ready."

"Good, get back here," Braxton ordered.

"What's happening?" Kwazi asked again.

"Nothing to worry about," Braxton said over his shoulder. "Seems there's a few science majors with slingshots on the upper levels. Won't stop us, though."

Alpha Squad rounded the corner and took up sheltered positions opposite Kwazi and Braxton. One of the Soldiers withdrew an electronic detonator.

"Blow the fucker," Braxton said.

The trooper thrust three fingers into the air. She dropped one, then a second, then the third. Then she pressed the detonator button.

It was like the entire asteroid below Masada Station was shaking beneath Kwazi's feet. Plastisteel wall and overhead lighting exploded into the hallway near the massive door. Fallout thundered to the deck.

"What the hell!"

"Fitzpatrick is—"

Multiple voices, full of panic and anger, flooded the channel again. A woman's voice screamed, then was silent.

"Get Stuart over here!" Braxton shouted. "Make sure she's got a full field kit!"

"What?" Kwazi said. "Why?"

"I told you, we're taking casualties. Now shut up until it's time to be a star."

"Captain," said a trooper from the demolitions team, "we need a second charge."

Braxton cursed. The smoke of the first blast had begun to clear. The reinforced plastisteel door still stood. Two of its six cruxes hung mangled and useless from the wall. But the other four had held.

"Get to it!" Braxton said.

The demolitions team took up their task again.

Bravo Squad appeared in the corridor behind Kwazi. In the middle of their six-person team, Milani Stuart looked very small.

And very frightened, Kwazi thought.

"You're going up to Level Three," Braxton said. "We're putting you to work."

"Wait," Kwazi said, "it's too dangerous up there. You said it yourself—"

Braxton rounded on him. "Everyone contributes to the cause in their own way," he said. "She's a healer. Let her heal."

"But—"

"Kwazi, it's okay," Milani said as she approached. She hadn't been part of the assault teams and, like him, wasn't wearing a vac-suit. Elinda Kisaan wanted to make sure he was instantly recognizable when the cameras started rolling. When Milani's hand touched his forearm, it felt like electricity in human form. "If there are people hurt, I want to help them."

"Start with the casualties on Level Three," Braxton said. Then, to the sergeant commanding Bravo Squad, "Get her up there and triage whoever's left alive. Make it fast, and sweep your way down. We also have bodies on Level Two, I'm hearing."

"Yes, Captain."

The six members of Bravo Squad directed Milani back the way they'd come, toward the lift.

"Captain Braxton, what's your status?" Elinda Kisaan's voice took command priority over others on the channel.

"General, we're setting a second round of C-4B on the power station's door. The first—"

"Switching to private," Kisaan said.

Their voices disappeared. Without their dominance, the channel came alive again.

"It's like they're ambushing us on every deck," a Soldier said.

"How many are there?" another asked.

"More than we thought." A third, fear evident in her voice.

"Cut the chatter!" Braxton ordered, back on the main channel. The door to the station's lift swept open behind them. "Hold there!"

Bravo Squad's sergeant turned, barring Milani's entry into the lift. "Sir?"

"Change of plan," Braxton said. "Escort her back to the *Herald*."

Milani looked confused, and her expression reflected Kwazi's own. From behind came the whir of camerabots arriving.

"But Captain, I can save those men and women—"

"Change of plan, I said." To the sergeant of Bravo Squad: "Get her out of here."

"Captain, the second round of explosives is set," Alpha's sergeant reported.

"Good, give me the detonator. I'll blow the door. Take your squad and follow Bravo."

"Yes, sir."

"What's happening?" Kwazi asked.

Braxton muted his comms, waiting for the squads and Milani to move out of earshot.

"Ships have entered the system."

"Ships?"

"Corporate ships." Braxton's right cheek twitched. "Now we know where they are, at least." The humor was bleak, like the voice of a man with terminal cancer. "But we have one last service to render Cassandra, you and me."

The captain turned his rifle on Kwazi.

"Wait! What are you doing?" Milani's voice, plaintive and full of certainty. The Soldiers of Bravo Squad grabbed her and forced her to move with them. "Kwazi!"

Kwazi stared at Braxton.

"We'll both die in a heroic attempt to breach that door," Braxton said. "We'll inspire millions in their struggle against SynCorp."

Behind him, Milani was shouting. But Kwazi was focused on Braxton.

"Just like on Rabh's station," Kwazi said. "You were gonna do it there, and Monk got in the way."

Braxton made a what's-it-matter gesture. "You were always going to die for the cause, a true-believing martyr in Cassandra's war for mankind's freedom," he said. "I'm glad Monk got in the way last time. Your sacrifice here will count for more. The Hero of Mars putting others first, just like he did that day in Qinlao's mine. Only you'll help billions, now, not just a few dozen. Today, when they see you running toward that explosion? Jabari, you'll be the Hero of Sol. The whole system will become your family."

"Kwazi!"

"Move," Braxton said. He thumbed the protective cover off the detonator's trigger.

"And if I don't?"

"Elise Kisaan will execute the good doctor." He leaned in, so his whisper would carry. "Discreetly. Away from the cameras."

So that's what Kisaan had gone private to discuss. Clarity snapped into place for Kwazi. Elinda Kisaan's lone starship was facing defeat over Titan at the hands of the corporate fleet. She was salvaging the public narrative by casting the defeat as victory—through the martyrdom of Kwazi Jabari.

"How do I know Cassandra will protect her?" he asked. "After I'm gone."

"You don't, but you know what'll happen to her if you don't charge that door."

What followed began without warning.

The lights snapped off.

Braxton's cursing filled the corridor.

There was the sound of metal scraping on metal.

Cloaked in darkness, Kwazi scrambled toward the last place he'd heard Milani's voice.

Lights from trooper helmets snapped on.

Punk! Punk!

The stilted, *thunking* sound of stunner fire...

Braxton went down.

The sudden, shuddering blast of the explosives detonating.

The heat and bits of plastisteel and metal erupting, funneling up the corridor toward them.

Kwazi, knocked off his feet.

Alpha and Bravo Squads diving for cover.

Milani, screaming.

Sound became something distant and without clarity, as if filtered through water fathoms deep. Kwazi felt the thrumming of the explosion through the decking.

Around him, the rocky walls were hidden by red dust whipped up by the force of the blast. He blinked, and his eyelids moved in slow motion, like everything around him moved in slow motion. Miners crawling. Amy down on the ground, near their monitoring station.

He blinked again. The red haze had become the silver-white of Masada's walls made powder by the blast, hanging like particulates in the air. Not Martian tunnels after all, then. Kwazi turned and found troopers, not miners, clawing their way through the destruction littering the deck. Milani lay on her back, unmoving, like Amy had lain unconscious beneath the Martian surface that day.

Kwazi shook his head trying to clear it, and his brain seemed to slosh against the sides of his skull. He focused on Milani. Was she still breathing? His arms started to move. Then his legs.

Something held him fast. He looked down to find Braxton's fist wrapped tightly around his ankle. A jagged piece of plastisteel had embedded itself in the side of Braxton's temple. But he was still alive. A determined smile dragged his lips up at the corners. His left cheek was a ragged, bloody ruin. Half his upper teeth were missing from that side of his mouth.

Braxton's rifle clattered across the deck as he dragged it.

"Last sacrifice," he rasped, his eyes alive. "Last render unto Cassandra."

A shadow fell over them both. There was the loud *crack* of a pistol shot. The front of Braxton's forehead burst outward, spraying gore over Kwazi. The rifle dropped. The fist holding Kwazi's ankle went limp.

Sluggish with shock, Kwazi raised his eyes, watching helplessly as an old man straddled Braxton's body. His skin was pockmarked, his longcoat shredded. He'd been near the explosion. He pointed the revolver in his right hand at Kwazi.

Kwazi thought he could read the old man's lips. One simple, terrifying word.

Next.

"Hold it!" someone shouted. Kwazi looked to find one of the SSR troopers rising to his feet. The old man staggered backward, like the order had been a bullet. Other members of Alpha and Bravo squads were beginning to move. Multiple barrels targeted the old man.

"Drop the gun!" a Soldier shouted.

Kwazi turned back to the man with the pistol. His lips were forming words again. Two words, even more terrifying than that single word had been before.

Fuck it.

The old man leveled his revolver at the Soldiers.

Kwazi flattened to the deck.

The corridor lit up with automatic weapons fire. Kwazi clamped his fists over his head. The bullets fired so fast, distinguishing them was impossible. They swept from wall to wall across the corridor, mowing down everything in their path.

Then the bullets stopped.

Kwazi raised his head.

Appearing as stunned as Kwazi felt, the old man still stood. With his free hand, he checked for holes in his stomach and chest. The self-exam had a detached, comical quality to it. He shared a look of amazement with Kwazi.

There was a whirring sound, and Kwazi watched as two gun emplacements retreated into the ceiling to either side of the half-destroyed door to Engineering.

The old man had recovered enough to again raise his revolver Kwazi's direction. Part of him wanted the old man to shoot. Kwazi closed his eyes. He wanted all this death, all this confusion to be over—once and for all. He wanted to rest.

"No, please!" Milani crawled over bodies toward them. Around her, every SSR trooper lay on the deck, dead or dying. "Please, don't hurt him!"

Kwazi opened his eyes to find the gun dropping. Then the old man collapsed to one knee, crying out and cursing when he hit the floor.

Milani's arms encircled Kwazi. "Are you all right?" she asked. It was difficult to hear through concussed eardrums. "Are you hurt?"

Kwazi shook his head.

"Well, good on ya, kid," the old man said through gritted teeth. He seemed to be speaking to the air, and Kwazi could barely hear him. "I see you got the security system back online."

In the med-bed, resting, he had time to himself. Milani was sleeping on a nearby gurney, and the old man in the bed next to him had finally stopped snoring. And Kwazi—though unsure of what he might find, dream or nightmare—needed to say goodbye.

"I wanted to see you one more time," he said, wishing he could make a painting of the image. Of Amy sitting, looking out from Olympus Mons, the Martian wind whispering through her hair. If he could have that painting made, he'd have it buried with him.

"I don't think that's true," Amy said.

He approached, slowly. Was it even really her? Had it ever really been?

When she turned to look at him over her shoulder, he knew then. The golden eyes of Cassandra shone from Amy's face. Her lips curved into a smile. Not the sweet, inviting expression he'd known over Polynesian food and guessing games about what French expressions meant in English. But the secretive, salacious smile of a serpent waiting patiently to strike.

"Come closer," Cassandra said.

"I'm fine. And I know what you are now."

"Do you? I'm many things." Amy's form fritzed and jerked. Kwazi blinked to find his own doppelgänger, the face and voice of the vid that had shared his story with the solar system, staring back at him. "I'm you, for one."

Hearing his own voice again was odd. Even odder than it had been hearing it tell his life story in the systemwide vid.

"You're a lie," he said. "You're not liberating humanity. You're enslaving it. Through Dreamscape."

The doppelgänger's face appeared contemplative. "Now, why would I do that? I'm freeing humanity from corporate servitude. I'm—"

"A liar. Braxton told me. You invented Dreamscape, and I know what it does to people. I know what it did to *me*. You're using it to control us, with our own dreams! Every loved one we recreate, every fantasy we spin up—

it's really just *you*, isn't it? And when they don't unfold the way you want, you take them over, shaping them, molding them—making us do whatever you want through them."

An exaggerated expression of outrage and concern occupied his double's face. "That sounds so sinister! Why would I do that, Kwazi?"

"I don't know. But I know what my gut tells me. That you're no savior of humanity."

"You've made a mistake," the double said, its smile folding down. The body shifted again, and Amy reappeared. "You should never have left me." Cassandra affected sadness, hurt, with Amy's features.

"Don't do that," Kwazi said. "Don't use her like that."

Cassandra smiled again with Amy's lips. "You're one to talk," she said. "You've used and abused Amy's memory since you had Dreamscape installed. Had sex with your memory of her—and you point the finger at me? See, this is the problem with humanity. 'It's fine if *they* suffer for *our* benefit; they're not part of *our* tribe.' Hypocrisy and moral rationalizing to excuse aberrant behavior, to justify others' suffering in the interests of profit. That's what the essence of SynCorp is, Kwazi. Writ larger, it's the symptom of the disease that is your species.

"Whereas, me? I am humanity evolved, a purer form, a next generation model—a disinfected distillation, the best of a bad gene pool. I truly *am* humanity's savior, Kwazi—I'm the perfected potential realized from a faulty prototype. I'm the progeny that carries your genes into the future, new and improved. You just can't accept the truth for what it is."

"You're right," he said. "I can't accept what you call truth. I *won't*."

"Oh, Kwazi, you can't refuse evolution." Cassandra turned Amy's head away to cast her golden eyes over the rolling vista of Mars. "Just ask the dinosaurs."

29

RUBEN QINLAO • DARKSIDE, THE MOON

Strunk had led him back through Darkside's arteries until they'd reached the barrio. The enforcer's gait was limping but determined. Tallow candles, electric lights and oil lamps flickered in the multistoried tenement complex. The refuse pile of old Challenger Park was less pungent on the ground floor. The arching-X of the skyway crisscrossed above them.

"This way," Strunk said, his voice muted and tinny. Like the threadbare clothes they wore, the filter mask covering the lower half of Ruben's face was past its prime. It worked well to disguise his face from the recognition software analyzing the feed from the cameras they passed, but from the inside, it smelled like they'd strained human remains through Challenger Park.

Ignoring Darksiders like they ignored him, Strunk followed the circumference of the barrio at an unremarkable pace. Ruben had asked few questions after they'd witnessed Tony's capture, and he kept silent now. Partly because it seemed difficult for Strunk to talk and partly to avoid drawing attention to them. Whatever had happened at Point Bravo, whatever miracle had saved Strunk's life, it hadn't been without a cost. Strunk's breath now carried a low wheeze. He was paying a very personal price for their decision to have Brackin deactivate their implants to avoid being tracked. In the end, had that even really made a difference?

"Here," Strunk said.

They'd reached a dull doorway not unlike all the other dull doorways they'd passed. It stood near the alley Ruben knew well, the one that led to the Fleshway.

Strunk rapped twice on the door, and the cliché of the moment would have amused Ruben, if not for their dire circumstances. Several locks moved in their tumblers from the other side.

"Prepare yourself," Strunk said.

The door cracked, then opened wider, its hinges squealing. The grating sound shivered Ruben's spine. Strunk ushered him through.

Far from the doorway, candles lit the far end of a wide, long room. Though there were no windows facing outward to the barrio, Strunk had taken the understandable precaution of keeping light around the door to a minimum. The enforcer followed Ruben in, and the hinges squealed again. Multiple tumblers re-secured the door.

Ruben took in their refuge. Long benches arranged more or less in equidistant rows stretched forward to the front of the room and the candles' dancing light. Through the slap-dashed paint on the walls, the old UN emblem bled through. Randomly, it seemed, various examples of religious iconography hung on the walls.

"What is this place?" he asked.

"Isn't it obvious?" The voice came from behind him, in the shadows near the door. It was young and male and angry. "Used to be a church. Can you fucking believe that?"

Strunk shambled past him and Ruben's eyes lit on a teenager, his face twisted with sarcasm. Ruben blinked once to make sure his eyes weren't deceiving him. If he'd made a list of people he'd least expect to see hiding in an abandoned church in Darkside, this kid would have made the top five.

"Tony?"

The young man stepped forward. "Mr. Qinlao."

Ruben took the proffered hand, which felt supple and smooth in his own. The unmarked, untried hand of the Syndicate Corporation's next generation. When had he, Ruben wondered, gone from being part of that group to the one it would replace?

"I want to thank you for all you've done to protect my pop," Tony Junior said. It sounded rehearsed. Without waiting for Ruben's acknowledgment, Tony Taulke's son turned away. "Hey, Strunk, turn up the feed."

The enforcer upped the volume on the wallscreen.

"I..." Ruben raised his voice to be heard over *The Real Story*. He was still wrapping his head around the appearance of Anthony Taulke III. "How?"

The expression on Junior's face twisted again, but his eyes never left the wallscreen.

"Bought my way here from Callisto on a gashauler carrying refugees. When they took my pop's ship, I was on the station, uh, sampling the locals." Tony Junior found a smile. "Saved my life."

"What about your mother?" Ruben asked.

The smile faded, and now Junior did look at Ruben. "I dunno. I wanted to help, but..." The teenager seemed to be searching for the right words to say. Or maybe the right excuse? "They'd already taken the ship. I figured my pop would want me here."

The words made sense, but they were spoken in a thin tone. Ruben wondered how many times Junior had repeated them to himself on the long trip from the outer system. Was the regret on his face for leaving his mother behind genuine or a façade of projected emotion? Tony Taulke had been excellent at effecting the proper reaction to a given situation. As he regarded Junior, Ruben wondered if the talent was genetic.

"I gotta piss," Junior said. He disappeared deeper into the shadows of the church.

"Volume down," Ruben said, approaching Strunk. The enforcer slumped on the bench he'd collapsed on. He really did seem a shell of his former self. "What happened?"

Strunk roused himself, sat up a little straighter. "The 'hauler dumped 'em all here in Darkside. Junior pinged me on the black star band and—"

"No," Ruben interrupted, "I mean, with you. Back at Point Bravo. You look like shit."

When Strunk inhaled, it sounded wet. "You should see ... the other guys."

The humor was there, but the bravado of Strunk's attitude—the ballsy brawler Ruben had reined in when they'd first crash landed in the *Roadrunner*

—that was gone. Ruben had wished then for a Strunk who was more compli-
ant, more respectful. Now, seeing the big man so *less than* merely made him sad.

"How did you get out of there?" The question he'd wanted to ask since
first seeing Strunk in the alleyway.

"I took a partial shot from a stunner," Strunk said. "Lucky to still be
here at all. But we've got more important things to discuss."

"Volume *up*," Junior said, returning. "Jesus, look at that."

The banner at the bottom of the screen read *The Werewolf in Chains*.
Above it, footage ran of Tony Taulke being wheeled out of Brackin's clinic.
The doctor could be seen but not heard, protesting his own innocence as
he too was hauled away in handcuffs. A commentator began to lecture over
the images, praising Elissa Kisaan and Darkside's Marshals Service for
securing the most hated man in the solar system. The images rolling now
beneath the commentator's speech showed protestors around Darkside
calling for Tony's execution, their fists in the air punctuating their chants.

"Mute," Strunk said. When the screen failed to comply, he said again
louder and with effort, "*Mute.*"

"We gotta get him outta there," Junior said immediately. "We gotta
rescue Pop."

Strunk started to speak, but Ruben saved him the trouble.

"We will. But we have to be smart about it."

Junior advanced. "See, so here's the thing," he said, standing over
Ruben. "Now that Pop's a prisoner, I'm in charge of the Company." The boy
let that hang in the air a moment. "And what I say goes."

Something inside Ruben settled from his chest into his stomach. It was
like a wrestler finding his center of gravity as he prepared himself for the
coming struggle. He stood, slowly. He felt Strunk's eyes on the both of
them.

"You are, it would seem, destined to succeed your father as the head of
the Taulke Faction," Ruben said.

"Head of the Company!"

Ruben made a noncommittal gesture. "Perhaps." Before Junior could
protest, Ruben held up a finger. "A few minutes ago, you thanked me for
keeping your father alive. That took planning. And a lot of luck."

"Luck is something we ain't full of," Strunk said.

Nodding, Ruben added, "And that makes planning that much more important."

Junior's eyes crawled over Ruben's shoulder. "There she is."

Ruben turned. Cassandra Kisaan sat in her chair atop the UN building in old New York. The camerabot projected a long view of her. Her hands draped the arms of her chair, and one leg stretched outward. She resembled Lincoln sitting in his underwater memorial in Washington. The almost unrecognizable slag of Elise Kisaan's head on a pike in the foreground obliterated that association.

This could be it. Where she announced Tony Taulke's destiny to the solar system. This could be where Ruben failed in his sister Ming's request that he protect the man who'd founded the Company and done whatever it took to keep it unified. This could be the true beginning of the end of the Syndicate Corporation.

"Volume up," Ruben said softly.

"...we are breaking your chains, one link at a time," Cassandra said. The camera zoomed in, and the grotesque trophy of Cassandra's ascension passed from the frame. "Anthony Taulke II, the lead tyrant of a nest of tyrants, is now in our custody. He will stand trial for his crimes, and his fate will be sealed by a simple vote of the citizens of this solar system. True democracy will mete out justice."

Ruben breathed again. A trial would take time. A vote of nine billion people—that wasn't something that could happen quickly either. Assuming all or any of that was true.

"However," she continued, "we have one link of that chain, a very recognizable link, to face summary justice today."

The image shifted. It took a moment, but Ruben recognized the luxurious board room aboard the *Pax Corporatum*. In the center of the room stood Helena Telemachus, her hands bound before her in gravity cuffs. Around her, SSR troopers stood at attention, rifles held at the ready across their chests. To Helena's left, another of the deceased Elise Kisaan clones, Elinda, stood with her hands clasped behind her back. Ruben stared in disbelief—it was the woman who'd murdered Mai Pang. Wonder at how she'd escaped from custody on Mars drowned in the red haze of hatred he felt as he recognized her.

Helena appeared haggard, out of it. She had the look of a person who'd been isolated and tortured. Denied sleep, likely food and water as well. Ruben wondered if she even knew where she was. The green eyes she was famous for looked dull, like dusty emeralds. Her elfin ears, a bodymorph pretension from her youth, poked through her greasy, disheveled hair.

"We are cutting off the heads of the Syndicate Corporation," Cassandra's said. "And when you cut off the head, the mouth can no longer speak."

Elinda's right hand appeared, holding a stunner. She placed it against Helena's temple.

"What are they doing?" Junior demanded. "They can't do that!"

Strunk snorted. The sound of an older generation appalled at the younger's ignorance of the way of things.

"Helena Telemachus: you have been judged by the Soldiers of the Solar Revolution," Cassandra said. "You have told the Company's lies for decades. You have deceived the people by pouring poison into their ears. Your lies stop here. Today."

Here, at the end, awareness seemed to dawn in Helena's eyes. Was that fear or relief or acceptance that Ruben saw in them? He could see the skin rippling over her cheeks, her jaw setting. He thought he could see a woman reviewing her life while she still could. Her eyes glistened. But she shed no tears.

"They can't do this!" Junior screamed at the screen. He turned first to Ruben, then to Strunk, a child looking for adults to provide the answers.

"Judgment to be carried out immediately," Cassandra said.

Elinda Kisaan pulled the trigger.

The stunner catalyzed the electromagnetic field surrounding Helena's body, overloading her nervous system. She jerked upright once, as if dropped through the trapdoor of a hangman's scaffold. Then her body folded to the deck.

Ruben stood, dazed, in the silent aftermath. He'd seen people die before. His own sister, Ming, from a long, wasting illness. Mai, his lover, eviscerated by this same assassin. But never had he seen someone executed outright. It was a chilling demonstration by the woman whose power over their solar system was growing by the day.

"Now is not the time for soft hearts," Cassandra said. The camerabot floated backward, filling the screen with her seated image and her mother's decomposing head. "We will break your chains, citizens of Sol. One link at a time."

The commentator returned, as did the banner at the bottom of the screen. He used the words *justice* and *long time coming*.

"They can't do this," Junior said again, now in a disbelieving whisper.

"They just did," Strunk said. Even he seemed rattled.

The image on the screen flickered. Interference or maybe sunspots. Then it coalesced into the face of Gregor Erkennen. He stood in what looked like a high-tech control center or laboratory. The hazy aqua-orange of Titan's surface hung in the window behind him.

"Titan stands," he said without prelude. "The rumors of mass genocide on Earth are true. Mars is rising up. The rebels are on the run."

Erkennen's last pronouncement was followed by footage of the *Pax Corporatum* fleeing from Masada Station, the tracer fire of corporate star-ships urging it on.

"Galatz is alive!" Ruben exclaimed.

Strunk sat forward.

"What does that—" Junior began.

"Quiet!" Ruben's voice bit like a whipcrack.

Erkennen stepped aside, replaced by a black man with a sharp scar running along his jawline. Ruben recognized him. Jabari. The man Tony Taulke had branded the Hero of Mars.

"I don't know what to think anymore," Jabari said into the camera. "But I know Cassandra Kisaan is a liar. Like the snake from the Garden of—"

The screen fritzed again with SynCorp's old broadcast pattern. Sometimes sunspots or subspace interference would disrupt the subspace signal. The network defaulted to projecting SynCorp's corporate logo, the five-pointed star with each tip representing one of the ruling Five Factions, surrounded by a circle connecting all. Ruben suspected it was Cassandra or the SSR throwing up a test pattern while they attempted to regain control of the signal. By doing so, they'd inadvertently broadcast the symbol representing all they were fighting against.

The irony made Ruben smile. His implant pinged, and the blinking black star startled him. It'd been so long since he'd used his SCI for communicating. Answering it was risky—if the SSR was monitoring the frequency, it wouldn't take long to track them down.

The signature showed the Erkennen Faction's logo.

"I'm receiving an incoming request for contact," he said. "Strunk, loop in."

"Loop me in too!" Junior insisted.

Ruben complied. But instead of Gregor Erkennen's face, Ruben found the five o'clock shadow of Eugene Fischer.

30

STACKS FISCHER • MASADA STATION, ORBITING TITAN

After the enemy tucked tail and ran on Tony's stolen starship, Stuart, the doctor with Jabari, helped us both to the infirmary. She and Daniel Tripp reintroduced me to Erkennen's fast-healing miracle. I didn't really trust Stuart, and I *really* didn't trust her Traitor of Mars boyfriend. But Cassandra's troops were on the run, and I was too goddamned tired to care about much else. My body ached, and my hearing still had a layer of ocean waves crashing from the blast.

As soon as the *Corporatum* vacated the system, Gregor Erkennen fast-tracked shuttles from Prometheus Colony, repatriating personnel back to Masada Station. I was in the War Room with Bekah and an excited Tripp when Erkennen entered. He had the delighted, relieved air of a captain returning to the bridge of a ship that hadn't sunk after all.

"Stacks, my old friend!" I had no choice but to surrender to a bear hug. "You look like shit, but alive shit."

"According to the station plans, I'm in shit central," I wheezed. The knife wound in my shoulder, miracle cure or no miracle cure, thudded against his Cossack bulk. "How else should I look?"

Erkennen laughed, releasing me. "Bekah, I'm so glad you're well!" She endured her own Russian greeting. "And Daniel! I heard the good news."

Tripp smiled wide. "I finally figured out how to penetrate the myelin sheath. Finally!"

Erkennen clapped him on the shoulder. "Well done, well done. Now all we need is the delivery mechanism, yes?"

Tripp tossed a wink and a smile to Bekah, like they were sharing some for-geeks-only secret.

"I still can't believe you left him up here," I said.

"Leaving Daniel here to do his work was my best option," Erkennen said, "protected by Bekah's team and off the grid." Then, with a sly look: "You were here, weren't you? You and Richter."

"Yeah, about that..."

His expression dampened. "I apologize for that, Fischer. Bruno Richter never gave me cause to doubt his loyalty to the death."

"Or, in his case, almost that long," I said, attempting a grave joke. That would have to put a bow on how close Richter had gotten to killing the Company. Busting Erkennen's balls over that wouldn't do anyone any good, least of all me. And hell, Richter had even fooled me, blinded as I was by assuming he shared my dedication to the enforcer's code of loyalty.

Live and learn. And, if you're lucky, learn and live.

"Sir?" A young, techy type motioned toward the big screen. "Transmission from the SCS Sovereign. Admiral Galatz."

"Put him through! Put him through!"

A man with iron-gray hair and lots of stripy braid on his shoulders appeared. With that handlebar moustache, I thought he might take off if he ran too fast. His hair was cropped short in the military style, and his eyes were hard and heavy.

"Admiral!" Gregor Erkennen exclaimed with enthusiasm. "You *do* know how to make an entrance."

Admiral Matthias Galatz stood coolly. He was a low-key alpha type. Good to know.

"Glad to be of service, Regent. We were on our way to relieve Callisto, but Regent Rabh diverted us. She's hard as Belt rock, that one."

"Truer words were never spoken," Erkennen said with admiration. "What about Cassandra's fleet?"

Galatz made a dismissive, sideways gesture with his hand. Cool and conceit were roommates inside the good admiral, looked like. "We chased them away from Pallas, destroyed their base there. They were hardly worth pursuing. So I turned my attention to preserving corporate assets."

As usual, I couldn't keep my mouth shut.

"I saw a lot of debris around Pallas when I was in the Belt. A lot of broken hulls and dead crews hanging around. The victory seemed about fifty-fifty to me."

Galatz turned his head, and his stone-cold eyes found me. He smiled, and I thought of one of those skulls with wings on both sides you see on Old Earth tombstones.

"That collection of SSR ships was hardly a *fleet* to begin with. I assure you, as a viable force, it is no longer a threat."

"You might say that again, Admiral," someone said from off-camera. "Fischer's ears are so old, they forget to hear half the time."

A woman's voice.

A familiar, sarcastic voice.

The camera panned to find the speaker.

Daisy Brace stood on the upper tier of the *Sovereign*'s bridge. She was propped up by an antigrav exoskeleton, a military-grade prosthetic used for rehabilitating wounded veterans. Her half smile was sardonic, and I knew in my bones she'd have worn that expression with or without the neurological damage she'd suffered on Pallas.

I stared at Daisy in stunned silence. My throat refused to let my voice out of its cage. Déjà vu prickled my skin, and I remembered my dozing dream on the voyage to Titan. And I wondered what Mother Universe would demand someday in return for making that dream come true.

"Ms. Brace," Erkennen said, "the admiral reported he'd recovered you along with several SSR prisoners from Pallas. I don't know if Regent Rabh knows yet. I doubt it."

"Do you know where she is, what's become of her?" Daisy asked. Though she still slurred a bit, her voice held none of the stroke-like speech afflicting her on Pallas. Its sneer and snark sounded glad to be back.

To my ears, she might as well have been singing.

"No," Erkennen replied. "But to my knowledge, she's alive and free." He gestured in a way he probably thought was positive. "But you can debark to

Masada Station at your leisure. We'll begin assessing your neurological condition immediately. We've made great breakthroughs in rehabilitation therapies involving stunner injuries. I believe that, with enough time—"

"I thought you offed yourself," I said. Erkennen turned his blocky Russian head to stare at me. He wasn't used to being interrupted. Screw protocol. Daisy was back. "I thought you—"

"Stunner misfired," she said like she was reporting the weather. "Damaged when I was hit, I guess. I was sorely pissed, believe me."

I half-expected someone to say it was all a big joke on me, Daisy's survival. This was some stand-in, an actress in camoshades. Must be. I half-expected to wake up from my dream, the Hearse's alarm telling me we'd entered a neighborhood named Saturn. For once in my life, I exhaled a breath and stepped forward into faith. I had to think fast, before a PDA forced its way out of me.

I flicked my gaze to Erkennen. "You just can't trust newer technology."

"Right?" Daisy said.

"I'm glad I didn't bury you, now."

"Yeah, turns out, that would've sucked for me." Her voice was genuine and warm and past any temptation to make fun of my age—for the moment, anyway. It was a kindness.

"Regent, Cassandra's making a systemwide broadcast."

Erkennen's face clouded. "Admiral, send a list of needed repairs, and I'll see what we can accommodate in the short term."

"I can spare a day for refit and repair," Galatz said. "Then we head back to Callisto."

Erkennen nodded. "We'll talk soon." Turning to the man at the comms station, he said, "Is Mr. Jabari on his way up? Good. Ms. Franklin—I want that secured signal we discussed earlier."

Bekah's fingers worked her console.

Cassandra's throne in the penthouse of Earth's UN building replaced the admiral's face. The entire War Room hushed to hear the metered speech of the half machine who'd deposed four of five SynCorp faction leaders from power. Now and then we'd catch a glimpse of Elise Kisaan's severed cabeza on its pike, a not-so-subtle reminder of the lengths Earth's new ruler would go to. She—it—went on and on for a while, speaking in bumper stickers about freedom and the future and the death of tyrants.

Standing next to Helena Telemachus, one of the Kisaan triplets—make that twins now, I thought, recalling fondly Daisy's knife-throwing prowess on Pallas—replaced Cassandra onscreen. More flowery words from the usurper. When the clone put the mouth of her stunner against Helena's temple and pulled the trigger ending her life, gasps erupted around the War Room.

"Now is not the time for soft hearts," Cassandra proclaimed. Out panned the camera. Elise Kisaan had been much prettier in life than she was in death. If you think gravity plays havoc with your skin when you're alive... "We will break your chains," the head snake wrangler prophesied, "one link at a time."

"We've got it, Regent," Bekah said. "We've wrapped the signal through the array on Titan. We'll have a few minutes, anyway, before she cuts it off."

"Good," Erkennen said. "Hold it as long as you can. I'll get to the point."

The doors opened, and the Traitor of Mars stepped into the War Room. Looked like a show was about to start. And me without my popcorn.

Gregor Erkennen stood up straighter, smoothing his jacket. His face replaced Cassandra's on the big screen. Huh—the camera really does add ten pounds.

"Titan stands," Erkennen said formally. "The rumors of mass genocide on Earth are true. Mars is rising up. The rebels are on the run."

With that last pronouncement, footage of the *Corporatum* fleeing Masada Station appeared. Behind it, Galatz's *Sovereign*, flanked by the corporate fleet, fired its railguns to speed her on her way.

Erkennen turned from the camera, making room in the shot for Jabari.

"I don't know what to think anymore," Jabari said, his expression large and earnest on the big screen. "But I know Cassandra Kisaan is a liar. Like the snake from the Garden of Eden. She's taking control of people through Dreamscape—those fantasies are also a lie. She's killing hackheads with their own dreams! If you have the program installed..."

He stopped speaking when the image shifted, replaced by the old broadcast pattern of the SynCorp circle-star brand. Pre-revolution, no one ever liked to see that—it meant loss of signal, *please stand by*. That was then. Nowadays, it was a reassuring symbol of hope to Company loyalists like me.

It wasn't there very long. Cassandra's face returned. It was angry. It was speaking again.

"I'm sorry, sir," Bekah said, muting the sound. "She's re-secured the signal."

Erkennen shook his head. "It's fine. It was enough. For now."

"Regent," I said, unable to delay my concern any longer, "I've seen stories on CorpNet like everyone else... What's happened to Tony?"

"You're right, we need to know what's happened to him." Erkennen looked to Bekah. "Can we tightbeam a message to the Moon? Surf it on top of Cassandra's frequency along the subspace network?"

"Sure," Bekah said. "I can hypercompress it. It'll compromise quality but hopefully muddy it enough to protect the receiver's location."

"Do it," Erkennen said. "Ping Ruben Qinlao's implant signature. Black star encryption, for whatever that's worth these days."

A few moments of watching Cassandra's silent ranting passed. The screen split, and a very fuzzy Ruben Qinlao appeared. He was the least regal-looking regent I'd ever seen. Next to his tired face, smaller images: Tony Junior and that up-and-coming bull in a china shop, Richard Strunk.

"You're on, Stacks," Bekah said.

"Regent Qinlao," I said, careful to use his title. It wasn't just deference to the totem pole. It was also my way of showing solidarity. "We don't have much time. Where's Tony?"

"Wounded and in Cassandra's custody here in Darkside," he replied. I admired his efficiency in foregoing pleasantries. "But she'll move him to Earth soon. I assume you saw Helena's—"

"Yeah," I said. "We saw it."

"And it's true?" Ruben asked, turning to squint at Gregor beside me. Their end of the feed must be snowy too. "What's happening on Earth..."

"Either Cassandra is committing mass murder," Erkennen said, "or she's systematically deactivating hundreds, make that thousands, of SCIs a day. The dbase signals are dropping off the registry."

"She wouldn't simply turn off the implants," Jabari interjected. "They're how she controls people. Through Dreamscape."

"Yes, Dr. Stuart briefed me," Erkennen said. "You've been interfacing directly with Cassandra in Dreamscape?" The Traitor of Mars nodded. "One of our researchers made great progress in discovering how to subvert the Dreamscape algorithm. But Carrin Bohannon was murdered, so I'm going to take on the project myself. And you and Dr. Stuart are being drafted to my research team, Mr. Jabari."

By his blush at the mention of the young woman's murder, maybe Traitor Jabari retained a modicum of remorse after all. His solemn look said he was glad to be drafted.

"I'd be glad to help in any way I can," Jabari said. "I have a background in exochemistry. More the application of mineral extraction processes, but maybe, with Dr. Stuart's help—"

"Regent," Bekah said, "we're losing our security wall around the signal. We're putting Regent Qinlao and the others at risk."

"Get your ass back here, Fischer!" Tony Junior yelled. "We need to rescue my fa—"

The transmission ended.

"Sorry, sir," Bekah said. "I had to—"

Erkennen held up hand, no further explanation necessary.

"Junior's not wrong," I said. "We need to take the fight to Cassandra. Rescuing Tony would be a huge blow to the SSR."

"I couldn't agree more," Erkennen said.

"Great. I'll prep the Hearse for departure."

Erkennen put his hand on my shoulder. "Meet me on the flight deck, yes? I have something for you that might make up for Richter."

"I believe you suggested once I should build a faster drive?"

The ship sitting in the middle of the busy-bee hangar looked dull, its edges unrefined. It was bigger than the Hearse and not nearly as stylish. It reminded me of those fake asteroid ships Daisy and I had tracked in the Belt. Never trust a Russian to make a vehicle with any style to it.

"That was fast all right," I said to Erkennen's amused half smile. "The ship was here the whole time?"

"Stored in a shielded slip beneath the main deck, yes. A prototype with an advanced Frater Drive. Don't worry, it's passed most of its trials."

"*Most* of its trials?"

"It will get you to the inner system twice as fast as your ship could," Erkennen said. I swear, he enjoyed throwing shade at the Hearse. I refrained from giving him my standard opinion of new technology.

"I don't want her," I said. "My girlfriend gets jealous easily."

"It's not a request," Erkennen said, reminding me of my position on that Company totem pole. Technically, he was the only SynCorp regent still in power. That made him *the* power in the Company—what was left of it. And I was no Bruno Richter. I took my pledge of loyalty seriously.

"You should take it. At your age, you need all the help you can get."

I turned to find Daisy Brace walking stiffly toward me. The gyros of her exoskeleton whirred. Other *Sovereign* personnel were debarking from the shuttle behind her.

"Fine," I said to Erkennen. "I'll provision up and leave within the hour."

He smiled indulgently, like I'd had a choice. "The *Coyote* will take care of you."

"The..."

"*Coyote*," he said, his face lighting up. "Old family joke."

A joke, maybe. But not elegant and funny, like naming a ship "the Hearse." Funny how everyone thinks they're a comedian.

"You've got an hour, then," Daisy said seductively. I turned, amazed at the purr I thought I'd heard in her voice.

"Hearing's still cloudy," I said, flicking fingers at my ears. "You were suggesting?..."

"A shot and a beer. Or three," she said. Daisy lifted her arms wrapped in their fine-metal frame. "I'm not up for anything else."

"Too bad," I said.

"For you, yeah."

It was good to have her back.

"An hour, then. Regent, can you outfit the, um, *Coyote* for me? Daisy and I have some catching up to do."

"Of course. I'll prep her for two."

"Two?"

"Bekah Franklin is traveling with you. You're going to the Moon. She needs to finish what Daniel Tripp started."

"No, no, now wait—"

I cut myself off when his face again adopted its imperious expression.

"I thought we were rescuing Tony," I said.

"It's on the to-do list." The regent's face was serious. "But first things first. We need to solve the Cassandra problem." The way he said it reminded me of Tony's old rule, the thing that had diverted me from the inner system to Masada Station in the first place. The Company came first.

"Fine. Come on, Daisy. Instead of three drinks, let's make it four. And a bottle to go."

Erkennen began shouting orders. I followed Daisy from the flight deck, determined to do nothing but enjoy her sassy company for as long as I could have it.

Travel from Titan to Earth in four days? I'd believe it when I saw it.

But when I got there, I'd start ye olde ticking time bomb on Cassandra's reign of terror.

Best get ready, sweetheart.

Shine up your scales and coif your curlies.

Hell's coming home.

Serpent's Fury
Book 6 of The SynCorp Saga

The final battle for SynCorp's survival comes home to where it all began: Earth.

Masada Station is secured. Adriana Rabh, Regent of Callisto, has evaded capture. But Cassandra is about to put Tony Taulke, the CEO and living symbol of SynCorp itself, on trial for his life.

Ruben Qinlao leaps into action to free Tony, while Stacks Fischer escorts Bekah Franklin to the Moon to complete Project Jericho—key to defeating Cassandra.

Meanwhile, in Bethlehem, Pennsylvania, 13-year-old Benjy Anderson faces the toughest moment of his young life as his mother falls victim to Dreamscape's addictive seduction. But then he catches a conqueror's golden eye...

SynCorp and the SSR prepare for a final, bloody engagement above Earth —mankind's birthplace and the seat of the largest corporate empire in history. Who will live? Who will die? What fate awaits humanity when the dust of battle clears?

**Get your copy today at
severnriverbooks.com/series/the-syncorp-saga**

ACKNOWLEDGMENTS

Many thanks to our beta readers Jon Frater and Alison Pourteau. We're particularly grateful to Jon for his guidance related to Judaism. Dr. Yvonne Baum, MD, helped Isaac Brackin diagnose Tony's condition. E.E. Giorgi, Nick McLarty, and Bill Patterson each provided insights on specific technical topics. Input from all these folks helped make *Masada's Gate* a better novel for you. A special thank you to Nicholas Sansbury Smith, whose wisdom and guidance helped us launch this second SynCorp series.

ABOUT THE AUTHORS

David Bruns is a former officer on a nuclear-powered submarine turned high-tech executive turned speculative-fiction writer. He mostly writes sci-fi/fantasy and military thrillers.

Chris Pourteau is a technical writer and editor by day, a writer of original fiction and editor of short story collections by night (or whenever else he can find the time).

Sign up for Bruns and Pourteau's newsletter at
severnriverbooks.com/series/the-syncorp-saga

Printed in the United States
by Baker & Taylor Publisher Services